# THE FIFTH ANGEL

"Mark Stitzer was trained to fight his own kind of war," Major Stroup said. "In the event of conflict, he was to penetrate enemy lines, establish himself within the resident civilian population, and familiarize himself with the target areas."

"Then what?" asked the doctor.

"Then, at a given signal, he was to deactivate the area."

"Deactivate?"

"Gut it!" said Stroup. "Rip its insides out. I mean, kill it! He can come in, blow up the Bronx, garrote cops, poison the wells, then get away."

"He's insane," the doctor said.

Stroup shrugged indifferently. "That makes him all the more effective."

"Effective at what? What is he accomplishing?"

"At killing the largest city in the nation."

---

"Remarkably suspenseful . . . Wiltse works wonders with his plot and characters, building tension solidly from the first page."
—*Chicago Tribune*

# THE
# FIFTH ANGEL

## DAVID WILTSE

PUBLISHED BY POCKET BOOKS NEW YORK

This novel is a work of fiction. Names, characters, places and incidents are either the product of the author's imagination or are used fictitiously. Any resemblance to actual events or locales or persons, living or dead, is entirely coincidental.

 POCKET BOOKS, a division of Simon & Schuster, Inc.
1230 Avenue of the Americas, New York, N.Y. 10020

Published by arrangement with Macmillan Publishing Company, Inc.
Library of Congress Catalog Card Number: 84-26178

ISBN: 0-671-60605-0

First Pocket Books printing January, 1986

10 9 8 7 6 5 4 3 2 1

POCKET and colophon are registered trademarks
of Simon & Schuster, Inc.

Printed in the U.S.A.

To my beloved daughters,
Laura and Lisa

And the fifth angel sounded,
and I saw a star fall from heaven
unto the earth: and to him was given
the key of the bottomless pit.

—REVELATION 9:1

# Part One
# BURIAL

# 1979

TWENTY-FOUR MEN LEAPED from the plane into the black New Mexican sky, a double squad of highly trained saboteurs and assassins, the elite of a killing corps.

They fell out of the sky in one of the creases of the radar net, too far from the commercial airline routes to deserve any attention from the ground controllers, too distant from population centers to be noticed by civilians. The military saw the fleeting blip on their screens, but then the military was looking for them. The military had sent them.

The moon was a thin crescent and high in the sky, providing little light. The men fell with increasing speed until they hit terminal velocity, acceleration of gravity balanced by air resistance. They stayed in a circle, their hands linked, their limbs stretched out like wings. The wind roared in their ears and the cloth of their camouflage uniforms, tucked and tightened, nonetheless flapped like playing cards stuck in the spokes of a bicycle wheel.

One man disengaged from the circle, pulling his hands away abruptly. He tucked his knees into his chest, arched his back, and tumbled away from the falling ring of men at twenty-five hundred feet. It was too dark and too noisy for any but those next to him to realize he had gone.

The lone man straightened from his tuck, twisted his body to one side, and extended his arms and legs again. The force of the air pushed his limbs up over his body so he looked like a marionette dangling from its strings.

At two thousand feet the joined men released from one another and the circle widened like a rippling ring of water. Two seconds later they opened their chutes, floating black mushrooms, darker than the sky. To an observer on the ground, the descending parachutists would have been visible only as shifting shapes, temporarily obscuring one star cluster, then another, like so many unseen clouds.

At the referee's observation post, located atop hill 127, the chutists became clearly visible at last in the infrared viewers. The referee had tracked the plane coming in. When they were free-falling, the men had been no easier to pick out than shooting stars, tiny flashes of moving light against a background of other tiny lights. Only now, in the relative slowness of their canopied descent, did they take on a recognizable form. The dangling men, faintly green, their outlines blurry, swayed in the eyepiece of the bulky nightscope.

"I see twenty-three," said Colonel Parker, automatically counting the men again as he spoke.

Beside him, Lieutenant Colonel Meeson looked through his own infrared scope. "Twenty-three."

Major Stroup chuckled, making no effort to keep the sound to himself, even though he knew it would offend the others.

"There were supposed to be twenty-four," said Meeson, wheeling on Stroup.

"Twenty-three and Sergeant Stitzer," said Major Stroup, still scanning the night with his scope. He could not contain his grin. He moved his scope away from the clustered chutists, scanning to either side, knowing as he did so that he was probably already too late. Stitzer would have free-fallen longer, got down quicker, before the others could trip any alarm. Strictly against proper procedure, of course. Stroup continued to grin.

His billowing silk opened a bare thousand feet from the ground, just long enough to slow his descent before he smashed into the earth with the impact of a man falling from a three-story height. He landed more than four hundred yards from the others, fell and pitched forward in a roll, absorbing part of the impact with his back and shoulders as well as his knees. His arrival was witnessed by no one, friend or foe.

Operation Pretty Polly was officially under way.

While the twenty-three members of the double squad maneuvered together in the darkness, scraping shallow graves to hide their chutes under the sand and shale, counting heads, gathering themselves, the lone man, Sergeant Stitzer, was up and sprinting through the night. He ran toward the highest point, the jagged knoll that broke the horizon. If he got there before dawn, burrowed into it before the hunt began in earnest, he could watch the watchers. Like a leopard perched in a tree, he could pick his prey and dispatch it at his leisure.

The leader of the commando group counted his men a second time. "Where the hell is Stitzer?" he asked.

"He peeled off early, before we hit silk," said one of the men.

The leader grumbled briefly about the lack of discipline. It was a pro forma complaint. None of the men was surprised.

"He's probably already got a half mile on us," said another, voicing their real concern.

The leader checked his luminescent compass, oriented himself, then sent the men off in silent squads. They were the best men in all of airborne at infiltration, sabotage,

5

assassination. They were the elite corps. Stitzer was already eight hundred yards closer to the objective. Some were more elite than others.

In the referee's observation post, Colonel Parker kept himself removed from the bickering of Lieutenant Colonel Meeson and Major Stroup. Parker was the referee, the judge and final arbiter of the war-game exercise. He determined what lessons, if any, were to be learned from Pretty Polly. Meeson and Stroup represented the two opposing sides. Lieutenant Colonel Meeson was from the infantry. He had a battalion of men stretched out in parallel lines, "defending" a perimeter two miles long across the desert basin. They had been told only to expect an attempt at infiltration, but, by inference, they had a good idea of when and where it would come.

Major Stroup was the company commander of the elite corps, a group so secret they had no official status but served as part of the organization chart of an airborne battalion. They were known, informally, as the specialists, but few outside the company knew exactly what they specialized in.

"Two to one Stitzer makes it through your whole battalion," said Stroup.

"You don't even know he jumped," said Meeson.

"He jumped."

"We never saw him."

"He didn't want us to."

"*If* he jumped, he might be a grease puddle by now."

Stroup gave Meeson a sharp look, fighting an impulse to bark at him. Some matters were not joked about in a paratroop unit.

"He cuts it fine, but not too fine," said Stroup.

"There's always a first time."

"He'll pass through your battalion like a fart through khaki, Colonel."

"He won't last till noon. One man alone in that desert? Crazy."

Stroup grinned again and Meeson turned his back on him, looking out at the night. He intensely disliked Stroup's bony, angular face with the ears that resembled a dog's, protruding and bent at the tops. He looks like an enlisted man, Meeson thought with contempt. Meeson scanned the darkness. While they had been talking, the specialists had vanished; he could see only his own troops hunkered down in their defensive positions. Wake up, you bastards, he thought. He could feel Colonel Parker watching him with amused detachment.

"You think quite highly of this Sergeant . . ."

"Stitzer," said Stroup.

"Stitzer. He's a favorite of yours," said Parker.

"Not a favorite, sir. Can't say I know him, he's a hard man to know. But he's the best I've ever seen. He's an absolute natural. What we call a carnivore, sir. With due respect, Colonel Meeson's boys are way over their heads. It's almost not fair."

Before Meeson could respond, the silence of the night was broken by a high-pitched *wheel*, very faint, very brief, followed by a pop. The desert was suddenly bathed in an intense, flat white light. A phosphorus flare floated down on its tiny parachute.

One of the infiltrating squads hit the dirt a half second late. An infantry listening post saw their movement and radioed their position. Another flare went up, followed by a distinctive concussive sound that was more felt than heard, like a sudden convulsive but silent intake of breath. It was followed rapidly by another, then a third. The first mortars crashed within twenty-five yards of the infiltrators as they hugged the ground. The observers called in corrections, walking the shells across the desert until the last two hit in the middle of the men. When the shells landed their thin

7

plastic casings shattered and released a pressurized blast of noctilucent pink dye. By the rules of the game, an infiltrator marked by the dye was considered a casualty and out of the exercise. Five of the elite corps were out fifteen minutes after hitting the ground, their uniforms glowing pink.

Sergeant Stitzer lay motionless ten feet from the mortar crew, his body half-concealed by a slight depression. When the flares went off, he froze, one eye closed to retain his night vision against the glare. The mortar crew, looking to their front, never suspected his presence. When the first flare died, the sergeant inched one hand to his belt and removed one of the dye grenades attached to the webbing. He froze again during the second flare, while the mortar crew hurriedly adjusted their coordinates and loaded their weapons.

The "grenade" was nothing more than a sophisticated water balloon, a plastic bag within a tougher outer bag. Sergeant Stitzer activated it by releasing a mild acid solution that ate through the outer bag within seconds. When it landed among the mortar crew, it burst with a splash. The men, officially dead, looked around, cursing, to see who had killed them. Sergeant Stitzer was already gone.

He moved through the darkness with the assurance of a cat. Once past the first mortar crew, he moved entirely on his belly, but with speed. From his low vantage point he could see every bump and rock that rose above the surface. The helmeted heads of the defenders stood out in sharp relief, their silhouettes too regular for nature to have formed them.

He destroyed a second mortar crew ten minutes after wiping out the first, and fifteen minutes after that he removed a machine-gun crew from action. None of his victims knew he was there until the grenade hit them. None of them saw him afterward.

He moved straight forward, deviating from his path only to accommodate the contours of the ground.

By the time the sergeant had passed through the second parallel line of defenders, the "casualty" reports had painted the picture clearly for the observers in the referee's post.

Meeson was livid. A dotted crimson line on the map cut a swath straight through his troops, each dot a casualty. Stitzer had penetrated his men to the depth of a quarter of a mile in less than an hour.

"He'll be all the way through by daylight," said Stroup.

"No way," growled Meeson. He scanned the desert with his scope. It was impossible to tell if any given glowing dot was Sergeant Stitzer or one of his men. He was so close among them, why didn't they see him, why didn't they hear him?

Stitzer pulled himself forward, his weight on his toes and fingertips, his breathing the only sound. He paused and took a thin block of wood from between his teeth. Placing the block on the ground, he pressed his ear to it, holding his breath. Far to his right, he heard the sound of many footsteps—a patrol. They knew he was among them then, and were actively looking for him now. The sergeant gripped the block once more with his teeth and continued to move forward, as soundlessly as a lizard. If anyone was listening for him, he would give them precious little to hear.

After twenty-five yards he placed his ear to the block again. This time he heard a rustle, something below the ground. Someone close by had shifted his weight in a foxhole. The sergeant relaxed his body, melting into the earth. His eyes looked in the direction of the sound, casting quickly from side to side, looking only to either side of the object he wanted to see, using his night vision. After two minutes he heard the rustling noise again. Men were close by, waiting for him in silence as the patrol moved noisily toward them.

Finally two shapes materialized out of the darkness. Two helmets, only the top thirds showing above the ground. The men were dug in well, practically impossible to find by sight alone. They were less than two arms' lengths away from the sergeant. He moved his hand slowly toward his belt.

The patrol was moving rapidly toward him, walking with little attempt at noise concealment, secure behind their own lines.

"Skyhawks!" one of them whispered hoarsely.

"Skyhawks," came the reply from the foxhole.

"Molino, that you?"

"What are you doing running around?"

"There's been casualties in Alpha Company. We're going up to replace them. You heard anything?"

"How'm I supposed to hear anything when you're clomping . . . oh, no!"

A luminescent dye sprouted from the ground in front of the patrol, splattering all of the men. The one called Molino ducked into his foxhole, but even as he did he could feel the warm liquid seeping through the back of his shirt.

Passing through the second line of defense, the sergeant finally became visible to the observers in the referee's post. A single shape moved slowly but delicately between the two lines of defenders. Stroup checked his watch. Half an hour to first light. With luck, Stitzer would make it. Stroup urged him on silently.

The radio crackled. Colonel Parker moved to the map with his red grease pencil.

"Eleven more casualties," he said, trying to keep his voice flat and unemotional. "Infantry."

Meeson felt his face flush to the roots of his close-cropped hair. He kept his eyes focused on the moving dot of greenish light in his nightscope. He did not trust himself to speak.

Sergeant Stitzer sensed the coming of the light before he saw it. The atmosphere seemed to change first, as if the weight of the night had to be lifted before the sun could pry its way underneath. He was fifty yards from the last line of defense. He might make it with a dash, but he doubted it.

He began to dig. Using his hands, he scooped up the loose, sandy earth, spreading it on either side of the growing hole, then smoothing it out so no telltale mound grew up to give him away. The digging was easy and very quick, although he did it soundlessly. Once in his shallow grave, he lay on his back and covered himself with sand and rocks. A clump of scrub grass broke the shape of his face, which rose higher than his body. The sand under the surface was cool and slightly moist.

An experienced Apache tracker might have spotted him when the sun rose. It was an old Apache trick, after all. More than one bewildered cavalryman had sworn Indians had disappeared and reappeared by magic out of the ground—and more than a few had lost their scalps because they had not seen it happen. But there were no Apaches among the infantry that day. The sergeant was not detected, and after the sun's heat had worked for less than half an hour, the moister sand around his hiding hole was baked as dry as the surrounding desert. He lay within a stone's throw of several hundred troops on the barren desert floor in the full light of day, invisible.

They looked for him in earnest. Reconnaissance patrols traced his path through their ranks with ease, each cluster of embarrassed, dyed, "dead" soldiers pointing like an arrow to the next kill. At the second line the path stopped. They patrolled between the second and third line repeatedly, looking for any sign that he had passed. More than once they walked within a few feet of where he lay. He heard them talking, cursing; heard their guesses as to where he had gone, how he had done it. He was no more apparent to them than a lizard under a rock—less so, because the lizard had to come out eventually to hunt. The sergeant had but to wait till nightfall.

But the sun accomplished what the soldiers could not. By

noon the temperature on the desert floor was 103 degrees. With only a thin covering of sand to protect him, the sergeant lay supine, absorbing the rays like a sunbather on a beach. The hole became an oven. Sweat dripped from his body and gathered in tiny puddles in the lower folds of his uniform. The sun streaked through his closed eyelids like a red flare. The sand over him became fiercely hot to the touch, each grain seeming to burn into his exposed skin like a glowing coal. The cloth of his camouflage uniform was sodden on the bottom where the sweat collected, baked to his skin on top. Still he did not move.

He tried to sleep to conserve energy, but the sun made it impossible. By midday he was no longer sweating. His throat was so dry it seemed to have sealed shut. His breathing became harsh and shallow, increasing in intensity until he was panting as his body tried desperately to cool itself. Suddenly he felt cold, he began to shiver, and the sergeant knew he was suffering from sunstroke and dehydration. It never occurred to him to quit.

In midafternoon, when the heat was at its worst, a mess truck toured the lines, distributing water and salt pills to the troops who were lying under sunscreens formed of ponchos and shelter halves. The truck halted at the foxhole nearest to Sergeant Stitzer, screening him from the men; he crawled under it and grabbed the spring suspension. When the truck drove off, it took Sergeant Stitzer with it.

From the rear area where the mess truck finally stopped, Sergeant Stitzer snaked his way to the edge of a bluff on which the temporary motor pool stood. Two feet down the slope, he found the opening to an abandoned coyote's den. One large boulder balanced on two others, forming a natural arch at the entrance. The sergeant squirmed in headfirst, his shoulders barely squeezing through the entrance. Inside the tiny cave, the feral scent of the desert wolf was overpowering. A pile of small bones littered one end where the bitch had fed her pups. The sergeant could see nothing, but he could feel the toothmarks on the bones as he ran his thumb across the jagged edges where they had been gnawed in two.

The coyote's cave was barely large enough for him to roll over, but it was cool, and because of the elevation off the desert floor, a slight breeze made its way past the entrance. The sergeant was thinking of backing out and turning around so his head would be in the breeze, when he heard the rumble of heavy engines above him. The trucks were on the move in the motor pool. One of them rolled directly over his head. A thin trickle of dirt sprinkled down on him. He felt a shifting in the earth, a strangled cry of anguish from the rocks. Too late he realized what was happening. Before he could scramble out backward, the damage was done. An armored personnel carrier had maneuvered too close to the edge of the bluff. The heavy treads tore at the earth over the sergeant's head, seeking purchase. The boulder that formed the arch of the entry was forced down. Twisting as it fell, the boulder wedged tightly in the entrance, sealing the cave.

Not a ray of light entered the sergeant's sudden tomb. The breeze stopped abruptly. The only sound he could hear was his own blood pounding in his ears.

Staff Sergeant Mark Stitzer, best of the elite corps, was buried alive two feet underground, trapped face down in a hole no wider than his shoulders. He would have had as much room in his coffin.

*Part Two*
*ESCAPE*

# Chapter 1
## 1984

NEW YORK STATE HIGHWAY 511 is a truncated slice of narrow asphalt that begins just beyond the town of Speculator, where a road sign suddenly proclaims that the local road leading from the town center is now, by official designation, a state thoroughfare. There is no increase in the size of the road. The same yellow stripe runs down the middle, the shoulders on either side still nudge timidly against the trees that crowd in. The only difference in the road is the sign, and not even that lasts for long. The highway meanders upward, into the Adirondacks, never making demands of the forest, taking the easiest route through the mountains, following contours. No tunnels were dug for 511, no bridges erected. It is a very timid road; it seems almost ashamed to be there in a landscape where all else is wild or raw. After a short run it peters out as inconspicuously as it began. A sign appears, announcing that the highway is now 511 and 513. Two miles later, another sign declares the road is State Highway 513. That is the last of 511.

The landscape along the length of 511 is deciduous forest, with piney woods asserting themselves at the higher elevation. There was once a logging industry there, but that yielded years ago to the more efficient practice of managed forestry in Georgia and the Pacific Northwest. The lumber industry was followed by a short-lived tourist industry in the days when the very wealthy would ride up from New York City in their private rail cars. The hotels are gone now, and most of the railroad track as well. When the rich summer people left, the area collapsed in upon itself. Here and there farmers still try in vain to wrest a living from a soil better suited to trees than crops. More of them go bankrupt every year, their farms lying idle, the buildings slowly rotting, broken and abandoned equipment turning orange with rust. A few scattered towns eke out a life-style of poverty. One hundred miles from Manhattan, it seems more like the Ozarks than New York.

But the forests surrounding Route 511 are a good place to hide. Deer hide there. There are reports of bear, an occasional claim of a mountain lion. Several packs of wild dogs, relics of the faded farms and the shrinking villages, roam beneath the oak and beech and maple. Geese and other wild fowl frequent Lake Pleasant.

A few miles past the lake a building lies hidden. It is euphemistically named the United States Army Pleasant Hospital. Pleasant Hospital is not a hospital, it is a mental institution—and it is certainly not pleasant. It is one of several places where the military conceals its mistakes.

The main building is a converted luxury hotel. Built in the 1900s, it is typical of the period, with carved balustrades on the sweeping front porch, dormer windows peering out from under sloping eaves, and a startling number of red brick chimneys. From the outside, it still looks very much like a nice place to spend a few days, warmly inviting in the turn-of-the-century manner. Inside it has been gutted and rebuilt. The interior decoration is of the government-issue variety—functional and uncomfortable. There is a heavy accent on bars, double locks, and steel mesh windows.

The lawn around the hospital is enormous, even larger than the original green verge on which the wealthy played croquet and lawn tennis and sauntered in the sun. The surrounding forest is kept rigidly at bay and the lawn is as free from obstruction—or hiding place—as a free-fire zone in a combat area. Anyone escaping from Pleasant Hospital has to make a very long dash across open ground before he hits the trees. Once within the trees he must scale a ten-foot high Cyclone fence topped with barbed wire. The fence is deliberately concealed by the trees so it will come as a surprise. It is one of several surprises in store for anyone trying to escape.

Carl Thorne approached Pleasant Hospital with the usual mix of depression and guilt. He came every thirty days, making the three-hour trip on the first Saturday of every month, more than sixty trips so far, and yet the feeling never changed. Only the first time had been different. It had seemed an idyllic setting then, and he was glad to see that his uncle was living in a place where gentle deer might be glimpsed timidly venturing out of the woods. He had not noticed the fingers sticking through the upper-story meshed windows like talons; he had not at first felt the weight of all those crazed malicious eyes. But then Carl had gone inside, and ever since then the surrounding woods had taken on the menace of a Grimm's fairy tale. Pleasant Hospital throbbed with foreboding in Carl's mind like a house from Poe.

There were two sets of watchers at Pleasant Hospital, Carl learned. The first were the inmates, staring out the windows with God-knew-what deliriums of violence. The second set were the firm-jawed men atop the roof on the flat widow's walk with a full 360-degree view of the surrounding lawn. They watched the watchers, their stun guns discreetly out of sight. How many of the firm-jawed men were there, Carl wondered, because of his uncle?

Long before he got there Carl felt the place calling to him like a silent scream. He had had too much to drink last night in anticipation. He would drink too much again tonight in an effort to forget.

Passing the guard at the gatehouse with a familiar nod, Carl kept his eyes on the driveway, not glancing up at the windows. He could feel their eyes on him anyway. As always, an involuntary shiver ran through his body.

He checked in at the registration desk and Dr. Michaelmas was sent for. Slack-mouthed, glassy-eyed men moved slowly by, dressed in pajamas and slippers, escorted by orderlies. Drugged to the brim, they walked like zombies, doing the Thorazine shuffle. These were not the dangerous men. They were "personality disorders" of an easily manageable type. Career-soldier alcoholics, full colonel kleptomaniacs, veteran amputees who had never adjusted to the loss of limb. Embarrassments to their families, they had disgraced the Army and themselves. This was the safe side of the hospital. It was at the end of the corridor, on the other side of the double steel doors, that madness crouched.

Dr. Michaelmas shambled toward him, a large, heavy, sad-eyed man dressed in a gray business suit. Every other employee at Pleasant Hospital wore the white medical smock; Michaelmas's suit was his own uniform, his mark of distinction.

"Mr. Thorne. How nice to see you again." He extended his big hand. The fingers were unusually short and wide and the palm was fleshy, broader by half than Carl's own. Carl thought of it as a paw rather than a human hand, and he had difficulty not staring at it. Self-consciously, the big man kept his hands tucked away in his pockets most of the time. Occasionally they would drift out, as if on errands of their own, looking rather lost and bewildered in the open air. Michaelmas would catch Carl's eyes wandering toward them and move them quickly out of sight once more.

A strangler would have hands like that, Carl thought. In another context he would not have made the comparison. It was Pleasant Hospital that forced such thoughts.

"How is he?" Carl asked.

"The same. Much the same. Very calm, very lucid." They walked toward the double steel doors.

"That is entirely to be expected, of course," the doctor continued. "Any change is most unlikely."

"I know."

"Most unlikely." They walked in silence. After so many visits, there was little left to say to each other. How strange, Carl thought. Over the last five years I have seen more of Michaelmas than I have most of my friends, and I know nothing about him. That was not altogether true. In the beginning Carl had made a point of finding out about Dr. Michaelmas, to assure himself that his uncle was getting the treatment he needed. He had made inquiries—and before long he had a picture of Dr. Michaelmas. A promising beginning, a degree with honors from Columbia Medical School, psychiatric education at Johns Hopkins, private practice, then a whiff of scandal, something vague, no charges filed, no records kept, no direct witnesses. Michaelmas had applied to and been accepted at Pleasant. Beyond those sketchy facts, Carl knew little else. What drove a man to immerse himself for ten years in this kind of bedlam? Carl thought of the peculiar hands, Michaelmas's compulsive hiding of them. In the end, it had been nothing more than another futile attempt to assuage his own guilt. Competent or not, Carl was stuck with Dr. Michaelmas. They both knew there wasn't a private therapist in the country who would come within twenty yards of Carl's uncle.

"I saw your article on the racehorse," Michaelmas said. Carl wrote by-lined features for a New York City tabloid. His newspaper had the largest circulation in the country; millions of people read everything he wrote—today's paper ran a story dealing with a three-year-old Thoroughbred filly that had broken its leg and been put away; he made it sound like high tragedy—and yet few readers admitted to anything beyond "I saw it." He had learned to take it as a compliment.

They stopped at the first steel door. Michaelmas looked at the closed-circuit television screen overhead. The screen showed the empty hallway of the restricted ward. Michaelmas waited patiently until the camera tilted slowly on its axis, revealing the space under it, immediately on the other side of the door. No one lurked there. Not until the machine had told him the corridor was clear did Michaelmas bother to crane his neck and look through the porthole-sized windows cut in the steel. The doctor unfastened two separate locks on the first door, swung it open, and he and Carl stepped into an alcove two feet wide. The heavy steel door swung closed behind them, the locks clicking automatically. Only then did Michaelmas unlock the second door.

The sound of the insane ward was always a shock, but one that faded quickly. There was something familiar about the angry mutterings, the terrified screams, the violent cursing. It was the stuff of horror movies, a staple of late-night television; the real thing seemed almost a caricature of the skilled artifice of films. And by now Carl had learned to save his fear for the men with intensely reasonable tones. The dramatically mad ones, the ones who shrieked and screamed, were dangerous mainly to themselves. It was the men who were in control who had to be feared.

It was the smell of the ward that he could never get used to. There was no preparation in the films for the stench of men for whom personal hygiene had long since lost all meaning. The fetor of human wastes and vomit was mixed with another odor, a high acrid stink that caused Carl's skin to crawl and the hairs on the backs of his hands to stand up. Michaelmas had explained to him long ago that it was the reek of fear, oozed out in sweat and breath by most of the inmates. Science would isolate the particular pheromone one day, Michaelmas had said. He seemed to think it mattered.

They could hear the sound of his uncle from a distance. The steady *thwonk thwonk thwonk* penetrated the other noises. Carl heard it as if someone had called his name in a crowd. Each cell had its own distinctive noise. A bellow of rage came from Corporal Rafe Campbell, an infantryman who had killed once too often then snapped, turning his M-16 on his own men and blazing away until he ran out of ammunition. From Major Michael Brent, who had shown up one day to inspect his battalion without his pants on, there came the impassioned grunts of masturbation. From others there were whimpers, pleas for help, or hatred-charged silence. From his uncle, there came the *thwonk, thwonk, thwonk*.

At the end of the corridor Carl and Michaelmas stopped outside the cell of Pleasant Hospital's star boarder. The hollow percussive sound stopped abruptly. He had heard them coming. Carl glanced at the closed-circuit screen over his uncle's door. He was the only man in the restricted ward who warranted his own private television camera. His uncle glanced up at the camera, then held up his hands, palms outward. Slowly he turned them, showing the backs, then, in a magician's gesture, feigned rolling up his sleeves. He was naked to the waist. With his hands still in front of him, he backed slowly away to the far wall and sat on the fold-down bench that was bolted to the wall. A brief look of contempt for the security procedure played over his features.

Michaelmas unlocked the outer steel door of the cell and swung it aside. A barred door inside the steel barrier remained closed. It always did.

"Hello, Uncle Mark," said Carl.

Staff Sergeant Mark Stitzer looked at his visitor.

"Hi, kid," he said.

Carl glanced around the room. His uncle's cell never changed. The bench on which he sat doubled as a bed. A table folded down from the side wall, where it served as a platform for the Ping-Pong games the sergeant played with himself, slapping the ball first with one hand then the other, his right hand versus his left, the ball moving with incredible speed, and the hands even faster. The ball rested on the table now; it would be replaced in two days. A pile of books was stacked neatly in a corner. They would be changed in five days. The sergeant read eight hours a day, one book per session, and the range of his interests was staggering—but then it was his only diversion after he had put in his eight hours of exercise.

In the early days, Michaelmas had given Stitzer a television set. Three days later the sergeant had managed to get the set to ignite. When two orderlies had come in to put out the fire, Stitzer had shattered the collarbone of one man and garroted the second with the television cord. Michaelmas had learned a great deal since then. Now Stitzer received his toilet paper in loose sheets—the cardboard roll could be used as a weapon. The sergeant ate with plastic cutlery, which was returned after every meal. His furnishings were limited to the bench/bed, bolted to the wall, the table, bolted to the wall, the books, the Ping-Pong ball, and a scrapbook, the contents of which were carefully clipped from the newspaper and presented to him one page at a time. No one was ever to step over the dotted yellow line that bisected the hallway, more than an arm's length from the door, unless Stitzer was seated on his bench at the far wall. It was a rule that had been forgotten only once. An orderly had slipped the dinner tray through the grille when Stitzer moved. The man was fast and had jumped back as soon as Stitzer lunged—it was almost soon enough. He had felt practically nothing, just a scratching sensation, and he actually had made it halfway to the double doors before he realized his carotid artery had been severed by the jagged edge of a broken plastic spoon. The man had survived. The surgeons considered him lucky. Michaelmas wondered if it was the sergeant's way of showing mercy. He could as easily have taken the man's eye.

Stitzer shifted his weight on the bench and Michaelmas moved back instinctively across the line. Stitzer smiled knowingly, mocking the doctor. His torso was drenched with sweat from his workout with the Ping-Pong ball. He was forty-four, but his physique looked like that of a man fifteen years younger. It was a gymnast's body, shoulders sloping away from the powerful neck, his chest flat, not bulging like a weight lifter's, the waist narrow, and the stomach rippling with muscles, each one etched in detail, like the midsection of a romanticized Greek sculpture. The body was not bunched and showy but lean and wiry, a blend of strength and agility. The body of a circus acrobat.

"Aunt Pauline sends her love," said Carl.

Stitzer looked back at him evenly, showing no response. Carl wondered if he even knew who Pauline was. He had shown as little reaction two years ago when informed that she had divorced him.

Carl tried again. "How's everything with you? The food all right?"

"He doesn't eat it," said Michaelmas.

"You've got to eat, Uncle Mark."

Stitzer chuckled silently, his head bobbing briefly down, then up. His scalp was bald, shaved to the skin every three

25

days by electric clippers that were plugged into an extension cord outside the cell. Carl could see the tiny brown birthmark in the shape of a leaping squirrel that rode the sergeant's hairline. As a child, Carl had been fascinated by it.

"It lives in the forest," his uncle would say, holding Carl on his lap. "It's very shy, but maybe it will come out for you." He would sweep his hair back with one hand, and the squirrel would appear as if by magic, suspended in mid-jump, half in and half out of his uncle's hair. Stitzer would wink at Carl's father.

"He likes you," Stitzer would say, laughing. When Stitzer carried him on his shoulders, whooping and leaping about the house, Carl would clamp his hands around his uncle's forehead, imagining he could feel the tiny squirrel, soft and furry against his palm.

"Mark, be careful!" Carl's mother would admonish. "You'll hurt him." Stitzer would rein in for a moment, humoring his sister, but his energy was too great to stay in check for long. Soon he would be bounding and whooping again.

"You're scaring him," Carl's father would say gently, intimidated himself by his wife's younger brother.

Stitzer would twist his head toward the youth on his shoulders, astounded at the suggestion.

"Am I scaring you, Carl?"

Timidly, frightened in a most delicious way, Carl would shake his head no.

"You see? He's not afraid of anything."

"All the same, let's let him rest for a while."

Carl's father would slip his hands into the soft pockets of his cardigan, rummaging by habit for the tobacco he had given up years earlier. So Carl would sit while his parents fussed around him, checking his temperature with hands pressed to his brow, listening for the first sign of labored, asthmatic breathing. He would sit quietly until the excitement passed, trying not to laugh aloud at the winks and comic faces his uncle sent his way when his parents' backs were turned.

You're scaring me now, Uncle Mark, Carl thought, looking into his glittering brown eyes.

"Is there anything you need?" Carl asked.

"How about a three-day pass, kid, can you arrange that?"

"He has what he wants," Michaelmas interjected. "His needs are few, his health is good, isn't that right, Sergeant?"

"How's *your* health, Doc?" Stitzer asked. Carl could feel Michaelmas suppress a shudder. Stitzer had not moved an inch, but somehow the force of his hatred seemed to leap across the cell. Carl had felt the same tremor of fear once in a zoo at a tiger's cage. The giant cat had appeared to be sleeping. It opened its eyes suddenly without moving its head, and the glower of malevolence had been there immediately, boring into Carl's eyes.

Carl spoke for a few minutes more, asking questions that were not answered, groping for words to fill the space between them. Stitzer sat, listening with interest, but saying nothing. His head was cocked to one side, eyes squinting, studying Carl. The younger man faltered. There was never a right thing to say. Stitzer seemed equally interested in everything or nothing. He was lucid, Carl knew he was lucid, but somehow he could never connect, he could never get his uncle to respond for more than a sentence. What constituted conversation for a madman? How did you exchange pleasantries with a man whose sole desire was to rip out your throat?

Carl struggled through several minutes, then ground to a halt. He felt exhausted.

"You're good, kid," said Stitzer suddenly. "You're a good copy, they did a good job with you."

"I'm not a copy, Uncle Mark. I really am Carl Thorne."

"I wish I could believe that."

"You can. I'm really your nephew."

"Really?"

"Yes. Yes!"

Michaelmas touched his elbow, a warning.

"You look so much like him."

"I *am* him, Uncle Mark. I'm Carl."

"Mr. Thorne," said Michaelmas.

"If only I could believe you."

"You *can* believe me."

"Mr. Thorne . . ."

"Wait a minute," Carl hissed, shrugging off Michaelmas's hand.

"What was your dog's name?" Stitzer asked.

"Skippy!"

"He's playing with you, Mr. Thorne."

"What kind of dog was he?"

"A schnauzer. Mostly schnauzer, anyway."

"His tail?"

"White. No, part white. It had a funny kind of streak near the tip."

"You could have seen that in a picture somewhere."

"Only Dad could make him heel, remember? I couldn't find that in a picture."

"I'm confused," said Stitzer. He pressed his hands to his temples.

"Don't let him do this to you, Mr. Thorne . . ."

"Will you get *away* . . . Uncle Mark, do you remember where he slept, remember where Skippy slept?"

Stitzer looked up, a smile slowly creasing his face.

"In the closet. In the goddamned hall closet!"

"Oh, Jesus. You're really him, you're really him!" Stitzer cried.

"Yes!"

Stitzer, smiling, held out his arms.

"No!" said Michaelmas.

"It's *me*. You *do* recognize me!"

Carl stepped toward the barred door, put his hand through.

"NO!"

"Carl! Carl!"

*"Get back!"*

Later, Carl could remember none of it. He had never seen him move. One second his uncle was seated on the bench, his arms outstretched in welcome, smiling; the next second Carl was pressed back against the wall, safely behind the yellow line with Michaelmas gripping him around the waist. Stitzer, still smiling, was standing at the barred door. If Michaelmas had not grabbed him before Stitzer started his move . . . The smile had looked so real. Warm and sincere. Only the tiger's eyes gave it away. Even after Michaelmas had swung the outer steel door closed, Carl could feel the weight of the eyes. The *thwonk, thwonk, thwonk* began again before they reached the end of the corridor.

"You mustn't blame yourself," Michaelmas said. "He can be very plausible. He fools me all the time."

The doctor splashed cologne on his huge hands, then patted it on his cheeks and neck. For the first few visits Carl had wondered at the habit until he realized that Michaelmas did it to cut the stink of the incurably insane.

"He didn't want to harm me," Carl said. "He didn't really try to hurt me."

Michaelmas looked at him in silence.

"Maybe he really did recognize me."

"As I say, you mustn't blame yourself."

A bank of monitors stood next to Michaelmas's desk. With a flick of the switch he could observe any area at Pleasant that was covered by a camera. The screen in the center showed Stitzer's cell. The sergeant was doing pushups, supporting the weight of his body on fingertips as strong as spikes.

Carl counted the pushups as his uncle's body moved up and down with the regularity of a piston. When the sergeant was nineteen and Carl was seven, Carl would count them aloud, jumbling the numbers, skipping some, getting lost over thirty. Stitzer could do over three hundred then. Doing them on fingertips was something new. Carl stopped counting after fifty.

He turned away from the screen to find Michaelmas studying him.

"What do you mean he's not eating?" Carl asked.

"He eats enough to stay healthy. Obviously. But he is very Spartan. He never eats a bit or drinks a drop beyond what he needs. Less than he needs, I would have thought, considering the energy he burns up, but then he clearly knows better than I." The doctor paused, his hands on his desk. When he saw Carl's eyes flicker toward them, he put them quickly in his lap.

"I asked him about it once. He told me about the Eskimos. It seems that when they used to live in the old way—before the skimobile and the government checks—they would have good years and bad ones, in biblical cycles, almost, but the cycles would last longer than the seven years which afflicted Pharaoh. Good years, when there was plenty of seal, plenty of whale, plenty of everything, would last for a long time. Often for longer than a generation. But the elders among the Eskimos would never allow their people to eat more than their near-starvation level. They would deliberately keep things as harsh as possible because they knew that sometime—even if not in their lifetimes—the lean years would return. I don't know if it's true, but your uncle says he read it. I believe him."

"You think he's keeping himself ready for hard times?"

"Yes, I do."

"What hard times? How can they get harder than what he's got now?"

"Mr. Thorne, your uncle does not have it hard. This is his home. You would do well to adjust to that."

"I've seen his home," said Carl. "I've lived in it with him. This is his jail."

Michaelmas paused, looking at the monitors. In the center screen Stitzer was doing tumbling exercises. With a bound he would cross the cell, take two steps up the wall, and flip over backward through the air, landing on his feet. Carl had seen Gene Kelly and Donald O'Connor do the same thing on a movie screen. His uncle had taken him to see those movies.

"I don't think of myself as a jailer," Michaelmas said at last.

"I'm sorry. I didn't mean it that way. I realize it can't be easy for you."

Michaelmas raised an eyebrow.

Carl swept a hand around the room, meaning all of Pleasant Hospital. "This. All this." Meaning exile. Meaning madness.

The doctor shrugged, keeping his hands below the desk. "Well."

"What hard times do you think he's preparing for?"

"I don't know. A mission of some kind. That's what he was trained for, wasn't it? Missions of some kind?"

He glanced again at the screen.

"He's still in training."

"You think he intends to escape?"

"Of course."

"Why?"

"Because he's never really tried."

"He's nearly killed three men."

"Mr. Thorne, your uncle was buried alive for three days without food or water or light. He drank his own urine. He dug himself out using sheep bones that were in his cave . . ."

"I know."

". . . and when he had worn the bones to nothing, he used his fingers. The plastic surgeons at Walter Reed are very proud of the work they did on his fingers. After he dug himself out he still had strength enough to attack and nearly kill three soldiers who were trying to locate him. He did kill two dogs they were using to track his scent. German shepherds."

"I was never told about the dogs."

"Possibly because they didn't want you to know the way he killed them. That was a wolves' den he had been buried in. He began to identify with the wolf. He still does."

"A coyote . . ."

"A coyote is a wolf. He attacked those men because he thought they were the 'enemy' trying to keep him from completing his mission. He still thinks that. You heard him today. He thinks you're a copy. He thinks we're all copies of one sort or another, frauds, joined in a giant deception to make him give up. He thinks he's behind enemy lines right now. Attacking a few orderlies is not the kind of escape effort I would expect from a man like that. Would you? I think he's biding his time, the other incidents were just exercises. He was testing the bars of his cage."

"You really think he's going to escape?"

"No," said Michaelmas. He looked again at the monitor. Stitzer was lying on the floor on his back. He gave the appearance of being completely at rest. With a sudden convulsive jerk his back arched, his knees jackknifed toward his chest, and he was on his feet. His hands never touched the ground.

"But I certainly think he's going to try," Michaelmas continued.

"What's he waiting for then?"

"I don't have any idea, Mr. Thorne."

Both men fell silent as they watched the monitor. Stitzer lay down again. He could have been asleep. Suddenly he was on his feet. He lay down once more. Then up. Carl tried to see him preparing, tried to find some movement that would serve as a warning. If there was any, he could not detect it. It reminded him of nature documentaries he had seen showing the strike of a praying mantis. One moment the mantis was still, the next it was devouring its victim.

When they looked away from the screen again, neither man had anything left to say. Carl Thorne went home.

# Chapter 2

CARL DROVE FROM PLEASANT Hospital directly to Boylan's, a bar at Forty-second Street and Lexington Avenue on Manhattan's East Side, which was frequented by reporters from his newspaper. Carl seldom went to bars, seldom drank, but he drank after his visits to Pleasant, and he welcomed the company of his colleagues. He did not want to be alone.

Later in the evening he called Marissa.

She was as tall as he, which had been disquieting when he first met her. He was used to leaning down to kiss, bending the woman backward slightly in his arms. It was, he felt, a masculine approach. But with Marissa, if he tried to bend her backward their knees collided. She hung there, awkwardly, trying to accommodate him, until she began to giggle.

"You've been drinking," she said when she met him at the door of her apartment.

"Yes. A few."

"You've been to see your uncle again?"

He moved past her, into the apartment. He was struck again by her size. She was a dancer, and he pitied her partners.

"You don't have to see him every month, Carl. There's no law."

"There's a law." He sat heavily on the sofa. She would have to pick at him before they made love, and the prospect wearied him.

"If he makes you feel so guilty, why do you do it? You look like you've been wrung out. I don't know why you put yourself through it."

Carl shrugged. "Duty."

"Duty is a very outmoded concept. Our duty is to ourselves."

"You're probably right."

"You know I'm right. You only say things like 'duty' because you're a Presbyterian."

"I'm not a Presbyterian. I'm an agnostic."

"You were born a Presbyterian," she said. Marissa believed that religion was a matter of birth and heredity, not faith. Although she could explain anyone else's actions according to this theology, she was vague about her own religious beliefs. Carl suspected she worshiped the Dance.

"I was born a baby," he said.

"The Protestant ethic is dead," she said, sitting next to him and stretching out her legs. They seemed to stretch halfway across the room. A dancer's legs, they were lean yet muscular, with the tensile strength of a cured oak barrel stave. When she wrapped them around his neck, he silently prayed for mercy.

"I do it for love, then," he said.

Marissa snorted. She did not believe in love, except between parent and child. She believed in sex. She believed in pair bonding. She believed, if pressed, in companionship. She thought love was an inaccurate description of emotional distress, mostly guilt. She accused Carl of being sentimental.

"You only come to see me when you've been drinking," she said.

"That's not true. I *always* come to see you when I've been drinking, but I come other times, too."

"Only when you're in need of something."

"I'm *always* in need of something," said Carl.

"You just want the sex."

"I want the sex," Carl agreed. "I need a lot more."

He fluffed her hair, spreading it on her shoulders. Most of the day she wore it in the tight dancer's bun that gave her face such a severe look. When he saw her that way, the skin of her face seemingly stretched taut by the tension of the bun, feet splayed to the side, hands defiantly on her hips, he thought she was another person. She looked not so much like a dancer as Dancer, stepped out of a poster. He was secretly pleased that she was a dancer. Although no balletomane, he liked the paraphernalia. He liked the silly, formal tutus for performance, but he also liked the heavy hip-length woolen leg warmers she wore to practice, the sleek leotard that emphasized the sharpness of her hipbones and showed her nipples while pressing her breasts into spreading mounds. He found her exercises erotic. The long, unlikely stretch of her leg over her head, the chilling ease with which she slid into a full split; the sweat, the effort, the maintenance of exquisite control despite the contortions and the exertion. Invariably it made him think of what she might be capable of in bed. Long after he had explored her limits there, he continued to fantasize when he saw her working. He liked what she did, on stage and off; if he did not like *her* better, it was not from want of trying.

With her hair down she assumed a gentler look, and Carl's attitude toward her softened. She let him carry her to the bed. He tried to do it without straining, remembering the seeming ease with which her partners toted her on stage. Even though he knew the real strength of those lean young men, he did not relish appearing less robust than a male dancer. He put her on the bed, dropping her the last few inches. She reached up her arms, and he suddenly thought of his uncle's image on the monitor, convulsing upward from his back to his feet like a spring let loose.

The orderly studied the monitor above Stitzer's door and watched the sergeant play Ping-Pong against himself. The orderly, whose name was Coombs, was amazed at the speed of the man. What would those hands do to you if they had a weapon in them, he thought. He rapped once on the steel door and watched Stitzer's image on the screen walk to the bench and sit down. Coombs unlocked the heavy outer door and swung it open, his eyes still on the screen. Coombs was new to Pleasant Hospital, but Dr. Michaelmas had briefed him long enough to be sure he was properly afraid before allowing him to go near the restricted ward. As always, Stitzer had merited a separate lecture.

Now watching the sergeant through the barred door, Coombs slipped a newspaper clipping through the grille. He stood behind the yellow line while Stitzer retrieved it.

"What is that, another story by your nephew?" Coombs had started to read it but found his attention wandering. Something about a horse. Coombs did not read much.

Stitzer smiled at him. "My *real* nephew."

Coombs nodded. He had no idea what a real nephew was, but the other man seemed so reasonable that Coombs wondered if the fat doctor knew what he was talking about. This one wasn't howling at the moon, at least. He wasn't cursing or ripping at the walls or pounding his pud. What made him so dangerous?

Coombs pulled the dinner cart closer. The sergeant was standing by the bench, his back to Coombs, reading the clipping. The orderly picked a food tray from the cart.

"You've got your foot over the line there, Coombs," Stitzer said without turning.

Coombs looked down at his feet. The toes were four inches beyond the yellow line. Stitzer was not looking at him. Coombs did not think he ever had. He quickly backed away from the line.

"Technically you're not supposed to be over the line unless I'm sitting down," Stitzer said. He put the clipping on the bench, turned to face Coombs, and sat down. He smiled. "Michaelmas can see you on the hall camera. It doesn't matter to me, but I wouldn't want you to get in trouble."

"Thanks," said Coombs.

"Silly rule, but you don't want to lose your job. Jobs are hard to come by these days, I understand."

"That's for sure," Coombs said. He held the tray uncertainly in his hands. Was he permitted to cross the line if the sergeant was talking?

"Did you have trouble getting *this* job, Coombs?"

"Some," Coombs admitted.

Stitzer nodded sadly. "I had a man like you in my platoon in the Nam. Best damned man in the platoon. Smart, brave, loyal. Do anything for a friend, and the last man you'd want for an enemy."

Coombs bobbed his head unconsciously. It seemed a fair comparison.

"But for some reason none of the top brass appreciated him. He wasn't articulate, Coombs, you know what I mean? He didn't have a whole lot to say unless it was really important, but that didn't mean he wasn't thinking. That man was thinking all the time. But you had to get to know him to realize he was a lot smarter than he seemed."

That's for *damn* sure, Coombs thought.

"What happened to him?" he asked.

Stitzer turned his head to one side, as if having trouble following the train of thought.

38

"What happened to the guy who was like me? You said he was in—uh . . ."

"The Nam."

"Yeah, in the Nam."

Stitzer smiled. "I saw to it he finally got what he deserved," he said. "You want that banana, Coombs? You're welcome to it. I'm not going to eat it."

With a quick glance at the camera at the end of the hallway, Coombs slipped the fruit from Stitzer's tray into his pocket.

"The cupcake, too," said Stitzer.

Coombs hesitated.

"Go ahead. Give it to your wife. Otherwise the kitchen staff will take it home."

"I don't have a wife," said Coombs. He felt a quick wave of self-pity.

"She left you? Jee-sus. Women don't appreciate a good man when they have one."

"That's for *damn* sure," Coombs agreed. Actually, he had been glad to get rid of her, she was always wanting something from him, but it sounded better the way the sergeant put it. Abandoned and unappreciated. That pretty well summed him up, he thought.

Coombs slid the tray through the door, palming the cupcake as he did so.

"You can give it to your dog or cat," Stitzer said.

"I got dogs," Coombs said. "But I don't feed 'em *cupcakes.*" The idea amused him and he chortled.

Stitzer laughed with him. "A couple dogs will eat a lot," said Stitzer. "Especially a good-sized one, like a terrier."

Coombs snickered. "Shee-it. A terrier? I got six *hounds.* Eat a lot? Shee-it!"

When Coombs wheeled the tray away it was with a growing feeling of injustice. The sergeant might be crazy, but Coombs had never known him to show anything but respect, interest, and a keen judgment of character.

Damned if he could say as much for anybody else around here. Especially the staff. Especially that toad Dr. Michaelmas.

When Coombs was gone, Stitzer sat on his bench and reread the column with Carl Thorne's by-line at the top. He read it slowly, careful to let his face reveal no emotion. He was always aware of the watching camera and tried never to show excitement of any kind. It was hard; he thought of himself as an emotional man, but he dared not give them anything to use against him. He was close enough to cracking as it was. He felt himself teetering toward the precipice every day. It would only take a push and he would topple over, tell them everything, give in. Give up. But he maintained the facade of strength and they never pushed him that little extra bit.

Being careful to give no sign that this clipping was any different from the others, he placed it in his scrapbook. He went back to the Ping-Pong. It was important to maintain the regular schedule. He could begin to review his plans when he began his study period. The plans had been completed long since, of course, but he would run through it all again one more time. He had just thought of an interesting variation. By dinnertime tomorrow he would begin. By the time the other inmates were smearing their desserts on the walls, he would be gone.

Marissa stopped shuddering, the tension in her powerful legs relaxed. Carl rolled off of her. By the time he was lying back he was no longer thinking of her.

"What are you thinking about?" she asked a few minutes later, her voice dreamy.

"You," he said automatically.

She rubbed her foot against his under the covers. She had a dancer's feet, ugly, misshapen from the toe work, flattened by the years of leaping. The torture of her discipline showed only in her feet. A long ridge of callus beneath her toes rasped against his instep.

"No, you're not," she said evenly. "Are you brooding again? You look like you're brooding."

He had been twelve years old again, his parents suddenly dead, together, at once; coming back from the movies while Carl awaited them at home, proudly, his first time of babysitting for himself at night. He waited until the police came and told him he must wait forever. A truck, the police had said, trying to beat a stoplight at the bottom of the hill. No pain, they assured him. No pain involved. They did not mention Carl's pain. Then, three days later, baffled even more than grieving, Carl at home following the funeral. Solicitous neighbors gone, the empty house resonant with the voices of those no longer there; the door opened, no knock, no ring. His uncle stood there, Green Beret tipped rakishly on one side of his head, OD trousers bloused into the tops of shining boots, looking ready to storm the citadel, leap from a plane, fight a war. Not at all ready to become an instant father.

"Hi, kid," he had said. Carl had burst into tears for the first time since his parents died.

"You like guilt, don't you, Carl?" Marissa asked.

"No. But I'm big on gratitude," he said.

"It's not your fault your uncle is in that place."

"No."

"And it's not your fault that you can't get him out."

"No."

"You've got to get used to it eventually," she said.

"That's what I'm afraid of," Carl replied.

Stitzer sat perfectly still, extracting the last benefit of relaxation. After the next few minutes he would have no real rest for a very long time. The Ping-Pong ball was in his hand, out of sight of the camera. In the hallway, the dinner cart was stopping outside the third cell. That would be Brent. The jack-off king, Coombs called him. The next stop would be Campbell, who would howl when Coombs approached his door. Stitzer knew them only by their sounds, but he could track their moods the way a wolf, crouched in silence, can tell the presence of his prey by the scrape of fur against leaf. Brent was worse today, more imploring. They must have jacketed him again, giving his abused member a chance to heal. Campbell was calmer. Not calm, he was never calm, but calmer than usual.

Stitzer took a deep breath and prepared himself. Everything was ready, his body, his mind. His only fear was the gag reflex, but he had worked on that as much as possible, practicing at night under the covers, his back to the camera.

Coombs unlocked the solid door and swung it away. Stitzer smiled warmly.

"How you doing, Coombs?"

Coombs grunted and gave the sergeant a nod. He did not want to get *too* friendly; it was better to stay a bit aloof so the man remembered who was in command.

"Want the pear?" Stitzer asked.

Coombs slipped it quickly into his pocket, then put the tray through the door. He was supposed to stay to watch the sergeant eat, then retrieve the tray and plastic spoon immediately. Coombs did not mind. The sergeant never took very long at his meals. The other inmates ate like children, whimsically, devouring everything or nothing, smearing the remnants about like finger paints. The sergeant was neat, clean, abstemious. Coombs approved.

When the orderly had backed safely beyond the yellow line, Stitzer took the tray to his table. He lifted a spoonful of mashed potatoes to his mouth and swiftly pushed the Ping-Pong ball back deep into his throat.

Stitzer stood up violently, clutching at his neck. Choking, he stuck fingers in his mouth. Coombs watched as the sergeant struggled. Mashed potatoes fell from his open mouth and onto his chin. He staggered, lurching into the table. Coombs glanced at the camera at the end of the hall, wondering if Michaelmas was watching. Shouldn't someone *do* something?

Stitzer was pounding himself on the back of the head, trying to dislodge something. Coombs could see he was choking. He needs that thing, Coombs thought. That thing where you squeeze the guy from behind and he coughs up whatever's choking him. Coombs had seen it done on television many times. It looked simple. He took a step over the yellow line, then quickly pulled his foot back, looking at the camera. Stitzer fell to the floor, still struggling as if locked in the embrace of an invisible giant who was crushing him to death.

"Hey!" Coombs yelled. He was not sure whom he was yelling to. No one could hear him through the double steel doors.

Stitzer's thrashing lessened. He was growing weaker, Coombs could see that. For Christ's sake, the guy's face was turning purple!

"Hey!" Coombs yelled again. He waved his arms at the camera, pointed into Stitzer's cell. "He's purple!" Coombs yelled.

In Michaelmas's office the images of Stitzer and Coombs were jerking on adjoining monitor screens. Coombs mouthed something to the camera, pointing toward the doctor's desk. The sergeant was out of sequence on the monitor. He appeared to be behind Coombs's back. He was lying flat on the floor, barely twitching.

Michaelmas looked up from his desk, glancing at the monitors. He saw Coombs's frantic waving first, then Stitzer. He saw Coombs touch the keys at his waist.

Stop, Michaelmas thought.

Coombs fumbled with the keys.

Stop!

Coombs stepped across the yellow line.

"Don't do it!" Michaelmas yelled aloud. He ran from his office, knowing he was already too late.

Coombs swung open the barred door. Stitzer was inert, his eyes half-open but unseeing, his face the color of a plum. Nobody can hold his breath that long, Coombs thought. No way he could be faking.

Coombs jerked Stitzer to his feet, put his arms around his midsection and jerked. He heard a single sharp cough, saw a Ping-Pong ball bounce on the floor, felt a hand grip his neck. The hand was squeezing, so hard Coombs thought maybe someone had slipped a noose around him. Coombs's eyelids fluttered, he saw the room swim in front of him, thought to himself this is very strange. He was unconscious by the time the karate chop cracked his collarbone and he slumped to the floor.

Michaelmas managed to get one guard to the double doors in time to see Stitzer running toward the camera. The sergeant leaped into the air and the monitor over the double doors went blank. The guard took up his position with the stun gun ten feet back, so the door would not impede his fire when it opened. Neither the guard nor Michaelmas considered going in after Stitzer. They knew he would be coming to them.

The wait surprised them. The guard looked toward the doctor, puzzled, shifting the gun on his hip. The stun gun was fat and squat with a truncated barrel. It looked more like a grenade launcher than a rifle. Designed to fire three electrically charged darts connected to the weapon by long wires, the stun guns had been adapted for Pleasant Hospital to fire six.

Michaelmas was not prepared when the door crashed open and all the inmates of the insane ward surged forward. The guard fired, and the first dart slapped into Corporal Rafe Campbell, who led the charge howling with rage. He twitched and fell; Major Brent, still in his straitjacket, leaped over the body, looking more bewildered than angry.

The second dart hit one of the jacket straps and bounced off. The guard retreated and fired again at Brent's legs. Brent kept coming for three steps, propelled by the bodies behind him.

Michaelmas vaulted a stairway railing, landing awkwardly on the stairs. He twisted his ankle but he was out of the way as the charge swelled past. He caught a glimpse of Stitzer, crouched low, herding the inmates in front of him like a cowboy taking cover behind a stampede of cattle.

A second guard arrived in time to fire two darts before the stampede bore him down. Four inmates burst from the doors of Pleasant Hospital.

Stitzer ran to the south where the lawn was the narrowest. One of the inmates followed him but was soon left behind, panting, as Stitzer sprinted away. The third inmate stopped, stunned by the open sky, the air. He stood there, bewildered and frightened by the freedom, until the guards reclaimed him. The fourth inmate was stopped by the fence. They caught him within two minutes, still staggered by the electrical charge in the barrier.

Stitzer made the trees with ease. When he saw the fence he veered to his right, leaped to catch the lowest branch of a maple, and scampered up the tree like a squirrel in flight. The trees had been barbered carefully. All limbs that came within three feet of touching the wire and causing a short circuit had been lopped off. Stitzer paused for just a second, finding the branch he needed. It was four feet higher than the barbed wire topping the fence and another five feet back from it. A large branch, capable of holding his weight easily, it was still supple enough to provide some spring. Stitzer backed up two steps, then moved forward, leaping up and out like a diver from a springboard. He cleared the barbed wire horizontally before tucking and flipping into a somersault that brought him to the ground on his feet. He rolled on his shoulder to break the fall, then vanished into the trees.

After the initial shock, Michaelmas responded efficiently. The two dog patrols were out and searching within ten minutes. It was a fast reaction, as fast as they had ever managed in a practice exercise. Michaelmas knew he would look all right when he filed the report; he would make a good showing on paper. He also had a good idea of what a man like Stitzer could do with a ten-minute lead.

The sergeant headed straight for the lake. The dogs did not worry him as long as the handlers had them leashed. If the big Alsatians had to tug a man along behind them, they would never catch a healthy runner who knew where he was going. The only peril would come if the handlers let the dogs run free. If they did it soon enough, they might catch him before he hit the water. Stitzer didn't fear the dogs; he knew he could kill them easily enough, but they would slow him down. He did not expect them to unleash the dogs, however; that was not military procedure.

Stitzer ran, an easy, steady lope that would maintain his head start without taxing him in the slightest. He could run this way for hours, had done so many times in his cell, trotting in place while in his mind calculating how far he had gone. After one hour he would be eleven miles away from the hospital; an hour and a half would see him passing through the streets of Speculator, heading for the main highway. He was not running on a highway now, of course, but if the underbrush and uneven terrain slowed him down, it hampered his pursuers as well.

He removed his pajama shirt and tucked it in the crotch of a tree, as high as he could jump. Half a mile farther he put his pajama bottoms under a rock. Running naked, he stopped when he could smell the lake. The sound of the guards was faint and far away when he urinated in a wide circle, marking trees and bushes like a wolf staking its territory. He did it as much to discredit the dogs as to delay them. They would howl at the pajama tops as if they had treed a raccoon, then dig like hogs after a truffle for the bottoms under the rock. When they hit the ring of urine, they would circle crazily, sniffing and barking at the scent, until their handlers hauled them off. If, later, the dogs found any of his trail, Stitzer knew the annoyed guards would be far less inclined to believe them.

Finding a boat was almost too simple. They were scattered along the shore with the implicit trust of a region where no one stole because there was so little worth taking. Stitzer untied the first skiff he came to. There were no oars, so he tied the rope around his waist in a quick loop and swam into the lake, pulling the boat behind him.

The water was incredibly luxurious. For five years Stitzer had been allowed only sponge baths because Michaelmas did not trust him to pass through the corridors to and from the showers. He had forgotten the weight of water against his body, the sensuousness of being bathed with it everywhere, all at once.

He swam with an easy but efficient pace, as he had run. Halfway across the lake he untied the rope from his waist. Diving under, he came up with both hands beneath the keel as he scissored his legs sharply. The skiff rose into the air, tipped, then fell back upside down. Stitzer swam faster now, pulling away from the boat, his wake forming a rapidly fading crescent. As he reached the shore half a mile from where he had entered the water, he could hear the dogs barking madly at the circle of urine. He was well into the woods before the first handler emerged and saw the capsized rowboat halfway across the lake. The guards assumed, as Stitzer intended, that the sergeant had been heading across the lake when the boat tipped over. They would try the far side first before dragging the lake in search of his body. They would not get to the point where Stitzer had left the lake until the next day, and by then his scent, already faint because of the bath, would be too weak for even the dogs to be sure.

Their voices carried over the water as if amplified. Even

as he hurried away he could hear them shouting to each other. Their voices diminished as they made their way around to the other side of the lake, away from Stitzer. They had taken the bait, and the sergeant was free.

Alone and unwatched for the first time in half a decade, Stitzer began to cry with relief and joy. He stood in the forest, his hands over his face, muffling the sobs. He was laughing as he wept, the higher pitched sounds of happiness mixed with the heavy sobs. His eyes still wet with tears, he started running again. He knew that he had a long way to go before he reached safety, but now he knew, at long last, that he would make it.

*Chapter 3*

"YOU CRIED OUT AGAIN," said Carl. Marissa shifted her weight against him in the bed, cuddling. She was too thin to cuddle well, she seemed to have no flesh at all on her hipbones. Thorne worried that someday she would break through the skin and he would be held responsible.

"Did I?"

"Yes." She cried out frequently when they made love. She was a very vocal sex partner, which she claimed was because she was uninhibited. Carl suspected it was overcompensation of some sort. He liked spontaneity and energy, but he would have gotten along without the yelling; he found it distracting. Whenever she moaned his name, he was inclined to ask, "What?" When she called out someone else's name, he found it even more dismaying. Tonight she had been crying out for her last boyfriend, once removed. Carl did not know if she did it unconsciously or to punish him for his inattentiveness. He had asked her once and she had vehemently denied it, so he had not pursued the matter.

The telephone rang and he groped for it. His voice was thick with apprehension when he said hello. He was never sure whether he should feel smug or embarrassed when discovered in bed with a woman—even by telephone—so he erred on the side of safety by acting guilty.

"Mr. Carl Thorne?"

Carl resisted an urge to deny it. He thought he recognized the voice.

"Yes."

"Mr. Thorne, this is Dr. Michaelmas at Pleasant Hospital."

"Yes?" Carl felt his throat tighten, his stomach lurch. He's dead, he thought. In the instant before Michaelmas could draw breath and speak again, Carl's mind raced through possibilities: heart attack; hanging by using his own pajamas as a noose; bleeding to death, his wrist gnawed through in fierce determination. My fault, he thought. My fault. I couldn't reach him. I quit trying.

"Your uncle is missing," said Michaelmas.

"Missing? How could he be missing?"

"He escaped, Mr. Thorne. We haven't found him yet. That makes him missing."

"Yes, I see." As if to clarify everything, Carl turned on the lamp on his bedside table. He squinted against the sudden illumination. Marissa groaned and pulled the sheet over her head.

"What can I do?"

"We'd like very much to talk to you," said Michaelmas. "We feel you may be able to help us locate your uncle."

"Yes," said Carl. He had no idea what the man meant.

"Could you come up to Pleasant to confer with us?"

"Of course. I can drive up in about three hours."

"There's a helicopter waiting for you at the heliport," said Michaelmas.

"A helicopter?"

"Do you know the heliport on the Hudson?"

"Certainly. I can be there in fifteen minutes."

"Good. Thank you, Mr. Thorne."

Only after the line was dead did all the questions come to mind, but Carl knew they would answer them soon enough. At least those they chose to answer. He wondered who "they" were, but he knew instinctively they existed. Michaelmas did not send helicopters on his own authority.

For most of the trip, the helicopter pilot dispensed with the need for navigation and simply followed the New York State Thruway north. Carl could follow their progress by watching the shadow of the craft on the ground as it swept with indifference over cars, houses, people. When they encountered a tall building, the shadow would elongate and climb the structure like a formless amoeba oozing past in fast motion. Just beyond Speculator the pilot veered sharply left until he could see the tip of Lake Pleasant. They shot across the lake while their shadow stayed ashore, keeping pace on dry land, bucking along the tree trunks like a wagon on a corduroy road.

"Down there," said the pilot, his words sounding strangely distant in Carl's earphones although the man sat beside him. The voice startled Carl. It was the first time the pilot had spoken.

On the lake below, several small motorboats surrounded an overturned skiff. The pilot hovered for a moment and Carl saw a man in scuba gear surface, remove his mask, and say something, gesticulating with one hand while clinging to the side of the boat with the other. The pilot was watching Carl closely. Carl glanced at him, then nodded. He had no idea what he was expected to say. The men on the lake never looked up.

The copter darted forward again, over the lake, then over the forest. From this height it looked to Carl like the scalp of a man with thinning hair. Impenetrably thick to the eye at ground level, from above the trees gaps showed in the canopy. The forest was not a jungle after all. The battle for space and sunlight was not as savage as it seemed when one was in the woods. Birds scattered from the trees as they approached, terrified by the noise, struggling against concussive blasts of the propwash. Carl imagined his uncle, also terrified, crouching as the copter passed overhead, digging himself into the humus-thick soil like an animal. But it didn't fit. He could not think of Sergeant Mark Stitzer as terrified, ever, by anything.

They landed on the lawn of Pleasant Hospital. Sucked from the ground, tiny darts with immensely long, thin wire tails danced grotesquely in turbulent wash like mutant wasps. Michaelmas gathered up one of the stun gun projectiles in his huge hands and carried it back toward the hospital with Carl, calmly winding the wire around his doubled arm like a cowboy looping his lasso.

After two hours had elapsed and Stitzer had not been found, Michaelmas had followed the established procedure and notified both military intelligence and the FBI. They would decide later when, indeed if, the local police authorities should be alerted.

The two agents waited now in Michaelmas's office. Neither man looked like what he was. Tony Capello was of average height, but his stout frame made him seem shorter. His face lit up as if meeting a long-lost friend when Carl entered.

"I'm Special Agent Tony Capello," he said, beaming, advancing on Carl as if eager to embrace him. "How was your flight? Have you ever been up in one of those little military jobs? Like riding a kite in a high wind, isn't it? *Ffwwoop, ffwwoop, ffwwoop!* Next time I'm going to just send my stomach on ahead of time by rail and pick it up when I arrive."

Carl struggled to think if he should know this man. It seemed as if a reunion of some kind were taking place and

Carl had been invited by mistake. Capello was bursting with hair trying to get out of his body. Black tendrils squeezed from under his collar, curled from his earlobes, the insides of his ears, as if straining toward the sunlight from the brain itself.

Another man stood by Michaelmas's desk, studying the television monitors. He was dressed like a Virginia squire in a smoking jacket of Harris tweed, pale corduroy trousers, riding boots of deep sorrel, polished and buffed until they seemed to glow from within. He looked as if he had outfitted himself in imitation of a catalogue mannequin; none of the clothes had anything to do with the man. He seemed a farmer at a masquerade; not a gentleman farmer, a hardworking laborer. His neck had a reddish raw look to it, as if a dull razor had just scraped it clean, and his ears made Carl think of a dog, a Doberman pup, before its ears were cropped.

The man glanced briefly at Carl, then returned his attention to the screens. There was no activity whatever on the monitors. The hospital was holding its breath.

"Well, sit down, get your equilibrium back," said Capello. "How you feel?"

"I'm all right," Carl said.

"It always takes me a little while for the inner ear to settle down. You must be a good sailor." Carl could sense the agent's reluctance to begin. He imagined Capello was a diplomat among FBI men, someone who specialized in entertaining congressmen, cajoling important witnesses.

"What about my uncle?" Carl asked. He looked first for Michaelmas, but the doctor had taken a place in the far corner, near the window, as if removing himself.

"Well, now, that's the thing," said Capello. "What about your uncle?" He smiled, rubbing his hands together.

"Have you found him yet?"

"Ah, no," said Capello. "But we are following a

53

number of leads at this time . . ." He stopped, interrupted himself with a chuckle. "That's my public relations pose. Sorry, Mr. Thorne. The truth is, we don't have any leads."

"Did he drown?"

"Why do you ask?"

"I saw the divers in the lake."

"Yes, well, he did apparently steal the boat and capsize it in the middle of the lake. It's possible he drowned."

"He didn't drown," said the man watching the monitors.

"Which is one point of view," said Capello lightly. "All points of view are welcome. As I say, he may have drowned. We'll never know that for sure unless we discover that he did not, if you follow me. That is a very deep lake."

"Sergeant Stitzer is not about to drown in a calm lake in the middle of the day unless he's got an anchor around his neck."

Carl looked at the man. He sounded angry, as if the thought of Stitzer drowning were a personal affront. He kept his back to Carl, who wondered what could be so interesting on the screens where nothing seemed to move.

"Chances are that is true," said Capello. "I wouldn't worry, Mr. Thorne. Your uncle may be dead, but I doubt it."

"We'd all be better off if he was." The angry man turned, looked directly at Carl. There was no trace of apology in his face. "No offense," he said.

"I do take offense. Who the hell are you?"

"Stroup," he said.

"Major Stroup," said Capello, "of the . . ." His voice trailed off.

"I'm retired," said Stroup.

"He was your uncle's commanding officer."

"I was a lot of things I'm not anymore. Let's get on with this, Capello."

Michaelmas continued to stare out the window, straining to be out of it.

Capello arched his eyebrows, enlisting Carl in a conspiracy of good humor against Stroup's anger.

"Well, now," he said, again rubbing his hands, "what we need from you, Mr. Thorne, is some suggestion as to where your uncle might be heading."

"I haven't any idea."

"Before you say that, let's just think for a minute. Dr. Michaelmas tells me you visited him regularly, once a month. You knew him well."

"I knew him well before the accident. He raised me from the age of twelve when my parents died. I knew him well then. I didn't know him at all after the accident. He didn't even think I was his nephew anymore. He thought I was an imposter of some kind."

"The enemy," said Michaelmas, turning from the window.

"The enemy. He thought we were all the enemy. He thought everyone was conducting some sort of elaborate charade to . . . I don't know, get him to relax his guard, get him to tell his secrets. I don't know what he thought exactly."

"What secrets did he have?"

"I haven't any idea."

"I told you," said Stroup. "I told you what he's thinking, I told you what he's going to do. What are you going to do about it?"

Capello beamed. "Thank you, Major Stroup."

"Just Stroup."

Capello turned away from Stroup and, surprisingly, winked at Carl. Humor him, his expression said, but pay no serious attention. "The major has his theories and I have mine. There's room for more, I daresay. Now, Mr. Thorne, did your uncle ever mention going anywhere when he got out? Anything that seemed to be on his mind?"

"No. Nothing. He scarcely spoke. He seemed to be amused by me, that was about it. He would say encouraging things once in a while. Good job, kid. Things like that. He never believed I was his nephew.''

''Most escaped convicts—not that your uncle is a convict —usually go home. They're not that hard to find because sooner or later they go home.''

Stroup made a noise that might have been a laugh. ''Stitzer isn't the homesick type.''

''Where would home be, for your uncle? With his wife?'' Capello smiled encouragingly at Carl. Tiny dark hairs bristled in his nostrils. Carl had a fleeting thought of a fur coat turned inside out and all the fur struggling to get back outside.

''His wife hasn't even seen him in three years.''

''Oh yes?''

''It was too painful for her. She divorced him.''

''Yes. And was it painful for him?''

''Not that I could tell,'' volunteered Michaelmas. ''He didn't recognize her either.''

''So she just stopped coming?''

''We discussed it,'' Carl said. ''There didn't seem any need for both of us to go through it. I see her now and again to tell her how he's doing.''

''This is your aunt?''

''Well, technically. He married her when I was eighteen. He was thirty . . . She's moved out of their apartment, she lives alone. Maybe he'd go to her, maybe not, I don't know . . . I suppose his home would be with me.''

''You'd better hope not,'' Stroup said.

''Why?''

Stroup looked at Carl directly for a long time. ''Shit,'' he said at last.

''You may be right, Mr. Thorne,'' said Capello. ''It seems, however, he may have thought more of you than he let on.''

''Why do you say that?''

Capello turned to Michaelmas. ''Doctor?''

Michaelmas turned back to them slowly, as if with great reluctance. Thrusting his hands in his pockets, he led the way out of the office.

"You said my uncle isn't a convict," Carl said to Capello. "What is he exactly?"

"That's a difficult question. Technically, he's committed no crime. There are no outstanding charges against him. He could have been court-martialed for attacking the men who found him five years ago, I suppose, but he was not."

"He was a hero," said Stroup.

"There you have it," said Capello. "He was a hero. He still is. But it is in his own interests as well as the public's that he be—uh—confined, so his treatment can continue."

"Why not just put out an APB?"

"An all points bulletin. I forgot that you're a reporter," said Capello.

"I'm a feature writer."

"In fact, we would rather not have any unnecessary publicity on this matter."

"Why not?"

"It might reflect on Major Stroup's organization, which, I am informed, does not relish the limelight."

"What do you do, Stroup?" Carl asked.

"I'm retired."

"What did you do that you don't want the public to find out about?"

"That's nobody's fucking business," said Stroup.

They reached the double doors. Michaelmas unlocked them as the others watched the monitor over the door, already repaired.

"If my uncle's not a convict, what is he?" Carl asked.

"A mad dog," said Stroup.

Carl put his hand on Stroup's arm, gripping his bicep.

"I'm getting tired of your comments," he said softly. "Keep your opinions to yourself."

Stroup studied Carl for a moment, then, surprisingly, smiled, his lips stretched thin and white over horselike teeth. Without seeming to make an effort, he moved his arm and was free of Carl's grasp. He followed Michaelmas into the restricted ward.

Capello fell back and walked alongside Carl. "I wouldn't mess with that man," Capello said, his voice low, conspiratorial. "He taught your uncle everything he knows. Or so he says."

The smell of the ward was the same, but Carl sensed something different. It took him a few moments to realize it was the sound of the Ping-Pong ball that was missing. The *thwonk, thwonk,* like the beat of his uncle's heart, was gone from Pleasant Hospital, and Carl was not sure how he felt about it.

Stitzer's cell was as he had left it; the Ping-Pong ball, flecked with mashed potato, had come to rest in a corner. A residue of sweat and saliva outlined the area where the sergeant had thrashed on the floor. Only the books had been moved. They lay atop the folding table; Carl read their titles from the spines: a text on hydraulics; a history of New York City; a novel by Hugh Walpole; an anthology of American folk poems; a controversial study of IQ testing. Five books in five days. A book a day, every day, for five years. How much had he understood of such a wide range of subjects? Had he shown any preferences, did one topic engage his mind, another stir his emotions, or did he simply devour the words as a way of killing the empty hours?

"Was there any pattern to his reading?" Carl asked. "Did he ever keep a book longer than a day or ask to see the same one again?"

"I don't really know," said Michaelmas. He looked at the others defensively. "I didn't keep records of what he was reading; he read everything. Anything. I did try to keep track for the first year to see if there was anything in particular that obsessed him, but I detected no pattern. After a while I stopped bothering.''

The scrapbook lay on the table beside the library books. Carl reached for it, then hesitated, his fingers on the cheap vinyl cover. Capello nodded to him, waggled permission with his hand. Carl opened it and saw his own name on a faded yellow strip of newsprint.

''How did he pick the books?'' Capello asked.

''At first he did it by topics. He'd asked for something on—I don't know—gardening, and we'd just take one off the shelves at random. Later he would mention specific titles. I assume he was reading the bibliographies and learning about other books that way. I've never seen anything like the variety. It was as if he was trying to learn everything in the library.''

''He was constructing a world,'' Stroup said.

Carl looked up from the scrapbook, his finger marking his place.

''It's a prisoner-of-war trick,'' Stroup continued. ''We taught it to our men in case of capture. You build something in your mind, a house, a car, whatever you're interested in. You build it *all*, the plumbing, the foundation, the curtains, every screw, every nail. It occupies the mind, dampens the fear. The sergeant was lucky, of course, because he had access to books. You could build anything that way. A house, a city, a world. I had to do it by memory.''

They were silent for a moment. Even Capello's good nature seemed to fade. Carl realized how small the cell had become, its walls seemed to crowd in on all of them. He tried to imagine a life so confined, but stopped, feeling claustrophobic.

''Where were you a prisoner?'' Carl asked finally.

''Korea,'' said Stroup. His lips parted in a contorted, mirthless smile. ''I built a house and a barn and part of a tractor—but then I was only there thirteen months.'' He shrugged, the tweed settling unevenly on his shoulders. Stroup tugged at the jacket, trying to make up for a bad fit with constant readjustments. "It works. It keeps you sane."

"But he *is* insane," said Michaelmas.

"He doesn't know it," said Stroup.

Carl leafed through the scrapbook, turning each heavy thick page slowly as a mounting sense of sorrow gathered. Each page was laden with clippings of Carl's work. His career was there in the book, five years' worth of effort, stories on all events, important and trivial, that Carl had written about for half a decade. A lottery winner whose life was ruined by sudden riches; a nun who married a priest; a bitter politician's reminiscences; a lost child and his mother's grief; an immigrant family's struggle with the American dream; an invalid's battle for recognition as a human being. Page after page of easy sentiment, concluding with his latest piece on the dead racehorse. The clippings were secured by sheets of clear plastic that clung electrostatically to a black cardboard background, and Carl felt as if he were looking at his own efforts the same way, through a sanitized sheet of film. How many times had he told the true story? How many times had he even known what the true story was? He had written it all with a thick plastic overlay of bathos, and seeing it now all together, he could ignore the craft, of which he was proud, and view the substance. It seemed a waste. What had it meant to his uncle, saving it all, squirreling it away, all that schmaltz, that restrained scolding voice, calling out for sympathy for people who didn't need it, did not benefit from it. Was it just a way to follow his nephew's career, or did the sergeant read something more into it? Was it, finally, an act of love?

"I thought you knew," Michaelmas said.

"How would I know? You never mentioned it."

"He was very proud of you."

"He thought I was an imposter."

Michaelmas waved his hands impatiently, then, as if startled to see them, clasped them behind his back. "He didn't believe in the person who came to visit him, no. But I think he did believe in the Carl Thorne who wrote the articles. He made that distinction; he thought you were two separate people. The real one in his mind, of course, was the one he never saw. I didn't see any harm, so we clipped your stories and let him keep them. He seemed very interested."

"You just clipped them? You didn't let him see the whole paper?"

Michaelmas looked to Stroup.

"If you roll a newspaper tight enough, it's as dangerous as a three-foot length of bamboo," said Stroup. Capello nodded agreement. Carl felt inadequate next to these men. Was that common knowledge? Should he know how to use a newspaper as a weapon?

"Do you mean his only idea of contemporary events was what he read in my stories?"

Michaelmas inclined his head, sniffed as if offended. "What did he need to know?"

Carl touched the scrapbook, felt the cool plastic slide beneath his fingers. What a slippery lifeline, how tenuous a hold on the world.

Capello was smiling again. "So, Mr. Thorne, what do you think? Is there anything in there that might tell you where your uncle is going?"

"Not that I can see."

"You'll want to study it some more."

"All right."

"You'll want to think in terms of a trigger. Something that might have set him off. He was lying dormant here for years, he could have tried the same escape at any time. Why now?"

"I don't know."

"No, of course you wouldn't. I'm saying try to think along those lines."

"I told you where he's going," said Stroup. He seemed annoyed again.

"We have those roads sealed off," Capello said. "He's not going south by highway."

Stroup picked up the Ping-Pong ball from the corner. He tossed it lightly from hand to hand, watching it as if it might suddenly hatch. "He doesn't care about roadblocks. He'll *walk* to New York if he has to. He'll stay in the woods, take the back roads, go by night, cut through people's backyards. You're never going to get him with a few state troopers in squad cars."

"We do have several dog teams out searching the woods."

"Shit, Capello, he'll *eat* the dogs."

Michaelmas laughed nervously, then stopped abruptly, embarrassed. Stroup squeezed the Ping-Pong ball between his thumb and fingers, then dropped it, squashed, to the floor.

"I don't really know anything about his escape," Carl said. "Did he . . . did he kill anyone?"

"No," said Michaelmas. "He put out one of the guards somehow . . ."

"Carotid artery," said Stroup.

"And he broke the man's collarbone," Michaelmas continued. "He'll be all right after a few days in the hospital."

"Could I visit that man?"

"Coombs? I suppose so."

"I want to apologize, see if I can do anything for him."

"Don't waste any sympathy on an idiot like Coombs. He's the reason your uncle got out," said Stroup.

"Even so." Carl gestured lamely. He felt inadequate to the entire situation, wished he could just throw up his hands and walk away, leave it to the men who seemed to understand it. But of course he couldn't. His guilt wouldn't let him. If his uncle was beyond responsibility, then it all devolved on Carl to clean up after him. Very Presbyterian, Marissa would say. Calvinistic. Out of date.

Capello began to question him in earnest. Silly questions, Carl thought, irrelevant. No trail of inquiry led logically to any other trail; Capello was forced to skip about at random. The sergeant had barely spoken to Carl for five years, how could he, how could anyone, know his mind.

Stroup flew back to New York with Carl while Capello remained at Pleasant to direct the operations. Carl was cramped into the jumpseat behind Stroup and the pilot, giving up the comfortable place in deference to the older man. There was no headset for Carl, and he was excluded from the lengthy conversation Stroup held with the pilot. The pilot seemed uncomfortable, very proper, and Carl wondered if Stroup was pulling rank, even though he no longer had one.

"They won't find him," Stroup said as they parted at the heliport.

"Maybe they will."

"Not with dogs. Not with state troopers and FBI men. Give Stitzer a ten-minute head start and you wouldn't find him up in those woods if you had a whole tribe of Sioux tracking for you."

"Well . . ." Carl let his voice trail off. There seemed nothing one could say to Stroup to assuage his anger.

"Where do you think he's gone?"

"He's coming here," Stroup said.

"How do you know?"

"He's coming here. It may take him a while, he might choose to walk. But he's in no hurry, he'll get here."

"Why are you so sure?"

"Take my advice." Stroup stopped, as if he had suddenly decided not to give his counsel.

"What? What is it?"

"Never mind. You won't pay any attention anyway."

"I'd like to hear what you think. What's your advice?"

Stroup tugged at his jacket, resetting it into place. Carl thought it was as if the man's body were rejecting his clothes, sloughing off the graft of foreign tissue. He belonged only in uniform.

"Hide," said Stroup. "Change your name, go away. Hide."

Carl looked for some sign that it was a joke.

"You think he's coming after me? You think I'm in danger? Why?"

"First off, I think anyone in this city is in danger. Second, you know him, you can identify him. When he gets here, it won't be long before one hell of a lot of people will be looking for him. If I was in his place, you and his wife would be the first to go."

"What exactly is it you think he's going to do?"

Stroup spat, as indifferent to his surroundings as a farmer in his field.

"Never mind. Probably nothing. It's none of my affair anymore, I'm out of it. I was just there today out of courtesy. Probably your uncle will get lost in the woods and end up in Canada. Maybe he'll stub his toe and call for an ambulance to take him back to Pleasant. Don't worry about a thing. So long."

Carl was glad to see him go. He walked home in the city twilight. The sun still hung just above the buildings, quivering, as if afraid to descend into the dark. Carl hoped that Marissa would not be in his apartment when he got there. She was not.

# *Chapter 4*

THE NIGHT CREPT DOWN from the mountains, darkened the trees that formed the panorama seen from the center of Speculator, then slowly crept out of the forest and into the town itself. The few streetlights came on, their cones of illumination hugging tightly to themselves, as if they knew any stray light would be immediately sucked up and devoured by the surrounding black. A wind blew off the mountains, adding a continental soughing sound to the night. Limbs moved in the breeze, casting shadows within the shadows, shifting shapes of darkness. Stitzer came with the night, his nude body blackened with dried mud, moving like a wraith through the shadows, unseen, unheard.

Where Ridge Street joined with Forster, a medical office occupied the corner lot in a modern building masquerading as Dutch Colonial, the architectural style favored by Speculator. An internist, still called a GP by his patients, had the office in the northern half of the building. A dentist's office occupied the rest of the space. The names of the two medical men flapped in the wind on a plain white shingle in the front yard. Stitzer came in from the back.

He came into the dentist's office from the window, slipping over the sill in a suspended leap, gliding into an interior even darker than the night. He located the X-ray machine and its timer control switch immediately. Working in the pitch black, the film took him a few minutes longer. He located the lead dispenser, removed two foil-wrapped packets, and slipped them into the bite-wing loops. He placed one of the paper loops in his mouth, clamping it into place with his molars. He adjusted the nozzle of the X-ray machine by touch, pressed the button. The machine hummed softly for less than a second. Stitzer repeated the process on the other side of his mouth, holding very still while the machine photographed through his cheek and gums and into his bones. Two minutes later he slid out as quietly as he had come, everything back in place, all drawers closed, the window snugly closed.

He trotted on the highway, following the path he had run in his mind so many times in his cell. Twice cars passed, but he saw the lights far in the distance and he was deep into the trees, pressed to the forest floor, long before the vehicles reached him. He was no more apt to be seen at night than a fox on the prowl, less so; he was warier, he knew the ways of men better.

He approached the house through the woods, leaving the road three miles early and curving in behind. If anyone was in the house, they would be watching the front; but there was no one in the house. He paused at the edge of the woods, taking in the smells, letting the animals get accustomed to his. When he passed the wire fence, he was greeted with the shuffling of paws, the sound of whimpers. He slipped past them, satisfied, and leaped up the trellis adjoining the back porch in three quick steps. He leaped from the porch roof to the window, catching the sill with his fingers and pulling his body up with the strength of his arms. The window was open, as he had left it, from his visit hours earlier, and he entered the house silently. Again he paused, breathing slowly, listening for any sound of life. There was only the occasional creak and groan of an old house settling, protesting against the stresses and burdens that never eased. Outside, the wind continued to sigh. He moved farther into the house, completely at ease in the darkness.

He settled in the small bedroom, lying on the throw rug made of rags. The musty smell of old wood mingled with dust from the baseboards and assailed his nostrils. It was the smallest of the upstairs rooms, intended once for a child's room but long since abandoned. He felt confined there, and he preferred it. He was not yet accustomed to open spaces, he had lived too long without them. He liked to be able to feel his boundaries with a few steps in any direction. It gave him a sense of dimension and security, it defined his world. He was used to it.

Sergeant Stitzer lay quietly in the darkness, waiting. In the dead of night he dozed at last.

He awoke certain that something was in the room with him. His body tensed, ready to spring, but he did not move. There was another sound, as faint as an insect's wing on a spiderweb, but Stitzer was aware of it. His nerves screamed with tension. Fur brushed his foot, and the sergeant relaxed. The cat rubbed against his shin. He could feel its jawbone through the fur, nuzzling against him. The sergeant swept the cat up in one hand and lowered it gently to his chest while it protested with a single mew. He stroked it and the animal settled down on his warmth, purring. Stitzer left it there, but did not go back to sleep.

In the morning, before the sun was up, he left the house, running easily, leaving a trail for the dogs to follow, curving wide through the countryside, and ending again in Lake Pleasant. He did it once more in the afternoon, working on the other side of the lake, giving them plenty to follow, making no secret of his passage, but doing it all a day before they would return to the area. They had swept through this quadrant before, would not return until they had tried everywhere else. They were military, he knew how their minds worked. He completed that trail, too, in the lake. At night he returned to the house, traveling the route he had gone before, knowing the trackers would think the dogs were repeating themselves. He laid new trails for two days, approaching many houses, circling them closely so it would appear he had been peering in, seeking food. He worked in a double-cloverleaf pattern centering on the lake. Plenty of exercise for the pursuers, plenty of frustration. Each night he returned to the house, stroking the cat, and lying still in the smallest of the bedrooms. Waiting.

On the third day he went to the highway and jumped a ride on a passing farm wagon, his body slung between springs stressed by the weight of three cords of firewood. The dogs would lose his scent there. The trackers would assume he was in a car, heading away from Speculator, long gone. After a mile he left the wagon and disappeared into the woods once more. He could have left, could have gone south at any time, but he was not ready yet. He continued to haunt the house, waiting. The whimpers when he passed the animals at night grew more urgent, but that was all right with him. The longer the better. Their wait would be over when his was.

On his third night in the house, Stitzer indulged himself. He wandered through the rooms by moonlight, touching everything. Shapes and textures that he had not known for five years thrilled his fingers. A cheese glass on the bathroom sink, the smooth surface punctuated by crisp edges of a geometric design. An old bedspread covering the sofa, the nap woven into thousands of tiny cobbles. The glide of linoleum that covered floors in kitchen, dining room, living room. In his host's closet he found clothing and rubbed his face with coarse flannel. For five years he had had nothing against his flesh but the frayed cotton of his pajamas. For five years he had felt very little—inside as well as out. Now, as his senses were liberated at last, his emotions, too, yearned for freedom, but Stitzer fought them.

He found the shotgun resting on two wooden pegs over the fireplace. Stitzer broke the chamber and sniffed. A faint whiff of cordite greeted his nose. The gun had been fired recently but not cleaned for some time. Stitzer put it back on the pegs, disapproving.

There were magazines in the host's bedroom, stacked in a pile by the narrow bed. *Playboy, Penthouse,* and a variety of lesser imitations, their pages ruffled and slightly swollen, as if they had once been soaked and dried, the covers icy slick to the touch. On a favorite poster taped to the wall at the foot of the bed, a young woman wearing a Santa Claus hat and a bit of gift ribbon around her neck lounged on a white rug beneath a Christmas tree, her legs apart, her breasts huge, pink nipples erect. Stitzer imagined his host lying on the bed, staring at the sultry young woman's image in the moonlight, the springs creaking, as he made love to the poster. It was like reading the man's diary.

In the kitchen, he intended just a taste but gorged himself instead. Going indiscriminately from bottle to jar, he tasted it all, dipping with his fingers into mayonnaise, ketchup, peanut butter, processed cheese. He bit directly into a head of lettuce, fished olives from salt water, assailed a piece of fried chicken, cold and dry. Unable to stop himself, he tipped his head back and let the juice of canned pineapple flow down his throat, over his chin. He was astounded at the level of excitement, he was panting, reaching for the next sensation before the last was finished. He found chocolate and tried to let it melt in his mouth but could not wait. He devoured it and sought frantically for more. It was too much for him, he wanted to stuff himself, rub the food into his body, wallow in it.

Finally, feeling sick and ashamed, he sat in the rocking chair in the living room and rocked back and forth hypnotically until his crisis passed. The cat, an old male, one eye partly closed by a wound, sat in the ray of moonlight that came through the window and watched Stitzer, squinting. Stitzer pursed his lips and made a smacking sound to the cat, which paused, then jumped into his lap. While the cat washed itself with rasping tongue, Stitzer ran his fingers through its fur. A stray, like me, he thought. After a time Stitzer wept silently, then stopped, still rocking.

Later that night the cat made him a present of a dead mouse.

# Part Three
# THE HUNT

# Chapter 5

Pauline moved through the class, fingering the buttons on her smock, aware of all the eyes flicking at her then back toward their canvases. She paused behind the easel of a scrawny young woman, barely more than a girl, whose hair hung down limply to her shoulders as if it, too, were undernourished. The girl's skin was nearly as oily as the pigments. Another "artist," Pauline thought hopelessly. Why did they all equate personal sloppiness, eccentricity, bad habits with art? The young woman, determinedly aloof, continued to stir the paints on her palette as if the teacher's opinion did not concern her. The others nearby strained to hear.

"The shading there is nice," said Pauline.

The young woman looked where Pauline pointed as if seeing the shading for the first time and surprised to find it there. She said "ummmm" through her nose, accepting the compliment without acknowledging a need for it. A hush hovered over all as Pauline continued to look at the young woman's work. She tried to think of something further to say of a constructive nature, but her imagination seemed thin tonight. Normally she was quite good at seeing virtue where none existed, but not this evening. She moved on without another word and the hush moved with her, enveloping each student in turn as she moved toward them, a relieved sigh and stirring of bodies sweeping in when she had passed. Why did they all want it so much, she wondered. She tried to remember herself at this stage, aching to know if she had any real talent, eager to listen to anyone who said she might. It seemed so long ago.

Pauline dismissed the class and shrugged off her smock. As she tucked in her blouse, the waist of her slacks bit gently into her flesh, a reminder of the inch she had promised herself to shed. At forty-two, diet was still her only concession to vanity. Her hair was graying, and she liked the way it looked. It seemed to add dignity to beauty.

As the students prepared to leave, Pauline noticed one of them, a man with a curly shock of dark hair, watching her. His attention made her feel self-conscious and she busied herself at her locker, turning her back to him. When she turned again, the curly-haired student was standing in front of her, pumping the smile that remained boyish despite his age. He's probably as old as I am, Pauline thought. Why does he insist on dressing like a boy?

"Thank you, Mrs. Stitzer. It was a good class. I see what you mean about the shading. Your suggestion really helped."

"Good," she said, knowing he was lying. He resented every bit of advice she gave him, his resistance palpable in the set of his shoulders, the grim line of his lips. He had no talent but lacked the wit to know it. A genius could make his own rules, she had told him once, but the rest of us must master the basics. She knew because she was no genius.

He rubbed at his hands with a cloth, smearing the oily pigments into his skin. Messiness was a badge of the beginner. They prided themselves on the stains on flesh and clothes as if they were Purple Hearts to be displayed. Pauline could work all day and never get a drop on herself.

"Feel like a cup of coffee at all?" the man asked.

Pauline tried to remember his name. Blatsky.

"That's a nice idea, Mr. Blatsky . . ." She knew she had it wrong. He winced, struggled to keep his smile afloat. Their egos were so frail, she thought.

"Blatty," he said. "Adam Blatty."

"I'm sorry, Adam. I knew it was Adam, of course." She hadn't. She thought of him as the angry resister with the curly hair. There were a lot of angry resisters, so she had to distinguish. It amazed her how many adults would come to an art class, pay good money to learn from a professional, then fight every bit of advice. "Art," she had decided long ago, "was the worst enemy of art. If only they would stop trying to be artists and learn a little fundamental craft.

"So, uh . . . we could have a drink if you'd prefer that to coffee," said Blatty.

Pauline seemed to have committed herself by not remembering his name. She did not really mind. He wasn't talented but he seemed to like her, and his smile, although practiced, was an undeniable improvement over a night of television watching.

The other students filed out, some of them murmuring goodbye, others sullenly slipping into the night as if a nod to the teacher were unconscionable flattery. Blatty stood with her, staking his claim. Pauline tried to decide if this was a pass or just a bid for extracurricular advice. There was a time when she knew a pass when she saw one, but in the past few years she had been reading—who could avoid it?—about the "new" relationships between men and women, and she didn't want to be so insensitive as to mistake a request for companionship for an advance.

She left the building with Blatty by her side. He took her arm as they started down the stairs, an act of gentlemanly solicitude that surprised her.

Carl Thorne stood on the sidewalk outside Cooper Union. "Hello, Aunt Pauline." There was something urgent in his expression that demanded recognition, as if she might decide to walk right past without noticing him.

"Hello, Carl," she said, surprised. "How are you?"

"I called you yesterday," he said. "I left a message on your answering machine. Two messages, actually."

Pauline smiled. "I haven't been home."

"All night? . . . I'm sorry, Aunt Pauline, it's none of my business."

She wished he'd stop calling her aunt; he was too old to have aunts. She felt too young to be one. Beside her, she could feel Blatty looking at her questioningly. She knew she should introduce him but she had forgotten his name again.

"I have to talk to you," Carl said. "Right away."

"We were going for coffee . . ."

"It has to be alone and it has to be now," he said.

He sounded forceful, but he rubbed one hand into the other as if he were cold, although the night was warm. What is there about me that makes men nervous, Pauline wondered.

"Well . . . perhaps we could have coffee another time?"

"Sure," said Blatty. "No problem."

"Family business," said Carl.

"Sure." Blatty hesitated for a moment, seeking a graceful exit, then finally walked away. He looks as if I criticized his paintings again, Pauline thought.

Carl ushered her into a cab, holding the door, assisting her with a gingerly, courtly touch on her arm. They rode in silence. She asked him once what it was all about, but he looked pointedly at the cab driver and seemed distinctly uncomfortable. A creeping sense of alarm began in her mind.

They went to her apartment because, as Carl pointed out,

it was closer than his. He hopped out of the cab and hurried around to open the door on her side. The cabbie beat him to it, reaching over the backseat, and Pauline was halfway out when he got there. He took one of her hands in his, put his other hand under her elbow. Was he always this much of a gentleman, she wondered, or did he think she was feeble?

He had always been difficult for Pauline to relate to. Carl had been eighteen when she'd married Mark Stitzer; she twenty-eight. She had never known him as a child, had no fond memories of teaching him to hunt, to fight, to grapple with the world as Mark had. To her he had always been an awkward, uncomfortable boy at the peak of sexual awareness who had tried to hide his desires by being formal in her presence. It had been only superficially successful. The first year they lived together, his last year in high school, it seemed to Pauline that the boy had a permanent erection. He could not rise from the breakfast table without trailing one arm, adjusting himself with his forearm beneath the table top. She wondered at the time if it hurt him.

Mark had laughed. "Hell yes, it hurts him," he said. "How would you like to be eighteen and suddenly have a sexpot move into your house? He's horny enough at that age without a constant reminder of what he's missing."

"I'm not a sexpot," she had said. She almost added, I'm an artist (this was before she had learned to think of herself as a painter, a craftsman). But she knew Mark would laugh even harder at this pretension.

"You are," he said. "But even if you weren't, he wouldn't know. At that age, every woman over the age of fifteen is a sexpot. I was in love with the super's wife once. She must have weighed three hundred pounds, but she brushed against me in the laundry room, and that was all it took."

"You were in the Army at eighteen," she said.

"So I loved my super's wife when I was sixteen. From

the age of twelve on, it doesn't make much difference. It's all the same hard-on.''

Pauline could not imagine the shy, awkward, courtly Carl Thorne in love with a three-hundred-pound super's wife. It was easy enough to imagine him in love with herself, however. She thought he always had been, although he became much better at disguising it.

He went away to college, and when he returned for vacations, his desire seemed less visible. He had discovered coeds and found them to his liking. Pauline had been relieved. They were able to be in the same room without her worrying how he would manage to adjust himself. It had been flattering, of course, all that flagrant desire, but it had also been uncomfortable—for both of them.

Soon thereafter Mark reenlisted in the Army. Pauline had visited him once at Fort Dix and then he was gone, shipped—voluntarily—to Vietnam. Pauline knew he was eager to go. He had left the Army when he came back to take care of Carl. The military was all right for him, he had said, possibly for a wife, but no place to raise a kid. He wanted Carl to have as normal a childhood as possible after losing his parents, and Stitzer spent seven years doing his best to provide it. He had worked as a cabbie by day, moonlighting as a karate instructor when money was tight, but taking nothing more permanent. He lived seven years as a temporary. Even after he married Pauline, she felt it was with his bags packed, one foot poised over the doorsill. When Carl entered college, Mark was gone at last. Carl had understood. He had always known his uncle would seek out his true love again one day. Stitzer found the true love in the jungles surrounding a hamlet called Ma Tok.

They learned of his Silver Star from the Department of Defense publicity people. Stitzer himself was already back in the jungle, working on the second oak leaf cluster. When the only successful attempt to rescue American prisoners of war was trumpeted joyously in the newspapers, they were not surprised to learn that Stitzer was with the rescue team; led the whole operation was the unofficial word, although credit was naturally ascribed to the major in charge. The citation merely cited his "conspicuous valor."

Carl Thorne had none of the ambiguous feelings that tortured the rest of the country during the Vietnam war. His uncle was over there, that was enough for him. It was not enough for Pauline. She realized Mark's need to be there, had always sensed the part of him that craved the darkness and chaos, but she did not understand it. She kept her feelings to herself, however, and never mentioned her doubts when the sergeant reenlisted for another tour of duty, and then another.

Mark would return home now and then, setting down in New York on little more than a flying tour and sweeping them both into his exuberant orbit. He passed them like a comet, fiery bright, pulsating heat and excitement, then streaking away, leaving a lengthening tail of fading joy behind. During those infrequent visits, Pauline understood why she stayed married to him, but during the long months in between the understanding would dim to confusion and, finally, recrimination.

Carl and Pauline served as family for each other while the sergeant crept through jungles thick with murder. She could see the boy trying to fill his uncle's place. In tones unusually solemn for one so young, he would inquire about her activities. Listening with gravity, he would gently chide her if she seemed too frivolous, murmur his approval if she appeared busy and slightly unhappy. Pauline did not take offense at his condescension. She knew he was acting out his own parody of marriage as he understood it. Stern husband, silly wife. He was young, she reminded herself, still only a college student. And, in truth, she rather enjoyed it. He was so somber she felt carefree, almost giddy, by comparison. And she liked the attention. The boy liked her. The episodes of his awkward erections had never been completely forgotten by either of them. He was no longer really a boy, for that matter.

He acted as her escort now and again, offering his arm with the same stiff formality when they entered restaurants, Broadway shows, receptions at art galleries—two of them for her own exhibitions. He was sweet, really, acting like a little old man. If it weren't for the tentlike projections that still occasionally stiffened his trousers at odd moments, he could have been *her* uncle. And, when she managed to loosen him up, he was fun.

As Pauline approached her apartment door and he reached reflexively for the key, she wondered at how little things had changed in the intervening ten years since he had graduated from college and moved into his own world. He still wanted so badly to be the man of the house.

Pauline unlocked the door herself and let them in. While she poured herself a glass of wine, Carl moved into the living room, then stopped, startled. The apartment had a fireplace, long since sealed off, which was valued by Pauline because of its heavy oaken mantel. Over the mantel hung an oil portrait of Stitzer, in uniform, beret cocked to one side of his head, his arm around Carl. Atop Carl's head, tilted to the other side as if to counterbalance Stitzer's beret, was the flat-topped mortarboard of a graduating college senior. She had caught the pride in Stitzer's face very well. Carl looked somber, as befitted the occasion, but somehow she had managed to convey the love in Carl's eyes. They seemed to wander, even as the viewer looked, away from the artist, who must have looked straight ahead, into a sidelong glance at his proud uncle. Carl was half a head taller, the difference accentuated by the mortarboard, but somehow Stitzer looked bigger. Both men were cut off just below the shoulders by a pale gray space, as if their heads were floating, disembodied, above the earth. It was her style, a trademark, that sometimes made the portraits seem unfinished. Carl never quite understood it.

"I did it from a Polaroid shot," she said, coming from behind him and offering a glass of red wine. She never asked how anyone liked a portrait because she knew it was the worst way to get an honest answer.

"It's startling to see yourself like that," Carl said. "I mean, unexpectedly. Why did you do it?"

She sipped her wine, looking at him over the rim, letting her answer lie in the calm stillness that emanated from her. Carl had never understood such calm, such self-assurance. He had never known anyone who seemed so complete in herself as Pauline. Not even his uncle; Stitzer needed a goal, a challenge. Pauline seemed to need only herself.

He looked at the portrait again.

"What a good-looking man," he said.

"Yes. Him too."

He turned, saw she was joking, and laughed. Then he remembered why he had come.

He made her sit down, then he told her everything he knew about his uncle's escape.

To her surprise, Pauline felt tears welling up in her eyes. It seemed so much less than she had at first feared. She had assumed he was dead. Escaped? She should probably feel good for him, out of that hellhole at last. She didn't know why she was crying. Release of tension, the anguish on Carl's face? Jealousy, perhaps? She envied the depth of Carl's affection for his uncle, his uncle's for him. She had rendered their love truly on canvas. That might have been why she had painted it, to torment herself with the reminder of what she did not have.

Carl put his arm around her shoulders.

"I know," he said. "I know."

Pauline did not feel sad, but she couldn't stop the tears.

Carl patted her shoulder. She tried to stop, started to protest her silliness, but a sudden sob burst from her and she wept even harder.

"It's all right," said Carl, leaning his head closer to hers. "It's all right."

She could feel his discomfort. She bent forward, turning her head from him, and felt the waistband of her slacks dig into her stomach. Rising slightly to readjust the slacks, her face brushed against his. Suddenly Carl was kissing away her tears. He murmured something low in his throat that she did not understand. He kissed her cheek, the side of her nose, the corner of her mouth where the moisture had gathered. It was so easy to turn her head, no more than a wish, and he was kissing her on the lips.

He did not pull away immediately; there was a pause, a moment in which he fought the battle with himself and his lips pressed against hers, soft, desirous. Then he got to his feet and stood in front of the portrait, his back to her.

Pauline could see he was adjusting himself.

"I'm going up tomorrow to visit this man Coombs," he said. His voice sounded untethered, as if looking wildly for something to cling to. "It seems the least I can do."

"It's not your responsibility, really," she said.

Carl was silent. When he turned back to her, she was smiling.

"I'm not mad at you," she said softly.

"The thing is, you might be in some danger. I don't really think that, but there's no point in taking unnecessary chances."

"Why would Mark want to hurt me?"

"Not you. He doesn't know it's you."

She nodded, but she didn't seem to understand. She had never understood Mark's insanity, he seemed so rational. Until he spit at her. Until he cursed her. She had stopped visiting after that.

"What I'm suggesting is that you move in with me until

82

he's found," said Carl. His voice was calm now, matter-of-fact. "I don't like the idea of your living alone here."

"I don't think that's necessary, Carl."

"Yes, I think it is. It's a sensible precaution."

"Thank you for your concern, but no."

"It's not just a suggestion," said Carl. "I insist on it."

Pauline smiled again. Little Carl, her protector. Man of the family at last. Not so little, of course. She packed a bag and moved into his apartment that night.

# Chapter 6

IT TOOK COOMBS A minute to realize he missed the sound of the dogs. They should have howled at his arrival. He hadn't been able to feed them since the day before he went to the hospital. Four days without food, they would be starving, but he didn't hear a sound. It occurred to him that they might have been stolen.

He could do nothing quickly because of his broken clavicle. Even driving with his left arm had been painful. They said they had immobilized the bones with the figure-eight harness that strapped him front and back and gave him the exaggeratedly erect posture of a West Point cadet; they assured him he could not feel the jagged edges rubbing together, but Coombs knew what he could feel and couldn't feel, damn it. They must be saving those pills to sell for their own profit, the way they were so stingy with them. Coombs liked the pills, liked the vague, detached feeling they gave him, but he didn't tell the nurses that. They would have misunderstood, the smug, snooty twats. If he said he was in pain, it was their job to believe him.

He eased himself out of the car and walked around toward the back of the house. Even if he had bothered to look, he would not have seen the eyes watching him from the empty bedroom on the second floor.

The hounds were there, all right, and they went frantic when he approached, but he could see now why they were quiet. Each of them was muzzled with strips of soft cloth. It looked like strips of his flannel work shirts. They leaped at the fence, their claws scrabbling ineffectually at the wire. They were wild to see him, hurling their bodies at the fence, the gate. Flecks of sputum flew from the corners of their jaws. They whimpered continually, sounding more like some strange species of cat than hunting dogs.

Abruptly they stopped and sank down, cowering, their ears flattened, tails wagging submissively, as if Coombs had raised a club to strike them. Their eyes looked past Coombs, over his shoulder. Coombs turned and saw a man standing on the roof of the back porch. He wore Coombs's faded blue work shirt, Coombs's jeans, Coombs's boots. Coombs's checkered hunting cap was on the man's head, and it was the cap that prevented Coombs from recognizing him instantly. The familiar bald skull was hidden. But as soon as the man swung down from the porch roof, his feet barely touching the trellis before he was on the ground and coming toward the kennel, Coombs knew it was the loony. He could feel his collarbone throb.

There was no point in running, he knew that much. Even healthy he could not hope to get away. With his right arm in the sling he doubted he could make more than a step or two before the sergeant was on him.

"There's only five dogs," Coombs said. "What'd you do with the sixth?"

"He didn't believe me," Stitzer said, raising a hand to point beyond the kennels.

A black mound seemed to move, then the swarm of flies lifted, rearranged themselves, and settled down once more on the furry corpse. It was the dog Coombs called Blue. Its throat was torn out.

"You believe me, though, don't you, Coombs?"

Coombs laughed, frightened.

"Yeah." Christ, yes. He believed he was crazy. He believed he'd kill him if he looked crosseyed.

"How's the collarbone?" Stitzer asked. He seemed genuinely concerned.

"You almost killed me," Coombs whined. "They thought you might have punctured a lung. They kept taking pictures of my chest, that's why I was in so long."

"I wondered," Stitzer said. "It's just as well. They could make you more comfortable than I could here."

"It hurts," said Coombs. "They just wouldn't give me enough pills."

"I have some painkillers."

Coombs stared at him.

"Novocaine. Pentothal. They'll put you straight in no time."

Coombs tried to smile, tried to look grateful.

"I was sorry I had to do it to you," Stitzer said. "But if I hadn't hurt you, they would have thought you were in on it. They would have suspected you of helping me. You would have lost your job."

"Hell, I ain't going back there anyway."

"I know you're not," said Stitzer.

Coombs laughed again, nervously.

"They won't expect you to, either. But this way they won't come looking for you. We'll be alone."

It sounded almost like a lover's expectant announcement. Coombs looked around, trying desperately to think of something to do. The trouble was, he was too damned scared to think straight. He wished he lived in town, wished he had some neighbors closer than a mile away.

"Let's go in," Stitzer said. He held out a hand. Coombs felt it tug at him even though it never touched him.

"What about the dogs?" Coombs asked. "Shouldn't I feed them?"

"Not yet," said Stitzer. He looked at the hounds appraisingly. They were still crouched submissively, tails switching.

"They're not quite hungry enough yet. We'll give them another day."

Stitzer walked toward the house, his back to Coombs. For a second Coombs considered making a dash for the car, taking his chances of angering the sergeant. Stitzer stopped, holding the back door open, waiting for Coombs. The moment passed and Coombs walked into his house, knowing already he had made a mistake.

The kitchen table was covered with a bath towel. Stitzer hooked a chair with his foot for Coombs, then with a flourish he whipped off the towel.

"Ta dum!" he said. He seemed playful, and Coombs took heart. Perhaps it wouldn't be so bad after all. He did not define "it" for himself.

"*Vazuki,*" Stitzer said.

Coombs looked at him blankly.

"Huh?"

Stitzer chuckled, shaking his head from side to side.

"Can't trip you up that easily, can I, Coombs? You guys are really good, I've got to hand it to you. I said take your pick."

On the table were a new comb, still in its sealed plastic container, purchased from a public-toilet vending machine, a pile of quarters, and a cigarette lighter with International Harvester stamped in red on the side.

"Take my pick?"

"Gifts. My way of saying I'm sorry. Take your choice."

Coombs reached out tentatively, took the lighter. He glanced at Stitzer for approval, making sure he understood. Stitzer smiled benevolently.

"Thank you," said Coombs.

"My pleasure. Take the quarters too."

"This is enough," said Coombs.

"What the hell. You only live once. Take the quarters too. Put them in your pocket."

Coombs pocketed the quarters.

"Now comb your hair." Stitzer opened the package, held it toward Coombs, smiling encouragement. Coombs took the cheap black plastic comb and ran it through his hair.

"It's hard with my left hand," he said.

"Looks good enough," said Stitzer. "Now put it back." The sergeant held the plastic case open and Coombs slipped the comb back inside.

*"Vstavay!"* said Stitzer. He waited. Coombs stood up, uncertainly. It had seemed a command of some sort.

Stitzer nodded approval. "You do understand just a little bit of it, don't you? Just a word or two?"

"What is it?" Coombs asked.

"Your mother tongue, you bastard. Upstairs, go on."

Three two-by-four-inch planks had been nailed together and laid in the bathtub, forming a ramp running from the drain to nearly the height of the door. When Coombs saw the ropes, he felt his stomach open up within him.

"Oh, God, no," he said, although he didn't know what it was.

"Get on it," Stitzer said.

"You shit, too," said Coombs. Stitzer rapped him once, lightly, on the collarbone. Coombs cried out and his knees buckled. He stepped into the tub and leaned back against the planks.

The bathtub was an old one with legs that ended in lions' paws gripping metal balls. The faucets were manned by levers, and a persistent leak from one of them had formed a deep blue stain in the porcelain around the drain. A stopper hung from a chain of silver-colored beads. A rubber hose looked more menacing to Coombs than anything else.

Stitzer tied Coombs to the planks, showing a curious solicitude when working around the injured collarbone.

"You've got the wrong man," Coombs pleaded. "Swear to God, I'm your friend."

"I don't have a friend," said Stitzer.

"Wasn't I good to you? Wasn't I? Didn't I try to save your life?"

Stitzer continued to work. He strapped a wide band of cloth across Coombs's forehead, securing his head to the boards. Coombs recognized another of his shirts.

"You wouldn't even be here if it wasn't for me!" Coombs was trying to keep from crying. "I saved you! Didn't I always talk to you? Didn't I? Didn't I?"

Stitzer wedged pieces of cardboard under Coombs's head and neck.

"Move your head," he said.

"I can't."

"I said move your head!" Stitzer leaned close to him, yelling in his face. Coombs struggled, trying to move. Stitzer tapped his collarbone. With a cry, Coombs jerked away from the pain. Stitzer adjusted the wedges, tightening the cloth strap.

"Okay," said Stitzer. "Okay now." His voice was low and calm. He kept repeating okay as if he were soothing a fractious animal.

"Holy shit," said Coombs. He was crying openly now, too scared to care. "Oh, holy shit."

Stitzer produced a block of wood wrapped in a washcloth. "Open your mouth."

Coombs clenched his jaw shut. His eyes bulged.

"You pick a hell of a time to resist," said Stitzer. He pressed Coombs's nostrils together. When Coombs opened his mouth to gasp for air, Stitzer placed the block of wood between his jaws.

"Now just relax," said Stitzer, and then he laughed, genuinely amused. "Don't you hate it when the dentist starts talking with his tools in your mouth? Now I know what it feels like.''

Coombs tried to plead with Stitzer, but only a prolonged *eeee* came forth.

''You were decent to me,'' said Stitzer. He held up a hypodermic syringe and a vial of clear liquid. ''I appreciated it. That's why I got the sodium Pentothal for you. I've added Valium; you'll sleep like a baby.'' He inserted the needle through the rubber stopper, sucked up the liquid, squirted some out the end.

Coombs tried to move harder than he had ever tried anything in his life. Stitzer watched, detached.

''That's bringing your veins up, you know,'' he said. He reached down and touched one in Coombs's bulging bicep. Coombs immediately let his arm go limp. He wanted to yell to Stitzer to be careful. You could kill a person with a needle like that if you didn't know what you were doing. Then he realized that might be the plan.

Stitzer froze, only his eyes moving. There had been a sound outside, something heavy on gravel. A car! Coombs tried to scream. Stitzer jammed the hunting cap into his mouth and moved out of the bathroom without a sound.

The doorbell rang. Coombs was alone, he had a chance! If only he could move at all, rock a bit, tip the planks over, make any kind of noise. He pushed frantically at the cap with his tongue. His voice sounded in his own ears as if it came from far underground. Could anyone hear it downstairs? His tongue pushed harder against the corduroy on the cap, willing it out, praying it out.

Stitzer slipped into the small bedroom, saw the car in the driveway, parked behind Coombs's Ford. He moved cautiously to the window, looked down. The visitor was hidden by the porch. The doorbell rang again. Stitzer climbed out of the window, his feet moving quietly even in the heavy boots on the porch roof. If he had to, he could swing down and kill the man in seconds. He hoped he wouldn't have to, he wanted to keep things simple.

Carl Thorne thought he heard a sound over his head. He looked up, saw the porch roof, grooved planks, drying, in need of paint. He listened, heard nothing more. Peering through the window beside the door, he could see nothing move. He knocked on the screen door, got only an unsatisfying tap. He opened the screen and rapped his knuckles on the inner door. A solid, resounding knock filled the empty house.

"Mr. Coombs!" he called. Carl paused, listening, waiting for some sign of response.

"Mr. Coombs?" He knocked again. He didn't know why, but he felt someone was in the house. He tried the door, thinking he might open it enough to call directly into the house. The door was locked.

Something drifted past Carl's eye, more motion than matter. He looked up again. A tiny rivulet of dust seeped down from between two of the planks. Was Coombs standing on the roof over his head? The idea seemed preposterous. If anything was there, it was more apt to be a squirrel. But would a squirrel's weight dislodge the motes of dust that sifted down, scarcely heavier than the air itself? Carl started to step off the porch and look up but the image of a man crouching up there made him stop. He pictured Coombs on the roof over his head, crouched in fear . . . Why?

"I'm a friend, Mr. Coombs," he said softly. The porch roof sighed, as if a weight had been lifted. Carl stepped off the porch and looked up. A squirrel, startled by his sudden appearance, leaped from one branch to another in a tree next to the house. Carl grinned at his foolishness and stepped back toward the house. The tiny motion in the upstairs window did not register on his consciousness, but it was noted by his nervous system. He whirled, his skin tingling, and stared at the window. His eyes grew accustomed to the darker interior. He could see a wall with flaking wallpaper in a paisley pattern. A darker square, once protected by a vanished picture from the bleaching morning sun, stood out amid the amoebic swirls. Carl realized his breathing was short, his skin flushed.

What am I afraid of? he wondered. This is not the enchanted forest. I'm not standing on the porch of the gingerbread house of the wicked witch. He removed his notebook from his pocket and wrote a note.

Stitzer crouched beneath the windowsill in the small bedroom. He was having trouble controlling himself. The guy playing his nephew was too good, he had troubled Stitzer from the first. The sergeant had almost given in to him many times. It had been all he could do to keep from embracing him, letting himself believe it was really Carl. When he looked at him, even now in this glimpse through the window, he could still see the little boy in that face. He could still hear the boy's voice crying, "Swing me, Uncle Mark! Play with me!" The others were easy, bad copies. The woman was too heavy, too old to be his wife. The doctor was no problem at all. He could talk to him all day and never give anything away. But the kid was difficult, he got to him. Even now it took a strong effort to keep from leaping down and killing him. Kill him or embrace him, either way let it be over. But he knew his real nephew was still alive, still writing for him, sending him messages, willing him to succeed. Stitzer would hold on to himself, let this one pass . . . It was so much harder to let him live than to kill him.

Carl slipped his note inside the screen door and was turning toward his car when he heard a sound from inside the house. A high-pitched *eeee*. He peered through the window and heard it again. It seemed to come from upstairs. Sunlight illuminated the south side of the open living room, leaving the north in shadow. A flight of stairs at the end of the room led to the second story, and sunlight flooded down from the head of the stairs as if poured from a ladle. The window through which Carl peered was coated with dust. Something white, bird dung, a dying insect, had streaked down the dust, leaving a curving trail like a worm casing.

Carl heard the *eeee* once more and then saw the cat standing at the head of the stairs. It stood there a moment, squinting against the light, then slinked down the stairs into the shadows. It crossed the living room, pausing once to stare at Carl with one eye, then continued to a sunny windowsill, where it curled, licking itself once before going to sleep.

Carl walked to his car. He felt eyes on his back but convinced himself it was the cat.

Stitzer watched the car go. When it was out of sight he vaulted to the porch, leaped up, caught the edge with his fingers, and pulled himself onto the roof of the house. He stood by the chimney for maximum height and watched the car weave through the woods. It was obscured by the trees almost immediately, but Stitzer looked toward a gap half a mile away, cleared to permit the high-tension power lines through. After a minute the car passed through the gap, flashing sunlight like a mirror. Stitzer waited five minutes longer, counting silently in his head to three hundred. The car did not return.

The note was brief: "Mr. Coombs, I missed you at the hospital. Sorry about everything. I would like to speak to you about my uncle and will return whenever you have the time." He had printed his name carefully and given his phone number in New York.

I would like to speak to you about my uncle.

I should have killed him, Stitzer thought. The dogs had not found him, the guards had not come close, but this imposter had come straight to him.

Will return whenever you have the time.

This one is dangerous, Stitzer knew. Dangerous because he seemed to read Stitzer's movements; even more dangerous because of the doubts he raised. I should have killed him now. I will kill him next time.

Coombs had managed to exhaust himself. The corduroy from the cap had caused his fillings to tingle unpleasantly. He heard Stitzer approach with relief. There was a certain comfort in not having to struggle anymore.

"Okay," said Stitzer, with the air of a man about to continue important work after an interruption. He pressed the needle into Coombs's arm, then watched Coombs's face, his eyes interested and benevolent.

Coombs tried to gargle another plea for mercy, then heard his voice fade as he drifted into unconsciousness. Stitzer removed the hunting cap from Coombs's mouth, then carefully picked out the bits of lint. He held the X rays of his own mouth over Coombs's face, glancing at them, then at the teeth of the unconscious man. After careful study, he dried one of the rear molars with a dishtowel and made a small mark on it with a grease pencil. He compared the mark to the X ray, adjusted its position by an eighth of an inch. Finally contented with the precision of his mark, Stitzer set to work.

They sat languidly, Marissa and Carl on the sofa, heads back, legs stretched out, balancing snifters of brandy on their laps. Pauline sat in the baronial wing chair, her face nearly obscured by the projecting sidepieces. The upholstery was a beige twill, contorted into dozens of little tufts by buttons set deep in the material. Several of the buttons were missing; Carl had pried them loose when still a child. It had been Carl's father's chair and then his uncle's and now it was Carl's. Much of the furniture had belonged to his parents. Carl could scarcely walk through the apartment without some piece or another evoking a memory.

"Everything all right, Pauline?" he asked. She had insisted he drop the title aunt if she was to live with him.

"Fine," she said. She took a sip of her Perrier. She had eaten cottage cheese and a wheat cracker while Carl and Marissa shared a sirloin, and she had seemed angry about it. Marissa, as usual, ate enough for two. She contended that after vigorous exercise her metabolism rate was so high that it would burn up anything. She had smiled at Pauline when she said it.

The two women had smiled at each other a good deal throughout the evening. Carl had hoped to lie back happily in their presence, like a sultan in his harem. His aunt, his girl. His women, his family. The women had smiled and addressed each other by name again and again, deferring continually to each other. Carl had seldom witnessed such hostility.

"Are we keeping you up, Pauline?" Marissa asked.

"No, Marissa, you're not. Am I keeping you from anything?"

"No," said Carl.

Marissa arched her back, lifting her arms above her head and stretching her legs out even further. She looked endless. Carl had one hand lightly on her shoulder. Her breasts rose to meet it under the thin T-shirt, and Carl jerked his hand away, embarrassed. An expanse of bare flesh revealed itself at her waist as the shirt crept up.

Thin as a slat, thought Pauline. She must be seven feet tall. Pauline felt even shorter than her five foot three. Marissa moaned, a long, soughing *ooohhh,* distinctly sexual. Probably more experienced than I am, too, thought Pauline.

"Actually," Marissa crooned, completing her catlike stretch by scrunching her head into her shoulders. She moved her head from one shoulder to the other, rolling it, and Carl could hear her neck vertebrae snapping. "Actually, I've had a rather long day. It must be so restful to just sit and paint, Pauline. I'll have to take it up someday.''

They smiled again.

''I think it's time for bed,'' said Marissa. ''Good night, Pauline. It was so nice meeting Carl's aunt.''

''It was certainly nice meeting you too,'' said Pauline. ''Carl had told me so little about you.''

Their eyes flashed, teeth glinted as they kissed the air beside each other's heads. It reminded Carl of the ritualistic posing of warring prairie chickens—much puffing of breasts, flaring of feathers, patterned skittering footwork— very little real damage done.

To his surprise, Marissa walked not to the door but into his bedroom. When he followed, she wrapped her arms around his neck, nudging the door partly closed with her foot.

''Not *here*,'' Carl protested.

''Why *not* here? We've done it here hundreds of times.''

''Not with my aunt in the apartment. We can go to your place.''

Marissa kissed him, holding him tightly with one arm around his neck, the other hand slipping under his belt. She began to moan, her breath raggedly excited. Not for the first time, Carl wondered about the immediacy and intensity of Marissa's response. What could there be about him that brought her rising so quickly to the surface of passion? He was not vain enough to think it was his own prowess that caused such a reaction. She pulled him toward the bed, locked her legs around him, and dragged him down. Carl held on, feeling, as he often did, like the boy on a dolphin, just along for the ride.

Pauline heard the yips and groans and startled sighs and tried to busy herself by converting the sofa into her bed. She arranged the throw pillows neatly on either side of the fluffier one she would use for sleeping. It made it look as if she were sleeping in a window display. There came a thump, louder than the others, followed by a shuddering exhalation that sounded like a soprano running down the scales. Loud enough to wake the neighbors, sniffed Pauline. She noticed that none of the sound effects came from Carl. The kiss they had exchanged in her apartment came into her mind. It was hard to associate that tenderness with the orchestrated display in the next room. There were so many ooh's and little squeals that it sounded to Pauline's biased ear like a convention of little girls being forced to view a pan of worms.

Pauline roamed the apartment restlessly, trying not to eavesdrop as Marissa so obviously wanted her to. She was damned if she'd give the showoff the satisfaction. So much furniture for such a small apartment—the wing chair that seemed to come from another era when learned men sat in their libraries and puffed pipes; a massive credenza of golden oak that threatened to take over the dining ell; a refectory table, chairs as heavy as tree stumps, upholstered in cracked leather held in place by bronze brads. Poor Carl, he had never been able to part with anything from his past. The entire contents of this apartment had once belonged in his family home—suitable for a bourgeois family, pathetically wrong for a New York bachelor. She wondered if he carried as much psychic lumber with him. Instead of silver serving bowls, pewter plates, or soup tureens, the surfaces of the old furniture held pictures: Carl's parents through the years, their early marriage, the beginning of their middle years caught in a variety of poses. Mrs. Thorne with the baby carriage, looking startled by the camera, her figure not yet fully returned after the pregnancy. Proud papa, holding a bundle of blue in his arms. Papa and Mama together, young Carl on their laps, laughing (was Stitzer the clowning photographer?). Carl alone, on a two-wheeled bike, looking frightened. Mark and Mrs. Thorne, brother and sister, arms around each other, the woman older now, her hair cut short in the first matronly bob. It seemed to add ten years to her age. Pauline touched her own hair, crimped close on the sides, barely covering the nape of her neck in back. Why do we do that to ourselves, she wondered; it's like an amputation. She heard a name being spoken, groaned, from the other room. She ignored it. Finally, only pictures of Carl or Stitzer. Few of them together—who would hold the camera?—until Carl's senior year in high school. Carl in his letter sweater—the high jump—and Stitzer in his cab-driving outfit. They held a football between them, each clutching an end, like two dogs with a bone. They looked so pleased with each other. Pauline had taken that one.

Carl seemed to be trying to construct a past for himself out of celluloid and artifact, she thought. These belonged in an album, fading and wrinkling in the back of a closet, not on display. The furniture belonged in a jumble sale. Poor Carl. Nothing wasted, but everything lost . . . She noticed there were no pictures of her.

The storm had subsided in the other room. Pauline slipped into her bed and promised herself she would go back to her own apartment tomorrow. It had been a silly idea in the first place; she didn't belong here. She was surprised that she had allowed Carl to talk her into it so easily.

The streetlights cast shadows on the ceiling, moving shapes of black on white. More ghosts, she thought. The whole apartment is filled with ghosts.

After the third day Stitzer withheld the Pentothal and Coombs came reluctantly to his full senses. He had awakened on the first day following the ordeal in the bathtub to find himself unbound in his own bed but too tired and woozy to move. Stitzer sat beside him, reading a magazine, and Coombs had lain silently, afraid to budge. His mouth was numb, and he recognized the paralyzing effect on his lips of novocaine. Probing with his tongue, he found a landscape of teeth drastically altered. One molar was missing and he could feel a hole as big as a trench, the gum flapping loosely inside it. Another molar had a filling in the side, still fresh enough to feel like aluminum on his tongue. There were other changes, more subtle, surfaces once jagged had been leveled, a tiny dent had appeared where his tongue had known only smooth surface before. Coombs felt as if he had been given another man's mouth.

Coombs kept his eyes closed, but he could hear the change in Stitzer's awareness.

"*Zdravstvni,*" said Stitzer. Coombs did not move. "Good morning," Stitzer repeated in English. "How you feeling?" Coombs tried to will himself back to sleep.

Stitzer held two fingers forming a V a quarter inch from Coombs's eyes. Coombs's eyelids flew open; the fingertips filled his vision. He gasped and felt a tug in the flesh of his arm like a stitch.

Stitzer pulled back his fingers and smiled.

"Hello, there, Sleeping Beauty. How about some breakfast?" Coombs sat up dizzily. A twinge reminded him of his collarbone, but it was not as sharp as it had been. He felt the stitch in his arm again and looked down to see the hypodermic syringe taped to his forearm, the needle still in his flesh. Two cc's of liquid were in the syringe, but a hair-thin line of blood had worked its way into the needle.

Stitzer fed him orange juice through a straw and cold scrambled eggs. His lips would not grip the straw properly and Coombs sucked spastically, fighting the novocaine. He was intensely thirsty and for a moment was able to concentrate completely on the spreading cold in his throat and chest and not worry about what was going to happen next. Stitzer spooned in the eggs himself.

"Chew on your right side, please," he said, as benign and disinterested as a dentist. The right side was where his teeth had been altered. Coombs felt grit abrade the new surfaces. He spat out the pale yellow muck, but without the support of his lips the eggs dribbled down his chin.

"They got sand in them!" he protested.

Stitzer lifted the plate in front of Coombs's face, as patient as a grandparent feeding a toddler.

"Chew on the right side, please."

Coombs clamped his jaws shut. He could feel the new fillings react unpleasantly to the grit. With his tongue he tried to excavate the hole where his molar had been. Goddamned if he'd eat sand.

Stitzer waited, the spoon in front of Coombs's mouth, not saying a word. Coombs looked into his eyes. They seemed so reasonable, so understanding, so tolerant. Stitzer was growing a mustache and the hair was coming in brown with flecks of white. A four-day stubble of hair covered his head like the bristling stumps of thousands of wheat stalks after the harvest. His head looked dangerous to the touch. A light brown squirrel, no bigger than a fingernail, was nosing into the stubble as if diving for cover.

"If you don't eat, you'll starve," Stitzer said. Coombs realized he meant it literally. He opened his mouth.

"The fuck you doing to me?" he demanded, his voice whining.

"Chew on the right side," said Stitzer.

"What about my dogs? You feed them yet?"

"In three days," said Stitzer.

"Shit! They'll eat each other before that!"

"Not quite." He presented another spoonful to Coombs's lips. Dutifully Coombs opened his mouth.

"I hate this!" Coombs said suddenly with an explosive sob. Little bits of egg fell onto his shirt. He had not meant the food. Coombs was surprised to hear the fear in his own voice; he hadn't known he was that afraid.

When Coombs finished the eggs, Stitzer gently pressed the plunger of the syringe and Coombs felt himself tumbling backward into sleep. He was relieved and gave himself readily.

"When you going to stop this?" he asked groggily,

already feeling the darkness welling up from his arm to his brain.

"In three days," Stitzer said.

At the second feeding Coombs tried to fight. He swung as Stitzer had his hands full with the plate and spoon. It wasn't even close. Stitzer blocked the blow with his left elbow and thrust with his right hand, the fingers doubled over at the second knuckle to form a wedge of bone. Stitzer withheld the blow an inch from Coombs's temple. Quivering, he slowly lowered his hand, the fingers still bent so they looked like a broad-nosed snake. Coombs realized the blow would have shattered his temple like glass.

"You're in a hurry," Stitzer said, his voice tight. "I thought you understood better than that."

"Sorry," said Coombs. He knew he had been an inch away from death, and he accepted the spoonful of cold egg with gratitude.

For three days he dozed, woke to eat—always the same gritty eggs—and dozed again at Stitzer's chemical command. He was aware, dimly, of Stitzer's ministrations, of being assisted to the bathroom and placed on the toilet like a child, where he would doze again. He could feel himself being lifted at times and carried back to his bed, and several times he perceived that Stitzer had pried his mouth open and was studying his teeth, probing gently at the new creations with some sort of pick. Coombs incorporated it all into his dreams, but they were strangely peaceful, filled with images from his childhood of his mother and, more surprisingly, of his father, a stern, cold man who had beaten him more than he had spoken to him. Yet in the dreams it was his father who tended to him during his long, lingering, mysterious illness that debilitated but did not threaten. The dreams were serene and nostalgic and Coombs would often leave them with a pleasant ache in his throat. It was only when he was awake that he was afraid.

On the third afternoon Stitzer withdrew the Pentothal.

"Your mouth looks good," he said.

Coombs nodded. His tongue had grown accustomed to it, the tingling newness of the fillings had gone, the shapes now seemed familiar. Even the excavation where the molar had been extracted seemed to have hardened and closed, like a hole filled in by the erosion of its edges.

Stitzer helped him to his feet and unbuckled the figure-eight strap from his chest and back. The clavicle was still tender but no longer hurt. The enforced rest seemed to have done him some good, although he was shaky on his feet.

"Have you ever broken any other bones?" Stitzer asked.

"My nose," said Coombs. Stitzer touched the tiny lump on the bridge of Coombs's nose. His fingers were cool and gentle. Coombs let his eyelids flicker closed. He knew Stitzer would not hurt him. He had come to trust him, to depend on him.

"How did it happen?"

"Got in a fight. Son-of-a-bitch hit me with an axe handle." His wife had struck him with the edge of a plate the day she walked out. His lie had been reflexive and Coombs regretted it. He knew it was dangerous to lie to Stitzer; it was also a betrayal. He felt certain Stitzer would not lie to him.

"Any other breaks? Even as a kid?"

Coombs thought hard and finally shook his head. Stitzer nodded and Coombs felt strangely pleased by his approval.

"How tall are you?" Stitzer asked.

"Six feet."

"How tall . . . exactly."

"Five feet eleven and a quarter."

Stitzer smiled. "I thought so." He tugged at his waistband, as if asking Coombs to look. Coombs stared dumbly for a moment, then realized how well his clothes fit the sergeant. The pants were a little bit long, perhaps, but Coombs was not particular, they might have been too long on him as well.

"Feel like a walk?" Stitzer asked. He smiled again. The mustache was coming in well. Seven days' growth began to look good above his lip, but it still seemed pathetically short on his head. Coombs realized that Stitzer was a good-looking man, would be handsome when his hair was full. It surprised him; it was not the kind of observation he normally made.

Still shaky, Coombs hesitated uncertainly at the head of the stairs. Stitzer gripped his bicep firmly. Coombs realized he would not let him fall; he would take care of him. Once in the living room, Stitzer released him. Squinting against the sun that poured across the room, Coombs still felt uncertain about his footing. He reached out once when he felt he might fall and grabbed Stitzer's arm. When he had steadied himself, he left his hand there. He was grateful that Stitzer didn't seem to notice.

They paused in the kitchen.

"Hungry?" Stitzer asked.

Coombs shook his head no. Above the refrigerator a spider had spun a web linking the top of the machine with the cupboard above. It was a scrawny web, no more than a few strands running vertically; the spider was nowhere in sight.

"No more eggs," Stitzer said. "No more pumice. You can have anything you want. Except your chocolate. I'm afraid I ate that. Sorry."

"That's all right . . . It's bad for my teeth, anyway." Coombs chuckled uncertainly, not sure if he could make a joke. When Stitzer smiled, Coombs knew it was all right. He had survived it, whatever it was, and something new had come out of it. Stitzer clapped a friendly hand on Coombs's shoulder, steering him out the door. No one had ever been so solicitous with Coombs in his life, so patient and caring, not even his wife.

The sun was blinding at first, but after blinking for a minute, Coombs looked up at the sky, as blue as a morning glory. The air was still at ground level, but high above, a cloud raced past as if being chased. Watching the cloud move made the earth seem to spin.

The dogs looked thinner than usual, their ribs seemed to be pushing through their hides. Still muzzled, they whined and keened, but lay down, their hind legs propelling them forward in supplication, when Stitzer raised his hand. Coombs remembered they had not eaten in a week or more.

"What was it all about?" Coombs asked Stitzer, his eyes still on the dogs. Their eyes looked crazed.

*"Molis,"* said Stitzer.

Coombs turned to see what he meant.

"Pray," Stitzer said in English. His hand, fingers formed into the serpent's head, crashed into Coombs's temple. The dogs leaped to their feet as the man crumpled with a wet sound like a trampled mushroom.

# Chapter 7

Blatty made it clear that he was not seeking matronly advice after all. From the moment they entered the restaurant he had shown her the small attentions of courting. Twice he picked imaginary bits of lint from her sweater. At one point he reached across the table and gently rearranged a strand of hair on her forehead with his little finger.

It was a small Italian restaurant so redolent of atmosphere that the food was an afterthought. They dined on escarole in brodo (a dish Pauline never would have ordered herself for fear of bits of green stuck between her teeth—but Blatty was being masterful and had ordered for them both), noodles Alfredo, veal piccata. Her stomach unsettled by excitement, Pauline picked at her food, trying to rearrange it sufficiently so that it would look eaten. She yearned for a crust of the Italian loaf, to dip it in the oil and sop it up like a sponge, then to devour it with slurping sounds. She drank too much wine and blamed what happened later on the extra glass. The alcohol made her retreat into stillness, the only activity she could trust.

"You're so calm," Blatty said, following a lull in the conversation.

"I've been told that," she said. "I think it just means my features aren't very mobile. Like a fish. You never know what a fish is thinking because nothing on the face moves."

"I would have said a bird of prey," he said. "A magnificent eagle, soaring."

"Me?"

"Sure. See, talons." He put his fingers lightly on hers, touching the fingernails. Pauline realized it was a practiced, calculated remark, but she should have had long fingernails to make some sense of it—hers were trimmed short. Blatty didn't seem to notice. He left his fingers on hers, their tips touching.

"I wonder what it would take to excite you," he said, his voice a full tone huskier.

This routine should not be working so well, Pauline thought. I'm a mature woman and this is about as subtle as a slap and tickle. Yet she wished he would stop talking and call for the check.

In the taxi he sat very close, his thigh pressed against hers. She could feel the heat of his body coming through the cloth. When the cab hit a pothole he moved even closer so he was half atop her. When he spoke his breath wafted into her ear. She smiled. Emboldened, he puffed tentatively, causing the hair beside her ear to ruffle like a cat's back, shivering. She wanted to tell him it wasn't necessary to seduce her. All she required was some sincere attention, and right now he was way ahead on points.

Her stomach growled discreetly, and in confusion he apologized.

They stepped from the cab in front of her apartment building, a converted brownstone on West Eighty-first Street. Garbage cans stood by the stoop, their lids askew. Blatty took her arm as the cab pulled away and turned her toward him. He held both her shoulders, pulling her body into his.

"This is going to be wonderful," he said. His nose was almost touching hers. His voice was so dry she wondered if his throat hurt.

"Yes," she said, smiling, hoping he wasn't expecting too much.

Carl Thorne rose from the shadows on the stoop.

"Aunt Pauline?" he said, his voice questioning, as if he could not quite make her out in the gloom. Or perhaps could not believe it was her in the grip of this curly-haired seducer.

"Oh God," said Blatty.

"I have to talk to you."

"Not again," said Blatty. Pauline touched his arm, trying to calm him.

"Does it have to be now?"

"Yes," said Carl. His voice was constricted.

"Tomorrow, my man," said Blatty.

Carl turned angrily toward the other man and his face came fully into the light from the brownstone window. The corners of his mouth were tugged down as if weighed. His eyes looked tired and faintly red. She wondered if he had been crying.

"I'm not your man. Why don't you go home?"

"Carl," she said, trying to soothe him.

"Why don't you, asshole," Blatty demanded. His voice was savage, trembling with possessive rage.

Suddenly they were grappling, clutching one another in a bear hug and aiming futile, awkward blows at ribs and backs. They fought like boys on a playground, plenty of fury and energy but no skill and little damage. It had sprung up so suddenly, as if they had both been primed for violence and needed only a spark to set them off. Pauline watched for a moment like a spectator, a doe witnessing the conflict of two stags. She had an interest in the outcome but no influence. They stumbled into a trash can and fell. Momentarily on top, Blatty struck at Carl's face, missed, and hit the sidewalk.

"Stop it!" she said sharply. "Both of you!"

They seemed eager to comply, as if they had just been waiting for any reasonable excuse. Carl stood up, but Blatty stayed down, doubled over, cradling his fist against his stomach.

"Aunt Pauline, he's dead," Carl said, his voice cracking.

For a second she thought he meant Blatty. Then she realized it was Sergeant Mark Stitzer who was dead.

"They wouldn't tell me what happened, not on the telephone," said Carl. They were in her apartment. They had come there simply because of proximity, but Pauline realized now that it was a good idea to keep him with her, away from the mausoleum of embalmed memories where he lived.

"What could be so terrible they can't tell me on the phone?" he asked. Her mind flirted with possibilities but she shut them out.

"Did they say he suffered?"

Carl shook his head mutely. His sorrow was overwhelming, like a palpable weight that slowed his every action and made it difficult for him to speak. Pauline's grief was insufficient next to his. She sat quietly beside him, holding his hand, waiting for him to speak again while she tried to think what she felt. Her mind refused to address the matter squarely; it would glimpse the shape in the darkness, then skitter off frivolously and occupy itself with trivia—the quality of light coming through the embroidered red dragon on the shade of her favorite lamp, a copy of a Chinese urn; the busy sound of silence in a city apartment, electric clock whirring, refrigerator humming, even the light bulb seeming to whine with heat at the threshold of hearing. Her mind would return, dutifully but reluctantly, to the death, then whirl away again, frightened. She remembered Blatty, a picture of frustrated lust, holding his fingers in his mouth for comfort like a child. He limped as if all injuries demanded a crutch, no wound significant if not observed by others. It seemed pathetic then, comical now, but she did not laugh.

"I'm going up there tomorrow," Carl said, breaking the silence and startling her. "Do you want to come?"

She looked at him, surprised. His eyes had the red-rimmed, dragged-down look of a bloodhound.

"You don't need to," he said. "I gather there's no body to identify."

"What do you mean?" she said, aghast.

"I don't know, I got that impression. I was too shocked to ask questions. I'm to gather his personal effects."

"Did he have any?"

"It's a formality."

She put her hand on his neck, trying to comfort him.

"I don't want to come," she said, after a pause.

"No," he said flatly. She couldn't tell if she was being judged.

"Mark died for me five years ago in a coyote den in the desert," she said. "I didn't know that man with the shaved head who prowled his cage like a wolf. That wasn't my husband, that wasn't your uncle."

"That was still him," said Carl.

"It wasn't, Carl. I prefer to remember him the way he was before."

"Prefer. Christ, yes, I *prefer* it too." He shrugged her hand off angrily. "But it's not that easy. He didn't cease to exist when he went insane. He *changed,* but he didn't die. He could still feel, he was still hurting inside."

"How do you know what he was feeling?"

"He was in constant torture."

"You don't know that."

"What do you think insanity is? He hurt. Right up to the end."

"Are you blaming me because I stopped visiting him?" Carl did not answer. "He spit at me, Carl."

"He spit at me, too. He did worse. He tried to piss on me once . . . I kept going."

"You've blamed me all this time, haven't you? Silently, smugly criticized me."

"No, I haven't."

"Don't judge me by your standards."

"I thought it was more painful for you," Carl said. "You were his wife."

"Don't be humble. You've suffered more than a mere wife could. You've made that obvious enough."

"I don't like it."

"You're very good at it, for someone who doesn't like it. Don't expect me to outmourn you, either. I'm no match for you."

He left the couch and moved away from her, his back stiff with reproach. Pauline was surprised at her bitterness. She wondered how much of it was due to guilt—for of course Carl was right, she recognized that even as she denied it; she should have suffered more. She should be bereft now, but he gave her very little room, his grief usurped the territory.

When she apologized later she went too far the other way, swinging past honesty into overpraising his faith and devotion, belittling her own. Either way was wrong, and she knew it but could not seem to find the middle ground.

The night stretched on with more silences than speech until at last she made him a bed on the sofa and retired to her bedroom. She did not want to be with him any longer; she knew she could not come to terms with her husband's death while Carl was around to watch her progress—but she did not want him to be alone tonight, either. He made no protest when she suggested he stay over.

Pauline slipped into a state that was not quite sleep. She did not direct her thoughts, they floated, but she was conscious of them all. Gradually her imagination, so fearful at first, began to come to terms with the reality of Mark's death. She saw it in her mind quite vividly, his death a dark shape, like a bear, but without feature, standing in the middle of space while around it played a tiny beam of light, seeking something recognizable within the darkness, some clue. Even as she saw it she realized she must be asleep, but she did not feel like it.

She awakened, startled, heart pounding, at the sound of her own sob. Her face was wet with tears. She saw the door of the bedroom open. A dark form stood in the doorway, silhouetted by the light of the streetlamps coming through the living room window. Carl approached the bed and sat on the edge, holding her hand. He was dressed only in his undershorts. She continued to sob, drawing shuddering breaths as if she were deeply chilled by a cold that would never thaw. He stroked the back of her hand, saying nothing. The light was behind his head and she could not see his face. She was aware how her bare shoulders would appear above the covers where the light passed his body and fell on her pillow. She touched his chest with her fingertips, felt the sparse, silky hairs on the firm breastbone. He sat for a moment and she knew he was trembling. Finally he lifted the blankets and slipped between the sheets. He was shaking all over, quivering against her body like a frightened animal. His erection seemed enormous, and when she put her hand on it, it felt familiar, as if she had known it for a long, long time.

There was no helicopter this time. Death had no urgency. Carl drove to Pleasant Hospital by himself, slowly, feeling as if he were leading a funeral procession of one. He did not allow himself to think of the night before.

The weather was hot and dry and everything drooped, beaten down by the remorseless summer sun. Even the vegetation in the surrounding forest had collapsed, as if the effort of holding leaf and branch erect was too much. Yet the green was startlingly bright, unnaturally luminous. It looked to Carl as if the plants were feverish, responding to disease with a febrile incandescence. He wondered if it were terminal.

Nothing moved. No breeze stirred the vegetation, no birds took wing; if there were animals at all in the woods, Carl imagined them burrowed into the cooler earth, hiding in what shade they could find, their mouths open, silently panting. He had no air conditioner in the car. Marissa called it puritanical self-denial. He contended it wasn't worth the money since he needed it only a few times all year. The result was the same—he sweltered in the heat. The wind from his open window only seemed to make matters worse, stirring the heat so it touched every inch of his body. Sweat dripped down his torso and accumulated in his socks, his shorts. By the time he arrived at the hospital, he felt as if he had been driving underwater.

"Terribly sorry. A dreadful thing," Michaelmas mumbled, shaking hands. "Dreadful. Most sorry." He withdrew like a funeral director, paying his professional respects, then discreetly removing himself so the real mourners could take the stage.

Agent Capello had his jacket off, hooked over his shoulder by a finger. His short-sleeved shirt was open to the navel, revealing hair on his chest and stomach thick enough to be fur. The hair was clumped and matted with sweat. Capello's normal ebullience was gone. He was restrained, almost depressed, but whether due to the heat or the occasion, Carl did not know. Only Stroup was unchanged.

He still seemed skeptical and angry, churning with an inner rage that had little to do with changing events.

They drove in Capello's car. The car was air-conditioned and Carl felt a shock when he stepped into the frigid air. As usual, the effect lasted only briefly and then the unnatural air seemed to lose all power to cool.

"He gave us fits, doubling, and redoubling on his tracks," Capello said. "To be honest, after the first day, the dogs didn't have a chance of finding him, he was too smart. If he had just left the area—in fact we thought he had—he would have been clean away. Oh, we would have caught up with him eventually . . ." Stroup snorted contemptuously. Capello steered a bit more carefully for a few seconds but otherwise did not react. "But for some reason he stayed around."

The car pulled into Coombs's driveway and Carl got out, bewildered.

"He was here?"

"We believe he stayed here until Coombs returned from the hospital," Capello said.

"I was here," Carl said. He remembered standing on the porch, peering through the window, the muffled *eeee* he had chosen to ignore. Had that been his uncle, crying for help?

"We know," said Capello. "We found your note to Coombs. It had your uncle's fingerprints on it."

"My God."

"You couldn't have known," said Capello.

"You were lucky," said Stroup. "I warned you. Did you have to go looking for trouble?"

"I was looking for Coombs."

"Damned lucky you didn't find him."

Capello led the way around to the back of the house. The kennel door stood open. A stench of rot hung over the kennel, kept low to the earth by the heavy air.

"It appears that Coombs killed your uncle," said Capello. "Or caused him to be killed. He may have shot him first with a shotgun. I rather hope so."

Capello stepped into the kennel. "We found a number of double-ought buckshot pellets in here. The shotgun had been fired recently. It may well be he shot him first."

"First? . . . What else?"

Capello glanced at Stroup, looked back at the ground trampled by the footprints of many men, as if even at this late date he might find another clue. "Coombs kept dogs here, Mr. Thorne. Hunting hounds. Five or six of them, we're not sure. Several of them, anyway. Big animals, vicious."

Stroup studied the sky, faded by the sun to a faint gray. He plucked at his shirt, pulling it from his body. He looked bored, disdainful. Capello shrugged his shoulders, lifting his arms from his torso for a moment and holding them momentarily like a scarecrow. Carl felt a drop of sweat break loose from under his arm and course down his side to his belt. The odor in the kennel was making him sick.

"When Coombs didn't come back to work for five days, the hospital sent someone around. He found some bones in there." Capello gestured broadly with both his hands, indicating they had been well scattered. "A shinbone of one leg, thighbone of another, pieces of smaller bones, ribs. They had been gnawed on by dogs."

Carl turned away abruptly. He pressed his head against a kennel post, squeezing his eyes closed. His stomach churned and he could taste bile in his throat, but after a moment he turned back to Capello.

The agent continued as if the interruption had never happened. Carl sensed it was hard for Capello to tell it and only wanted to get it over with and done with.

"They had to be absolutely starving to death to do that to a man."

"Where was the rest of him?" Stroup demanded.

Capello was taken aback by his directness, the anger of Stroup's question.

"The kennel door was open," Capello said. "The dogs had gone, they took some with them . . ." He glanced apologetically at Carl. "There are other animals in these woods, raccoons." He shrugged. "We're still looking."

A movement of black caught Carl's eye. He looked up to see a crow perched in a nearby tree, its mouth open from the heat. Carl had seen crows picking at the corpses of small animals killed on the road.

"How can you be sure it was my uncle?" he asked.

"There was a part of a jawbone left . . . I'm sorry, Mr. Thorne. I can't find a delicate way to put any of this."

"It's all right," Carl muttered.

"We compared the teeth with Stitzer's army dental record."

"Only part of a jawbone?" Stroup asked. "No head?"

Capello gave Stroup a look of disgust, his eyes urging some respect for Carl's feelings. Stroup didn't notice—or didn't care.

"A head is pretty goddamned big for a dog to carry off, Capello."

"We'll find it."

"How do you know this wasn't Coombs?"

"We have Coombs's dental records, too. It was Stitzer. Besides, we know Coombs is still alive."

"How?"

"Three days ago Coombs checked into a motel in Ossining. We have his license number on the registration and he left behind a comb with his fingerprints on it. Two days ago he spent the night in eastern Pennsylvania. He put some quarters in a vibrating bed. They had his fingerprints on them."

"Why?" asked Carl. "Why would he kill my uncle?"

"We'll know better when we find him . . ."

"And you *will* find him, of course," said Stroup.

*115*

". . . but at the moment it looks as if he shot him—I really do think he shot him first, Mr. Thorne—maybe in self-defense, maybe for revenge—your uncle did break his collarbone—maybe by accident, we don't know. Anyway I'd guess that Coombs thought he'd be accused of murder and panicked and ran."

Stroup spit in the kennel. "Well, that's fairly conventional, isn't it, Capello? Conventional and convenient. It's a lot easier to have Stitzer dead, I suppose."

"You don't think he's dead?" asked Carl.

"Well, Mr. Thorne, I don't know if he is or not. Let's say I have an open mind on the subject. But from all I've heard about this Coombs, I don't think a piss-ant like that could kill Sergeant Stitzer if he had a cannon."

Capello drove them back to the hospital. Stroup's anger seemed to have lifted and he appeared amused as he said goodbye to Carl.

"He may be dead. Let's pray he is. But I'll tell you one thing, if I was you, I'd keep looking over my shoulder for a while." Stroup smiled incongruously, his equine teeth touching his lower lip.

Capello watched Stroup drive off before he spoke. "Forget Major Stroup," he said. "He's a hard man, that doesn't mean he's right. Forget Stroup. Take my advice. Forget your uncle, too."

Michaelmas came running after Carl as he entered his car. The heat had built up and it felt like stepping into a sauna. The vinyl seatcover scorched his hand.

"Mr. Thorne," Michaelmas called, flapping one huge hand and puffing from the exertion. Beads of sweat had popped out on the doctor's brow like a row of silver rivets.

"I don't imagine we'll be seeing each other again," said Michaelmas.

"No, I don't suppose so," said Carl.

"I will miss your monthly visit," said Michaelmas. He wiped his brow with his forearm. "It was nice to have someone to talk to.'' He tried an uncertain smile, and for the first time Carl guessed at the depth of loneliness in the life of the self-imposed exile. Michaelmas put a large manila envelope in Carl's hands and trudged back toward the hospital. Heat rose from the asphalt driveway, and for a moment it looked to Carl as if the doctor were walking on water.

After he passed through Speculator, with the hospital and Coombs's horrible kennel behind him, Carl wrestled open the envelope with one hand. He upended it and a book fell on the seat beside him. Carl touched the cheap oxblood cover, ran his fingers over the pebbled surface. A scrapbook of his own writings—his uncle's only effects.

He drove back to New York through mirages of shimmering water. When he saw his first glimpse of the skyline, the towering buildings looked like rifts in the face of the earth, thrown suddenly skyward by subterranean pressures. The heat in the city was worse, and it felt as if the Big Apple were about to burst open in the sun.

# Part Four
# DESTRUCTION

# *Chapter 8*

MARVEEN WAS DUMB, WHICH was why Eastus had to hit her. If she'd been smarter, he could have talked to her and explained that if she ever tried to hold out on him again, he'd amputate her breast—and a whore with only one breast is going to do a greatly reduced volume of business—but Marveen was dumb, she didn't react to verbal threats, so Eastus hit her. He hit her carefully, though, didn't want to mark up the merchandise. Blows to the skull didn't show because of the hair but still hurt like hell.

Eastus was thinking of getting rid of Marveen anyway. She was not only dumb and strung out too far on her habit to be reliable, but she was getting old. He watched her now, strutting under the movie marquee, just the tiniest bit shaky on her platform multicolored clogs, the short shorts too tight on her waffled thighs. Her blond wig looked as if it were slipping. Or maybe it was the heat, the heat made everything look a little off center. He thought he'd replace her with a white girl, the whities were more appreciative of black men anyway. A sister would just take his milk-chocolate skin for granted, but the whiteys seemed fascinated by it, even the ones who'd been around. Black is beautiful, but brown takes the crown.

Eastus contemplated going to the Port Authority tomorrow to see if he could find any young whiteys coming to New York City on the bus. It was a challenge to recruit new pigeons, but in some ways preferable to taking over another pimp's property. The new ones had a longer shelf life. Eastus thought of himself as a businessman who had to tend to his inventory.

A white dude was approaching Marveen now. Looks like he just came off the farm, Eastus thought contemptuously. He sneered at the dude's scuffed boots, the work shirt with the sleeves rolled up to the elbows. His hair was very short, like he just got out of boot camp, but he was too old for that. Eastus had a quick flash of memory, seeing his own Marine boot camp. He would admit it to no one now, but he had enjoyed it. He'd liked all that running and sweating, all that effort, all that yelling. He'd liked the discipline, he'd loved the weapons. There was something about watching tracer rounds, following the gentle arc of trajectory, seeing them all converge on the target, slamming into it, ripping holes. That was before he got smart, of course. He wasn't about to let anybody tell him what to do now. That's why he carried the knife. That's why he kept the .38 Detective Special tucked into his ankle holster. It was a heavy weapon, he wasn't about to take a hike with it—he wasn't hiking in his platform shoes anyway—but it was mean. If you're going to have a weapon—he still thought of them as weapons, part of his Marine training—then it ought to be mean.

The farmer was saying something to Marveen and she was glancing at Eastus, looking more puzzled than anything else. Whatever the farmer wanted, it must be pretty weird to give Marveen a second's hesitation. Now they were walking toward Eastus. He hoped it wasn't trouble, but he was ready if it was. Once in a while he had to show some steel; not very often. He'd been forced to pull the .38 only once, but he hadn't had to use it. It called for very deep shit before he pulled the .38. That was the kind of thing the police got excited about. Eastus didn't like it when the police got excited—nobody on Forty-second Street did.

Marveen stopped a few feet from Eastus. She always tried to stand just out of his reach. Stupid. Didn't she think he could move if he decided to hit her?

"Said he wanted to see you," she said. She snapped her gum and backed off another step.

Eastus looked at the dude and raised an eyebrow. He put his right hand in his emerald green slacks. The handle of the knife seemed to nudge his fingertips reassuringly.

"I wonder if we could talk in private?" said the farmer. He looked at the Orange Julius stand timidly.

"You *in* my office," said Eastus. He was sure the dude wasn't vice. Vice never hassled pimps unless it was about six months before an election.

"This is kind of personal," said the farmer.

"It always is. What you want?"

"I'd be willing to pay for your time," said the farmer. He smiled shyly at Eastus and ran a hand over the stubble on his head. Eastus noticed a light brown birthmark at the hairline. He decided there wasn't any trouble from *this* farm boy, just something peculiar. Eastus's girls didn't like peculiar things, they had their specialties and stuck to them; but Eastus could arrange just about anything, given the right price.

"My time is expensive. You been saving up, farm boy?"

"Yes, I have. For many years."

Eastus laughed. "Get tired of molesting them sheep? Come on then, Farmer."

He led him half a block to the Hotel Mason. The farmer

paid the clerk twenty dollars and they went up a flight of stairs to a room. Eastus touched the knife again as he stepped into the dingy room. The farmer closed the door and leaned his back against it. Eastus didn't like the looks of that.

"What's your name again?" the farmer asked.

"You can call me bad news," said Eastus. He put his hand in his pocket.

"I think you're good news," said the farmer. He smiled at Eastus again, and this time there was nothing shy about it. The farmer looked like he'd grown an inch or two.

"What you want?" Eastus said.

"I want a loan."

"Say what?"

"I have certain business expenses," said the man. He didn't sound like a farmer anymore. "I'm going to need a steady income. Let's say fifty percent of what you make."

Eastus pulled the knife. The blade snicked out with a click.

"You out of your mind, farm boy?" Eastus waved his blade once, gesturing. "Get away from that door."

The man didn't move, but Eastus saw something shift in his face as if a gear had engaged and everything had suddenly been jogged just a fraction of an inch. The face seemed to harden, even the mustache looked as if it had tightened up. The eyes didn't narrow exactly; they seemed to come into focus for the first time. Eastus remembered his hand-to-hand combat instructor in the Marines, an evil gyrene who liked to take fresh boots apart just to hear them scream. He had stood like that in a demonstration ring, completely at ease but somehow coiled.

"Stand away now," Eastus said. He held the knife out in front of him, thumb up the thick part of the blade in the approved cut-and-thrust position. His left forearm was cocked in front of him, part shield, part weapon. The farmer never moved. He acted as if he didn't even see the knife, but Eastus could tell his attention never truly left it. Over the dude's shoulder, Eastus could see the sign advising guests to leave their valuables at the desk.

"The deal I suggest is for you to give me all that you have on you right now as a down payment. I'll come back every Monday and you can give me half of what you made during the week. Does that sound fair?"

Eastus laughed despite himself. The man had to be crazy. Eastus made a tentative move forward. Not close enough to cut him, just to test him. The man didn't move a muscle. Fearless or insane? It made a difference. If the man was fearless, he had to have a reason, and Eastus was in deep shit. If he was just crazy, Eastus would cut him and leave him, there wasn't any point arguing with a crazy man.

Moving closer, crouched over, left arm still up in front as a shield, Eastus came within striking distance. "Move," he said, his voice shaking with excitement. The man didn't budge. Eastus decided to go for his stomach—it was hard to move out of the way, it would scare him but wouldn't kill him. Eastus shot out his left arm, then slashed at the man's midsection. He felt a searing pain in his left elbow and screamed. His head crashed into the door; he could hear the cheap wood splintering.

Eastus scrambled to his feet, waving the knife in front of himself to ward off attack. The farmer stood in the middle of the room, his hands on his hips. He looked—bored. Eastus was amazed at how hard he was breathing. He felt as if he had run a mile already, but all he had done was make one unsuccessful lunge. He realized then that his heart was racing from fear. When he tried to lift his left arm again, he found it would not move.

"Naturally I will trust you about the fifty percent," the farmer said. "We will estimate your weekly income as four thousand, give or take . . ."

With his left arm useless, Eastus could not open the door without releasing the knife. He did not dare to let go of his blade. If he made a move, this crazy man was going to hurt him again, he knew that. It was like waking from a nightmare, afraid of the dark, but just as afraid of getting out of the safety of bed to turn on the light.

"I don't make no four thousand," he said, stalling till he thought of something, "I ain't got but two girls."

"You have four, Eastus," the man said. "I've been watching you."

That was the creepiest thing so far, Eastus thought. The farmer crossed his arms over his chest. Eastus lunged. When he rolled over, he could feel his kneecap was out of place. He dropped the knife and grabbed his knee with both hands.

"Let's start with the down payment," the man said. He didn't even bother to pick up the knife. Eastus was crying and sniffling, trying not to let the whitey see it, but, Jesus, the pain was awful.

Eastus reached into his pocket and pulled out his roll, secured by a diamond clip.

"I'm going to make you that loan," he said. He took out all he had, five hundreds and a fifty, and dropped the bills on the floor. The man didn't pick them up.

"Now the cash in your belt, Eastus." The man squatted in front of Eastus, his face on a level with the pimp's. The man smiled. It was the farm boy smile again, a little shy. "The money you keep for drugs and the payoffs."

"I think you busted my knee," Eastus said.

The man glanced at it. The dislocated lump was evident even through the shiny trousers.

"That's right," he said. "It's fortunate you don't work for a living. The belt now, please."

Eastus winced as the dude removed the three thousand in hundreds hidden in the special compartment in the belt.

"I keep some in my shoe, too," said Eastus. He reached for his ankle, felt the pearl-plated handle of the .38 in his palm, then looked into the man's face. For a second he reminded Eastus of his own father, waiting patiently as Eastus told him lies, giving the young boy a chance to do right, and ready to bust his head for him if he didn't take the chance. I'm probably not coming out of this alive anyway, he thought, and pulled out the pistol. He didn't remember anything after that until he woke up lying on the bed. The sheets smelled the way Marveen smelled after a day's work. When he moved his head it hurt so much he was sure it was cracked, split from one temple to the other. His knee and elbow seemed painless by comparison. The pistol and the knife were lying on his stomach.

It took the desk clerk the longest time to answer his cries for help, and then it was only because Eastus owed for the room for another hour.

Boylan's had been a bar before unmarried people were known as singles, before white wine became a substitute for a mixed drink, and before Perrier became a substitute for white wine; it had been a bar from the days when it was called a saloon with no slur intended or taken. It specialized in draught beer and rye and Scotch whiskey, with bourbon heavily favored as well. Peanuts were served in wooden bowls at the bar, and the only other edibles were jerked beef in a roll as long, thin, and corded—if not quite as healthy—as a hand-rolled cheroot, and hard-boiled eggs prepared by Quinlan himself and stored in a one-gallon glass jar that once held pickles and still lent an odor of vinegar and spices to the eggs. Quinlan was said to be a direct descendant of the eponymous Boylan, several times removed, but appeared old enough to have been the founder himself. The old man came every evening at seven and acted in relief while the bartender ate dinner, serving rye and Scotch and, with a grudging distaste, a limited number of mixed drinks—if he didn't know them, he didn't make them, and his memory was fading fast. Quinlan was so old that he had come to think of his own aged crotchets as picturesque; so old that some of his customers agreed. Quinlan's hands, along with his temperament, were a source of wonderment to his patrons—mostly the employees of the tabloid that had its headquarters two doors away—in that they were as begrimed as a sock tossed negligently under the bed and discovered years later in the sack of the vacuum cleaner. Dirt seemed to have been pulled into the very fabric of the hands as if by continuous suction. Some of the reporters suggested that the grime had adhesive qualities and that Quinlan never dared wash them for fear his fingers would fall off. Others suggested that Quinlan actually had no hands, what one saw were early prosthetic devices made from clay, cunning in their movement, ingenious in their imitation of the real thing, but abandoned by the medical profession because of their solvency in water.

Quinlan's tolerance of uncleanliness extended to the interior design of the bar. It was a dark, dingy place with high-backed booths made of shrinking pine whose original varnish was being replaced by the hair oil, natural and bottled, of generations of reporters. Even the interior of the light bulbs seemed dirty, for they gave off little illumination. The reporters liked the atmosphere. With the air of comrades during a war, they made virtues of necessity and exaggerated the faults of Boylan's until it appeared that they were rare people indeed to have survived it. Reporters, as much as most people, tend to think of themselves as a special breed.

Like any group of people laboring for the same employer, the reporters complained a lot. Their conversation was concerned less with the events that filled their written stories than with the slights rendered by the cretin on the night desk, the temper tantrums of the city editor, the parsimony of the publisher. They spoke, as the night wore on and they looked for reasons to avoid going home, of their dreams and ambitions. They dreamed of glories away from their job, the future was always somewhere other than their newspaper. One man had once authored annual reports for major corporations, and he spoke of returning to it. Clarke, a police reporter, had been writing a novel for seven years. One day, he said, he would do it full-time. The others were quietly respectful—they all had their own fantasies. A man who apprenticed to the regular food editor had sickened of dining out at the expensive restaurants he reviewed, and longed to establish a small restaurant of his own.

"With a different menu every day," said the food writer, whose name was Sheehan. "I'd cook whatever I felt like when I got up that morning, and I wouldn't take more than twenty customers a night." The others thought of all those expense-account meals he ate, compared them with their own lunches eaten on the street, on the run, and assumed he was crazy. But they were respectful of him, too.

Wistfully, the talk would turn in time to the latest work available at the *New York Times*. They all knew they would never be hired by the *Times*. Working for the city's largest-circulation newspaper had left them slightly tainted. Even the best of them suspected that it was an ostracism they somehow deserved. A man who spent years writing captions for pictures of the city's maimed and traumatized and violently deceased eventually lost confidence in his ability to write a balanced, reasoned appraisal of developments at a summit talk. An even larger stumbling block, however, was the *Times*'s Byzantine structure, which required "new" reporters, no matter how experienced, to undergo a lengthy apprenticeship. It was a sacrifice of seniority few established journalists were willing to make.

It occasionally happened that some of the mighty fell from their heights. A former music critic for the *Times,* his copybook blotted, had found himself working for Carl's paper, assessing the latest performance of Vivaldi just as blithely as if anyone in his new readership were likely to care. He was regarded by the others with a sort of contemptuous respect, like a former matinee idol performing daily on a soap opera.

Carl liked them all. He found them warm and funny and amazingly naive, and he assumed that he must appear the same way to them. But he did not think of himself that way. He was not a reporter, he was a columnist, a distinction he had worked hard to create and took some pains to maintain. Others reported the facts, he took the facts and squeezed them for the emotion. Carl sought out the small stories that would otherwise have gone unnoticed and revealed the "human interest." This day he had written a story about a man who had received a cornea transplant from a deceased heart patient. Seeing through the eyes of a dead man was how he put it. The recipient had been a perfectly ordinary man, who, after his initial moments of wonder, had taken the matter in stride. It had been left to Carl to invest the man with fulsome gratitude and to elevate his life to a sort of moral lesson. Carl took a craftsman's pride in his work, line by line, paragraph by paragraph, as if, in constructing a man by devoting enough attention to sinew and bone, he would capture the soul as well.

He was killing time after work until Pauline was finished with her art class. He knew they would spend the night as they had spent the last four, wrapped in each other's arms, gazing into each other's eyes, then making love again when silence was no longer strong enough to express their emotion. The intensity of his love was startling to him, and he found he needed these moments with his colleagues to relax from the passion.

"It's going to be about this guy who's a police reporter," said Clarke the police reporter. He frequently discussed his novel-in-progress—it was more fun than writing it.

"Faintly autobiographical, is it?" said Sheehan, the food critic.

"Just for verisimilitude," said Clarke. He resented any suggestion of autobiography, as if it implied a lack of imagination. "Do you want to hear this, or don't you?"

"No," said Sheehan, who had decided to have his menu scrawled in chalk on a blackboard in the front of his restaurant. In English, no pretension, no French. The patrons could study the menu before taking their tables, then give their orders when they sat down. No delay, higher turnover. He wasn't sure he liked the idea.

"He's covering this homicide and he thinks he knows who did it," Clarke continued. "But the cops don't believe him. He investigates it on his own . . ."

"You mean he leaves the cop house?" asked Feeny, a sportswriter. Feeny was a thin man who had an enormous potbelly the size and shape of a basketball. It looked as if it had been surgically grafted onto him.

"It's fiction," said Sheehan.

Clarke sank into a sullen silence, sipping his rye, until his detractors grudgingly ceded the floor once more.

"He discovers the murderer is his father, who left home when the reporter was only three years old," said Clarke.

"How could he be a reporter at three?" Feeny asked. "What a kid!" Feeny moonlighted by ghostwriting the autobiographies of athletes. He referred to himself, with a proud cynicism, as the Phantom. No one else did.

"Are you in love, Thorne?" Sheehan asked suddenly. Carl realized he had been staring vacantly into the middle distance over Clarke's shoulder.

"What?"

"You're either in love or constipated."

"He does look like he's straining inwardly," said Feeny.

Carl chuckled uncertainly. He liked the raillery of these sessions, the feeling of being amid a cloud of magpies swarming an owl with shrill but harmless insults; but he did not know how to react when it turned on him.

"Got a new girl, Carl?"

Carl shook his head, feeling his smile fade at the corners. He did not want to discuss Pauline with his friends, not even obliquely.

"Anybody want anything?" he asked, rising, starting toward the bar. Of course they all wanted something, but he felt it was a cheap price to pay to get away from the attack. He loved Pauline, but aside from that paramount fact, he had not yet decided how he felt about their relationship. He was certain he ought to feel guilty, but thus far he did not.

Quinlan served him, putting the drinks on a plastic tray next to the glass jar of eggs. Carl thought he could detect the faint smudges of Quinlan's fingerprints on the creamy shells.

"You got a brother?" Quinlan asked.

"Me? No. I don't have a brother. Why?"

Quinlan paused in midthought as he often did, his thoughts coming down as cautiously as the feet of a man moving over thin ice. As he grew older, the pauses lengthened, giving his conversation the rhythm of a Pinter play.

"Man was in here this afternoon, looked something like you," Quinlan said. He moved away to wait on another customer. Carl waited until he returned.

"You say he looked like my brother?"

"Something like that, not exactly. I could tell it wasn't *you*. He asked about you, so I thought he might be related."

"What did he ask?"

"Did you come in here, how long had you worked at the paper, stuff like that. Seemed to know about you."

"What did you tell him?"

Quinlan shrugged, then seemed to drift off. Carl feared that one day Quinlan would slip his moorings entirely, pause in midconversation, and never return. Not die, just slowly drift out of sight, like a leaf borne downstream on a gentle current.

"What do I know?" Quinlan said finally. "You cóme in here sometimes, you been doing it for years. I don't keep track."

"How was he dressed?" Carl asked. He didn't know what he hoped to learn from the question.

"He had clothes on," said Quinlan with a shrug.

"That rules out Lady Godiva," said Feeny when Carl returned with the drinks and told them of the visitor.

"Maybe it's a fan," said Clarke.

Carl chuckled wryly. In seven years he had received one fan letter. He had felt very flattered until it turned out that several of his colleagues had gotten similar letters. He was jealous enough to want his own admirer. He didn't value a fan who liked everybody.

Three days later Sheehan stopped by Carl's desk. He was passing out cold oriental appetizers, each individually wrapped in foil. The manager of a Chinese restaurant had penetrated Sheehan's halfhearted disguise and lavished him with the equivalent of a ten-course banquet for six. Sheehan had protested, but not too forcefully, as the hopeful restaurateur brought forth three kinds of dumplings, jelly-fish skins, pickled vegetables, shrimp toast, tea eggs, cold chrysanthemum leaves, and bean curd swimming in sesame oil. Sheehan dispensed the excess to his colleagues, sniffing grandly when they praised him for his good fortune, speaking knowingly of too much coriander, too little ginger, inferior soy sauce.

"By the way, I saw that mystery visitor of yours," Sheehan said. Carl stopped unwrapping his portion of cold spring roll, the once-crisp skin now the consistency of wet cardboard.

"Who?"

"The man Quinlan told you about. At least I assume it was the same man. He looked kind of like you."

"Where?"

"Here, in the building. Down by the lobby."

"Did he ask you about me?"

"No. He wasn't talking to anyone, just watching people pass. A nice-looking man, not as big as you are, but solid."

"And he looked like me?"

"Yes, sort of. Very short haircut, though. That makes him stand out."

Carl felt a chill. He didn't know if it was dread or excitement.

"When was this?"

"This morning," Sheehan said.

"If you see him again, let me know, would you?"

"Sure," said Sheehan. "What's the matter, did you misplace a relative or something?"

"Or something," Carl said. When Sheehan had moved on, Carl tried to think of the name of the man who had served as his uncle's commander.

Pauline dismissed her class five minutes early, fumbling with the buttons in her eagerness to remove her smock. Love was good to her figure; her slacks no longer pinched, the extra flesh at her waist had all but gone. For the past week she had treated herself to late-night sex rather than a snack. It had done wonders for her, she decided. When she looked at herself in the mirror, she now saw her body through the filmy overlay of adoration Carl had put upon it. It was no longer the body of a forty-two-year-old woman fighting, valiantly but with irreversible losses, against the demands of age; it was now the body that was nightly loved and cherished by a passionate young man. Her breasts looked firmer to her now, her muscles tauter, her skin smoother. Love had taken fifteen years off her age.

She got to his apartment before he did and even as she opened the door she could feel her loins tighten and tingle in anticipation. They had been lovers for a week, but she still felt pleasantly nervous every time. Pauline prepared herself in the bathroom, cleaning, scenting. There was an air of unreality to this ritual that troubled her slightly—could she be always coiffed, perfumed, breathing mint, and draped in a filmy negligee? She knew of course that she could not, that a time would come when he must see her with her face creamed for the night, a showercap on her head. That would be a truer test of their relationship than this elaborately artificial charade—but she saw no good reason to hasten that time.

In the bedroom she put on her negligee, a gossamery confection in blue, her most flattering color. It revealed enough to be enticing, hid enough to be flattering; she had bought it several years ago in anticipation of some sexual fantasy she had long forgotten. The negligee had remained in her bureau ever since, its charms stifled. Other lovers had merited cotton nightgowns or a black number that was frankly lascivious. There was nothing angelic about it, but then her other lovers had not wanted to sleep with an angel. She suspected that Carl needed more fantasy than most, but she doubted that she really needed to provide it; he brought his own supply.

The dresser was another relic from his parents' home. Large, heavy, oaken, it dominated the bedroom with its massive, brooding presence. On top of it were several more framed pictures of his family: mother, father, uncle. A large mirror that pivoted precariously on wooden dowels was attached to the top of the dresser. Pauline tilted the mirror to see herself full length and for the first time noticed a small snapshot tucked into the corner of the frame. She pulled it out and beheld herself, younger, much younger, smiling at the camera. It was a good picture, flattering more by accident than design, for it was clearly the work of an amateur. She was in the woods, fresh snow covered the ground and the pine boughs in the background; a white smirch on her shoulder might have been made by a snowball. Her cheeks were glowing red in the brisk air, her hair was much longer than now, flowing to her shoulders in a billow of black, like the dark water of a forest stream, shimmering with highlights as the sun caught it. For once in her life she didn't seem to be squinting into the sun or suppressing a yawn when the camera snapped. She vaguely remembered the scene, but not the photographer. It was before she was married, it wouldn't have been her husband. She looked twenty-five—younger.

Holding the photo between thumb and forefinger, Pauline looked at her reflection in the mirror, then at the photo, then back to her reflection. What a pretty girl I was, she thought. She did not look so very different now, except for the hair. She was clearly the same person, yet she would no longer refer to herself as pretty. She struggled for a moment, frowning unconsciously, as she tried to think of the word to describe her now. Too mature to be pretty; not beautiful, never that grand, yet attractive still. The word handsome occurred to her. A handsome woman. She had never liked that phrase, never understood it, but felt now as if it might apply. It was not what she would have chosen for herself, but surely it was better than any other epithets she could think of. She noticed the frown wrinkles in her forehead and immediately pressed the palm of her hand against her brow. When she removed her hand a distressing number of lines remained.

On the back of the photo, in a tight scrawl to fit the space, she had written, "To Carl, with my love, Aunt Pauline."

She did not remember giving him the photo, even less the inscription, yet here it sat, tucked into the mirror where he could see it whenever he looked at himself. Was this how he still saw her? When he took her in his arms, was he making love to Pauline the middle-aged artist or to Pauline the pretty young thing who had entered his life when he was still in high school? Or, worse, to a surrogate mother? Pauline was surprised to discover she didn't really care.

The phone rang just moments before she heard Carl's key in the lock. When she said hello she heard the sound of someone on the other end catching his breath, startled.

"Hello," she repeated. "Hello."

The line was not dead but absolutely silent. She could hear no movement, no breathing, but she sensed a presence, listening. Waiting?

"If you're there, I can't hear you. You'll have to call back," she said. Carl opened the door and smiled at the sight of her. She shrugged in dumb show about the phone call and felt her own face split into happiness at the sight of his smile. As she was putting the phone back on the cradle, she thought she heard the sound of a man's laugh. Less than a laugh, a chuckle, a slight, involuntary sound like the clearing of a throat. It was totally without humor, and Pauline hesitated for just a second. Minimal as it was, she felt it sounded somehow familiar. Then the phone was out of her hand and she held out her arms to Carl. The light behind her shone through the negligee and she saw his face change into the intense, troubled expression she had come to recognize as love.

They made love like old friends meeting again after a long separation. Tentatively, uncertain in their greetings, then with a growing confidence of shared emotion that grew into enthusiasm bordering on the boisterous.

Carl made love with great patience, his hands gentle, his fingers caressing her with a lambent, flickering stroke, like the touch of butterfly wings. His lips were soft and hungry but never greedy, never taking until she was willing to give. Afterward she would wonder where he had learned such patience. Remembering Marissa's whoops and hollers, she doubted it was from her. Carl did not make Pauline cry out; he drove her upward with a steadily building tension that revealed itself in long, shuddering sighs, lifted her until she thought she must stop or plummet, then gave her the courage to go still higher. Breathing in short, shallow gasps, her voice coming in barely audible mews, like a small animal, confined and frightened, she allowed him to lift her until finally, clinging to him, grinding against him, she flew apart and dissolved into the air. Afterward she would open her eyes and find him smiling down at her, his eyes shining with love. She had been so preoccupied with herself she scarcely knew if he was satisfied or not. She was amazed that he seemed to take so much pleasure from pleasing her. Stitzer had never shown that kind of love. Mark had made love with passion, with fire, but a fire of such heat that it could not last before it burned itself out. Sometimes Pauline would be ignited by it, sometimes not. If she was not ready, the flames would sweep right over her, leaving her singed but not consumed. Even as she compared the two men she knew she shouldn't, it was fair to neither of them, they were so different. Stitzer commanded respect, even awe and some fear and the excitement that came with it. Carl inspired love.

Reality, she knew, would come later, bringing with it the guilt, the cowardice, the reproach. But she would not hasten it. Let it come if it must, but in the meantime she clung to him in the dark, felt him stir against her, and realized he had only been waiting for her to show the first sign of willingness to be lifted again.

The phone rang again after Carl had drifted into sleep. Pauline stopped him with a touch as he lurched up, startled, and answered it herself. Again she heard the silence that was somehow charged with a presence. This time she felt a sudden chill of fright as if she had heard a footstep in an empty room. The silence had an element of hostility that she couldn't identify but couldn't deny.

"Wrong number," she said to Carl as she returned to his arms.

# Chapter 9

ROUTE 30 IN NEW Jersey is lined by oil refineries, their cracking towers jutting into the air like the elaborate skeletal structures of colossal dragons, frozen erect forever in agonizing cant, the scale and tissue long since burned away, but the mouths still breathing fire. The waste gases that issue from the dragons' mouths burn with an audible sound, a reptilian hiss that is passed from one smokestack to the next, teasing the ear as the dancing nighttime shadows from the orange flames taunt the eye with shapes that are not there.

Stitzer drove through the dragon boneyard at two in the morning, the beacon fires seeming to keep pace beside him, passing from torch to torch as if a relay of runners toiled invisibly beside him in the night. He drove in a stolen car, selected for its dark blue color as well as its accessibility. Stitzer found the access road between two fires and turned off the highway. He turned off the headlights, steering by the flickering lights of burning gas which made the buildings at the end of the road seem to dance and shift like a wraith.

He stopped alongside the Cyclone fence that bordered the warehouse and climbed onto the car's roof. Stitzer paused, listening, knowing he had to rely more on his hearing than his vision. The ceaseless sibilant hiss of the gas sounded in the background and he waited until he no longer truly heard it, consigning it to a background noise. He was listening for something closer and more erratic—the sound of men. Hearing nothing, he stepped from the roof of the car onto the fence, fitting the toe of his sneaker into the diamond-shaped hold, then kicking off and pulling upward with his arms. He cleared the fence and landed in a crouch, then ran toward the warehouse.

The locks were simple—there was not much here an ordinary thief would wish to steal. Stitzer worked with a penlight, picking his way among the stacks of bagged chemicals until he found the pile he wanted. He slashed the ends of the top five bags on the pile, letting the noxious crystals spill onto the ground while he shouldered an intact bag and made his way back toward the fence. The bag was a large one, intended for commercial use, and weighed fifty pounds. He paused at the fence, listening for the guards. This time he heard the sound of a foot hitting stone, but far removed, on the other side of the warehouse. Stitzer bent double, flexing his knees deeply, then straightened abruptly, hurling the fifty-pound bag up with the combined strength of his back, arms, and legs, jerking it into the air like a farmer with the dead weight of a bale of hay. It landed noisily on the other side of the fence, several feet from the car.

Stitzer paused, trying to hear the change in the pattern of footsteps. They stopped for a moment as the guard listened, then came more quickly. But not running. Stitzer knew he still had time. He slipped back into the warehouse. The slashed bags had nearly drained. He tipped them and shook out the last of the crystals, then rolled the five empty bags into a tight tube.

The guard had discovered Stitzer's car. He stood next to the fence, his flashlight playing across the auto, then the bag of chemicals that lay in front of it, then back to the car, as if hoping to find some connection between the two. He fingered the pistol uncertainly. There had never been any trouble before and his job was a formality, not a necessity. This was one of the many chemical-plant warehouses tucked in and around the refineries for convenient access to the carbon compounds they relied upon. The warehouse was well away from any normal flow of traffic. No one wandered by, no one just happened to be there, and most nights the watchman spent in reassuring monotony. He looked toward the warehouse, flashing the light, hoping to find someone—if he had to find anyone at all—outside in the open space between the building and the fence. The last thing he wanted to do was go into the warehouse.

"Who's there?" he called, his voice breaking with nerves. One of the shadows moved and the guard jerked the light toward it, at the same time shakily pulling his gun from its holster. The light found nothing. All the shadows seemed to move, dancing to the tune of the giant flames that burned in the distance, and he flicked his flashlight beam back and forth from one to the other.

The guard never saw the shadow that was Stitzer, nor did he hear anything until the tube of rolled bags hit him on the back of the neck. Stunned and abruptly angry, he tried to lift the gun, but something incredibly tight gripped his hand. He felt the fingers on his neck and tried to cry out before the dragon's flame fluttered out and all was darkness.

Stitzer tossed the tube of empty sacks onto the car and climbed up the fence in two springing leaps. By the time the guard came to his senses, the car had vanished into the night.

Stitzer lay very still at the base of a tree, listening. Any sound in Central Park after dark had to be considered hostile. The fifty-pound bag was strapped to his back and the ropes dug into his shoulders. He moved with infinite patience, shifting the ropes soundlessly, his ears still sorting out the night sounds. Two men were on the ground at the base of a bush twenty yards to Stitzer's right. They had entered the park a few minutes earlier, embracing first while standing, their silhouettes vague but recognizable against the background of buildings on the far side of the park, then they had eased to the ground with a frantic, urgent noise. Stitzer listened to them making love, uninterested. His attention was on the other men, three of them, he thought, who were behind the boulder fifteen yards to his left and lying between him and the reservoir. He could smell the water from where he lay, but to approach it he would either have to skirt the men behind the boulder or wait until they moved. He had never seen them, only heard the scrape of cloth against stone. He had lain still for the past ten minutes, sorting out the rest of their noises, trying to put form and reason to the sounds. He was fairly certain there were three of them, possibly four, and they were patient and calm. Like Stitzer, they were listening, and he could sense the tension in their caution, the same relaxed but ready air of an animal lying in wait for its prey. Stitzer assumed the two lovers to his right were the prey and the muggers had not yet found them, had not yet sorted out their scuffling love noises from the background noise of the city that continued through the night.

One of the lovers moaned softly and Stitzer heard the muggers move, then he saw them, sweeping from behind the boulder, moving in a crouch, two fanning out to one side, the other moving closer to the water so he could come around the victims from the other side.

Stitzer moved when the muggers did, knowing their full attention would be on their prey. He passed silently behind them toward the reservoir, the bag on his back, the tube of empty sacks held out in front of him for balance and as a weapon if he needed it. He could hear the useless pleas of the lovers as he slit the heavy bag and poured the crystals into the city's drinking water. He unfolded the other bags and scattered them along the edge of the water. Pausing a moment, ignoring the noises behind him, he cleared a path before him with his hearing. Content there was no danger there, he moved out of the park and into the sheltering city.

Capello shoved the newspaper across his desk at Carl, then jerked it back. He had been using the paper for emphasis for the last minute, jabbing his finger angrily at the article that ran across the bottom of the front page. It was Carl's tabloid. The scare headline crested a two-column photograph of policemen posing for the camera, two of them holding an empty bag in front of them like proud fishermen with their catch.

*"Maniac Poisons Reservoir!"* Capello shouted.

"I didn't write the headline," Carl said softly.

*"Maniac Poisons Fucking Reservoir!"* Capello continued. He had ignored all interjections since beginning his tirade. Helstrom, the managing editor, shifted his weight in his chair. Carl realized he was trying to control his temper, an act of prodigious and unaccustomed effort. Helstrom had taken the majority of the abuse since he and Carl had been summoned to Capello's office ten minutes earlier. There had been enough for everyone else, to be sure, but Helstrom had received the larger share, and, thus far, he had taken it in tactful silence.

"I feel we've covered this ground, Mr. Capello,"

Helstrom said, clipping each word off neatly, then lingering on the final *o* of Capello.

"Why didn't you say Flee for the fucking hills! Why didn't you just say Panic! Jesus Christ! Maniac poisons reservoir!"

Carl watched Stroup digging under one fingernail with another, his hawklike nose bent over his fingers. He had spoken to no one after grunting a greeting to Carl and Helstrom.

"New York City in the middle of summer—with a poisoned water supply!" Capello threw his head back suddenly and barked a horrible, unhappy laugh. "Why not just tell them to take to the streets and loot and burn, Helstrom? Why not just incite them to riot? What's the point in being so subtle about it?" He turned to Carl. "Why not write a story saying, H-bomb to explode over Manhattan tomorrow?"

"I didn't write the story. I didn't write the headline. I didn't know anything about it until I saw the paper today, the same as you. I don't know why I'm here. What does this have to do with me?"

Capello stared at him for a moment, and when he spoke again, it was as if all his anger had drained away during the silence.

"That ought to do it, Helstrom," Capello said. "Your publisher has agreed that you'll approach any other matters in this case with . . ."

"Circumspection," Helstrom offered.

"Yeah."

"We are always willing to cooperate in matters of security."

"Yeah, you've been swell."

"It appeared to be a straightforward news situation," Helstrom said. "We could hardly avoid giving it coverage."

"Which is just what he wanted," said Stroup, continuing to study his fingernails.

"So we have been apprised," said Helstrom.

"He'll do it again," said Stroup. "And again and again." He looked up and his eyes seemed to impale Helstrom with their anger. "He'll keep doing it until you won't be able to cover it with a five-acre tent."

"Surely you'll have him before then," said Helstrom, looking at Capello.

"We'll have him."

Stroup snorted, then returned his attention to his hands.

"You said he's one man," said Helstrom.

"We'll have him," Capello repeated.

"Did I come in late or something?" Carl asked. "What is all this and what's it got to do with me?"

Stroup didn't speak, but he raised his eyes until they were boring into Carl's with a radiant malevolence. If looks could kill, Carl thought, that man would be an assassin.

Helstrom was ushered out of the front door of Capello's office and Dr. Michaelmas was brought in through a side entrance. Surprised, Carl rose to his feet, took the psychiatrist's chunky hand in his own, and realized that the real meeting had just begun.

Stroup began without preamble. "The poison in the reservoir was Arbrin, a brand name for nicotine sulfate, which is used commercially for insecticides. It's strong and it's lethal, but there was no chance in hell of one man lugging enough to poison the reservoir. He was just trying to get the headlines. Which he did."

Capello raised a hand, stopping Stroup. He looked at Carl. "You realize you are here as a private citizen. Not a syllable is for publication."

Carl nodded, and understood for the first time.

"It's my uncle," he said.

"Of course," said Stroup. "I told you he wasn't dead."

"Possibly," said Capello. Carl noticed that much of Capello's energy seemed to have been lost in the tirade. Stroup was in charge now.

"Definitely. I told you no piss-ant guard is going to kill Stitzer."

"How can you be so sure he's alive?" Carl asked.

"Because he's doing what I taught him," said Stroup.

"What did you teach him?"

Stroup glared silently at Carl as if the question should not have been asked.

"I've got a right to know," said Carl.

"You've got a right to shit," said Stroup.

Michaelmas delicately folded his pudgy fingers, interlocking one with the other as if fearful they might fly away.

"If you want my help—and you wouldn't have me here otherwise—I have to know all there is to know. What did you teach my uncle? How do you know he's alive?"

"We found a head," said Capello. "In Lake Pleasant. A fisherman hooked it. Part of a head, actually. Judging by the dental records, it seems to be the man . . ." He looked to Michaelmas for help.

"Coombs," said the doctor. "An attendant at Pleasant Hospital."

Carl remembered the oppressive heat of the dog kennel in Coombs's backyard, the scent of animals. He remembered the long trip home, his final return from Pleasant Hospital, and the heavy weight of guilt and sorrow that had cloaked him for weeks.

"You said Coombs was seen in Pennsylvania, in a motel . . ."

"Not *seen!*" said Capello. "There was evidence that he'd been there, fingerprints . . ."

Stroup dismissed the discussion with an impatient wave of his hand. "There are ways," he said.

"I'm sure there are. Let's assume you're right and my

Uncle Mark is alive . . ." Carl felt his spirits rise as he gave voice to the thought. "I still don't know what you taught him."

"Major Stroup was the head of a special task force in the Army," Capello said after a silence. "You don't need to know much about it. It has been disbanded. Your uncle was a member of the group."

"What was the function of this task force?"

"Terror," said Stroup. His lips formed something akin to a smile.

"Guerrilla and insurgent warfare," said Capello.

"Terror," Stroup repeated, and Carl could hear the note of satisfaction in his voice. "Your uncle was trained to fight his own kind of war. In the event of conflict, he was to penetrate enemy lines, establish himself within the resident civilian population, and familiarize himself with the target areas."

"Then what?"

"Then, at a given signal, he was to deactivate the area."

"Deactivate?" asked Michaelmas.

"Gut it!" said Stroup. "Rip its insides out. I mean, kill it, Doctor."

"Yes," said Michaelmas. "Sorry."

"How was he supposed to do this?" Carl asked.

Stroup turned his gaze toward Carl. His eyes still burned with anger, but a note of amusement had entered his voice now that he was speaking to the innocent on the only topic that interested him.

"Have you ever heard of the death of a thousand cuts?"

Carl shrugged, realizing no response was necessary.

"It's a Chinese torture, and it means what it says. A thousand cuts, no one of them enough to kill, but taken together, over time, they leave you looking like the fringe on a cowboy's shirt. You are begging, believe me, begging, for the final cut. It was a technique that saw a few refinements in Vietnam. Your uncle was the best we had at it.''

"You don't mean that literally," said Carl.

Stroup looked at Carl in silence, his aquiline nose outlined more clearly as a raptor's beak by the humorless smile underneath.

"Of course not," he said at last. "Uncles don't do such things. Uncles take you to the zoo. Uncles give you piggyback rides. Uncles buy you big presents on your birthday."

"There's no need for that," said Capello.

"He's got to learn what we're talking about," Stroup said sharply. "Him and the good doctor. Stitzer can bring this city to its knees."

"He's only one man," Capello insisted. "How long do you think it could be before we catch him?"

Stroup looked at Capello in wonder.

"You don't understand either, do you? He can do whatever he wants and he can do it indefinitely. We were lucky this time. He wasn't trying to hurt anybody, he just wanted publicity. Terror can't exist without publicity; people aren't scared unless they know they should be. But next time, or the time after that, he's going to start leaving some bodies around. If you want to know how many he can kill before you find him, Capello, let me give you a fast estimate of several thousand. How many can he wipe out with a bomb in a theater? How about a couple of satchels of plastique at a rock concert? And he knows how to use it, let me promise you."

"He's one man, without allies . . ."

"Which means nobody can betray him. He can hole up anywhere in the city. How are you going to find him? He doesn't *need* anything. Whatever he wants, he can steal. How many thieves do you ever catch in this city? Ludicrous. Can you limit his movements? This isn't war, we can't put soldiers and roadblocks on every corner. Look how the PLO slip in and out of Israel, and that's an armed camp. This is his work; it's what he's trained for. He can commute in, blow up the Bronx, garrote cops, poison the wells, then go home to the suburbs! One man, working alone, without pattern. A thousand cuts? More, if he needs to. He'll shred this city.''

"You sound pretty proud of him," said Michaelmas.

"I am, Doctor. He's the best I ever created."

"He's insane."

Stroup shrugged indifferently. "That makes him all the more effective."

"Effective at what?" Carl asked. "What is he accomplishing?"

"At killing the largest city in the nation."

"He thinks he's at war," said Capello.

"He *is* at war," Stroup corrected.

"He believes we are the enemy, that we are all part of a deliberate ruse to confuse him. You remember that," said Michaelmas, folding his arms so his hands could hide in his armpits.

"But why New York? How can you be so certain?" Carl asked.

"Because New York is where I sent him," Stroup said. "It was his last assignment. We were running a war-game exercise. The objective of my group was to penetrate the defensive positions, that's really all it was about. The exercise was supposed to end in two days. To give it a sense of reality, though, we had to have an ultimate objective. Your uncle was briefed as if we were really at war and New York was his target area."

"He doesn't think of it as New York City, though, does he?" said Michaelmas.

"No."

"It would be difficult to simulate a killing rage against your own country, wouldn't it, Major?"

"Of course."

"So where does he think he really is?" asked Carl.

"I don't know where the hell he thinks he is," said Stroup. "I'm not his shrink. For all I know he thinks he's on another planet."

"You can do better than that, Major," said Capello.

"This is all classified," said Stroup.

"It's been cleared," said Capello. "You know that. I can call General Hayden again if you want to be reassured."

"Moscow," said Stroup. "If Stitzer thinks his briefing for the operation has come true, he thinks he's in Moscow."

"We have to assume he thinks it's true," said Michaelmas.

"Then, assuming that, he thinks he's in Moscow—after a nuclear incident. The plan called for seven men to be assigned to the city with him, but each would operate independently, on his own initiative."

"How could you contact him?"

"I couldn't. Nobody could. That's the whole point. He's on his own to do as much damage as he can for as long as he can."

"A suicide mission?" Carl asked, alarmed.

"Suicide my ass. Sergeant Stitzer ain't about to self-destruct."

"How was he supposed to get out?"

"What's the matter with you people? It was supposed to be after a nuclear conflict! If Moscow was still standing, that meant they won! He'd have to assume he was alone anyway."

"If they won, then what was your group trying to do?"

"Resist."

"Resist *after* it was over?" Carl demanded. "Resist what? What would be left to resist?"

Stroup shifted uneasily, his angry glare resting nowhere.

"That's why they were disbanded," said Capello, his

voice surprisingly mild. "They were after something beyond resistance, weren't they, Major?"

"Revenge," said Stroup. "Our purpose was revenge. And I'm damned if I see anything to apologize about in that."

"No," said Capello. "But Congress apparently did." The agent turned to Carl. "Major Stroup's unit, your uncle's unit, was called VG I. Vengeance Group I. As I said, it's been disbanded."

"Stupid," said Stroup. "Criminally stupid."

"I can't believe my uncle was involved in all this," said Carl. "He was a soldier, not an assassin. Not a terrorist. You're asking me to believe he would kill thousands of people just for *revenge?*"

"I'm not *asking* you to believe shit," said Stroup. "I'm *telling* you that Sergeant Mark Stitzer of VG I is about to rip New York City a new asshole, and there's fucking little anyone can do about it."

"We're doing a great deal already," said Capello calmly. "He has to live somewhere. We've got men with photos checking every hotel, motel, every flophouse, every single-occupancy apartment that's been rented in the last month."

Capello tossed a single sheet of glossy stock at Carl. In the center was the identification picture taken of Stitzer on his admission to Pleasant Hospital five years earlier. Surrounding the photo were an artist's renditions of the same shot with mustache, beard, longer hair, eyeglasses. The sheet looked like the audition portfolio of a character actor who specialized in different faces.

"If he's paying rent anywhere in the city, we'll find him," said Capello. "He doesn't know we're looking for him. As far as he knows, we think he's dead."

"That's your only edge," said Stroup. "He doesn't know you're after him. If you're lucky, you'll get one chance. You'd better hope you get him then, because if you don't, he'll go underground faster than a mole."

Carl resisted the urge to crumple the picture and toss it away. Was this really his uncle whose picture was being distributed to every cop and landlord in the city, his image made over into a rogue's gallery of criminal disguises? He believed them, of course; on one level his mind accepted the arguments of Capello and Stroup, the cruel certitude with which they labeled his uncle an assassin, the ease with which they assessed him a terrorist, his fate marked and doomed. But on a deeper level he rejected it all. The man in the picture might be Sergeant Mark Stitzer, accomplished killer, danger to the public welfare, potential mass murderer. But to Carl his Uncle Mark was none of these things.

Carl carefully placed the picture back on Capello's desk. "What will happen if he's caught?" he asked.

"*When* he's caught," Capello corrected.

"He won't get caught," said Stroup. "He might get killed, if we get lucky, but he won't get caught. He won't allow that."

Capello continued as if Stroup had not spoken.

"That determination will be made by the judicial branch. That's not our concern."

"He won't get caught . . . not alive," said Stroup.

"If he does . . ." Carl stopped for a moment. His throat had constricted and he waited for it to ease. He looked to Michaelmas, not knowing if he sought comfort or confirmation. "If he does get caught, he'd be back with you, wouldn't he?"

"At best," said Michaelmas. He stirred uncomfortably in his chair as if wishing to be left out of the conversation. "You may not believe this, Mr. Thorne, but there are worse places than Pleasant Hospital."

"You're right," said Carl. "I don't believe it."

"It doesn't matter where you put him," said Stroup. "He'll get out. If you want him to stop, you'll have to kill him."

"Or cure him," said Michaelmas.

Stroup laughed, an ugly bark that shocked everyone to stillness.

"To cure him, you've got to hold him."

"We held him for five years!" said Michaelmas.

"I wouldn't be too proud of that, Doc. He was just waiting for his trigger. He could have gotten out whenever he wanted."

"What was his trigger?" asked Capello. "What set him off after five years?"

Stroup shrugged. "I know what it was supposed to be, according to his briefing for the operation. What actually did it, who knows? The man's crazy."

"Crazy but with a purpose. What was supposed to happen according to your briefing?"

"It was a newspaper plant," said Stroup. "He was supposed to get to New York and wait for the repetition of the code-word trigger in the newspaper. But hell, he wasn't ever supposed to get to New York. All we really wanted to do was penetrate the ground defenses in New Mexico. The rest was just on paper."

"It seemed to have been awfully thorough if it was supposed to end in two days."

"Thorough is how you survive," said Stroup.

"What was the code word?" asked Capello.

"The same as the name of the operation. Pretty Polly," said Stroup.

"Pretty Polly?" asked Carl, straightening in his chair.

"Operation Pretty Polly," Stroup repeated.

"Does the name mean something to you?" Capello asked.

"I think so," Carl said slowly. "It's the name of a racehorse that broke its leg and had to be destroyed." He remembered the scrapbook his uncle kept of his clippings, remembered Michaelmas passing it to him through the car window on the last day at Pleasant Hospital. He pictured the heavy velour cover, the yellowing strips of newspaper pressed under the plastic. His uncle's final legacy to him—or so he had thought.

"I wrote an article about Pretty Polly," Carl said. "It was in my uncle's scrapbook."

"When did you write it?"

"Just before he escaped," Carl said. "I remember because it was still fresh in my mind when I saw it in the scrapbook." Carl paused and glanced out the window. The view took in the asphalt roof of a building across the street. It looked close enough to leap to. Heat waves shimmered up from the asphalt. He's out there somewhere, Carl thought. Is he lonely, is he afraid? Is he hurt? How can I help him? He felt his throat squeeze in upon itself again.

"My article on Pretty Polly was the last item in his scrapbook," he said, keeping his back to the others.

There was a pause, broken at last by Stroup. Carl did not need to turn to see the sneer on his face.

"Congratulations, Mr. Thorne," Stroup said. "You were the trigger."

# *Chapter 10*

THE BOY LAY ON the cinder horse path of the park, weeping. His cheek was pressed against the stones and one foot was still under the bike, his trouser cuff caught in the gear chain. He was aware that someone was watching him and he struggled to control his sobs; at ten he seldom cried in public anymore. He struggled to his feet, yanking the bicycle upright like a mother with a naughty child, criticism implicit in the violence of the jerk, placing the blame for his spill squarely on the bike. He knew the man was still watching, although he had not looked at him directly, and he continued to play his feelings more dramatically for his audience, tugging his pants roughly away from the chain. The cuff did not come free, spoiling the gesture, and when he bent to do it by hand the bike fell over again, pulling him down with it in an awkward fall of tangled limbs and metal. The pedal gouged into his thigh and he cried aloud.

When he looked up, the man was standing over him.

"Hi, kid."

The boy sniffed but did not speak.

"Yeah, I know all about it," Stitzer said.

He moved the pedal backward until the boy's cuff was free, then hoisted him effortlessly to his feet.

"What's your name?" Stitzer asked.

"Lewis," said the boy.

"Do you like your name?"

"I like Lew."

"So do I."

Stitzer pulled the bike upright and held it by the handlebars.

"I have to go," said Lewis.

Stitzer kept his grip on the handlebars.

"I'll go with you," he said, smiling.

Elaine heard the voices around her, but they had a strange quality, as if coming from a tunnel. I'm falling asleep, she thought, congratulating herself. She had been up until four the night before, waiting tables until the bar had closed and then helping Mr. Koster "with the books." That meant submitting to Mr. Koster's attention for half an hour, listening to him swear to the depth of his attraction for her, letting him kiss her while pretending to struggle. There was not much pretense necessary, actually. She didn't dislike him, he was kind as an employer, but she found his sexual needs pathetic. He never went beyond kisses—she was sure he thought of them as "stolen kisses"—and the occasional awkward rubbing against her breasts with his forearm. He made love to her like a teenager, frightened of going too far before he got his face slapped. After half an hour he would always break off abruptly, muttering, "We shouldn't, we really shouldn't." Still excited, radiant with the glow of guilt triumphing over lust—Mr. Koster was very conspicuously married—he would see her to the door. Unfailingly he would kiss Elaine on the hand, then the forehead. She had learned to leave quickly, eyes cast down, understanding and admiring him all the more for his decency. In truth, for all the predictability and artifice of her bouts with Mr. Koster, she left the bar feeling aroused. She was embarrassed to respond to what she knew was his fantasy, not hers, but at thirty-six she found herself getting aroused by far less attention than she used to—and being satisfied far less often. After Koster she went straight home. Sometimes she would spend the cab fare he pressed into her palm for a taxi, and sometimes she would brave the deserted subway, saving the extra money for emergencies. There were always emergencies.

Last night had been one of the frugal ones and she had paid for the extra money by an hour's anxiety wondering which of the men in the subway station would be the one who finally cut her throat or pushed her under the wheels of the oncoming train.

Lewis had awakened her early. He tried to be quiet, but the apartment was too small, she could hear the television no matter how low he put the sound. She needed just ten minutes' sleep, she told herself. It was important; if she weren't so tired she would be more patient with Lewis and feel less pity for herself. Just ten minutes. She really needed a couple of hours, but she would settle for ten minutes because it was the best she could do. Elaine had become quite used to settling for the best she could do, and frequently for less.

She awoke, aware that her mouth was open and the side of her cheek was wet. Lewis stood in front of her.

"Mom," he said again, impatiently.

She blinked, taking a second to realize she was still on the park bench, still thirty-six, still a single parent with no money and no man and no prospects. For part of that second she deeply resented her son for bringing her back to this reality. Then she noticed the man standing just behind Lewis, smiling, holding on to the bike. His hair was short, his mustache new, and at first it looked like the closely trimmed appearance affected by many in the gay community, but when his eyes made contact with hers, she dismissed the idea that he was homosexual.

"Your son fell off his bike," Stitzer said. "I thought you might want to take a look. That gravel can give a pretty nasty scrape sometimes."

"I'm all right," said Lewis.

"I'm sure you are," said Stitzer, but when he turned back to Elaine he said, "He fell on his knee. It wouldn't hurt to look."

Stitzer sat beside her on the bench as she examined Lewis's bruises. She murmured solicitously, taking more time than she normally would because of the witness. There was something very warm and considerate about the man that made her think of a father—not her own, there had been nothing paternal about her own father, nor about Lewis's father, for that matter—she had to reach out to television to find a model for the man's solicitude. He reminded her of the avuncular types on medical shows. Good men, good husbands, good fathers.

"Guess you'll live," Stitzer said when the examination was over. He relinquished his hold on the bike for the first time and Lewis moved off. "I guess I overreacted," Stitzer said to Elaine, smiling deprecatorily. "But I'm a parent, too, and it cuts me up to see kids cry."

"Oh, you're a father, are you?"

"I was," he said, and she could hear the pain. "I had a boy about Lewis's age."

"I'm sorry," she said. He nodded his head, looking at his feet.

"It was a long time ago," he said. He sounded so sad. Elaine touched his arm. He looked at her again, then away, shyly.

"You were resting," he said. "I don't mean to intrude."

"Not at all," she said, rather too quickly. She could sleep anytime. Elaine smiled at him, wondering if her breath smelled as stale as her mouth tasted.

"Do you come to the park often?" she asked.

He turned on the bench, facing her completely. A brown birthmark, shaped like a tiny squirrel, seemed to be fleeing into the forest of his hair.

"Quite a bit, since I lost my family," he said.

Elaine nodded sympathetically. She was no longer tired.

An FBI agent by the name of Harper entered the Hotel Marquise on West Fifty-eighth Street. It was one of a number of unremarkable hotels in the midtown area of Manhattan that thrived on their proximity to the Plaza, the Sherry-Netherland, and the other prestigious hostelries that bordered the park. The address was good, or nearly good, and the prices were reasonable, or nearly so, at least in comparison to the lofty cousins one block to the north. The Marquise was respectable, if not glamorous, and its clientele boasted the occasional dignitary among the business travelers, the odd film star who had arrived too late or whose luster was not quite high enough to merit a better hotel. It was, in a city already cloaked in anonymity, a good place to hide.

Harper approached the registration desk without expectation. This was his seventeenth hotel of the day and he was scheduled to cover eight more before dinner. Harper had entered the Bureau with some notion, vague but real, of glamour. Although he would never admit it to any of his fellow agents, he had dreams at one time of what he could only refer to as sleuthing, the sort of inspired guesswork that made Sherlock Holmes and Bulldog Drummond the heroes of his youth. Only gradually had he come to realize that police work, whether in the national service of the FBI or the uniformed blue of New York's finest, was dull, dogged, and unrewarding. It resembled nothing so much as doing inventory in a warehouse. Dozens of agents like Harper searched through the stacks, methodically checking items off the list, removing possibilities, accounting for every alternative. Winnowing and sifting. It was the surest way to find a needle in a haystack—Harper realized that—but it was terribly boring for everyone except the man who actually came up with the needle.

When the desk clerk said yes, he recognized the man, Harper's first reaction was that there had been a mistake.

"You're sure you've seen him?"

"Yes, certainly," said the clerk. He was young and Swiss and very positive. He placed his finger on the picture showing Stitzer with a mustache penned on. "It is this man. Precisely."

"How do you know him?"

"He is a guest."

"Here? In this hotel?"

The Swiss seemed impatient. "Yes, that is what I have said."

Harper fought back his excitement, which was unprofessional. He overcompensated so that when he spoke he sounded almost bored.

"What name does he go by?"

"I don't know."

"What room is he in?"

The Swiss shrugged. "I don't know."

"How do you know he's a guest?"

The Swiss was getting annoyed, his credibility was being questioned. "He passes by, through the lobby. I see him. Once a day. Twice a day. He does not ask for his key, he does not ask for messages, but he passes by. I know his face."

"Do you watch everyone who goes in and out?"

The Swiss gave Harper a wan smile.

"It is not active here. There is little excitement."

"I know the feeling," Harper said, but he knew his hand trembled as he took back the picture. He wanted to run to the telephone but forced himself to continue calmly.

"How long has he been staying here?"

"Several days. Perhaps a week."

"Has he paid the bill?"

The Swiss shrugged again. "I am reservations," he said.

"Do you know if he's in the hotel now?"

"This man is a criminal?"

"Would you know if he's in the hotel at the moment, Mr. . . ."

"Finkbeiner. I do not know."

"I thought you knew when he came in and out."

"I am not studying the man," said the Swiss.

"I'd like to see your registration book."

"The man is a criminal. This is certain."

"We're just trying to locate him," said Harper. "Can I see the register?"

"No."

Harper blinked. "What do you mean, no?"

"I am not allowed to show it."

"I am with the FBI."

"I am with the hotel," said the Swiss. "This is not permitted."

"Finkbeiner, don't give me grief."

"I *wish* to show you the register," said the Swiss. "But I am not permitted. You must ask the manager."

"I'm going to make a phone call," said Harper, trying to remain patient. "When I come back, I expect to see the manager standing right where you are. Is that clear?"

"Certainly, sir. Together we shall capture this criminal."

Not together, Harper thought as he hurried across the lobby. I want this one all to myself. I want to be the guy who finds the needle.

Capello was worried that he had not had time to get all the strands of his net in place. They had moved in immediately upon receiving Harper's call, but there had not been enough men available, too many were already out combing all the other hotels and rentals in the city. The call was out; if he had another hour or two, he could have enough manpower to cover the Hotel Marquise so tightly not even a cockroach could escape, but he was not sure he had the luxury of time. Stitzer could return at any time—or he could never return at all.

Capello sat in his car, which was double-parked across the street from the hotel. It was too obvious for his taste, even in a city where double-parking was epidemic, but he had lacked the time to set up anything else. Harper was in the lobby, behind the registration desk, serving as desk clerk, and the real clerk sat next to Capello, watching pedestrians flow past the hotel.

"That is not him," said the Swiss, indicating a man with a movement of his head.

"Just tell me when it *is* him," Capello said resignedly. He had been trying for several minutes to get the young man to shut up, without noticeable result. Finkbeiner's running commentary was inspired by nervous excitement, a condition Capello shared, but his response to nerves was to become more quiet, to shrink away from his natural good-natured garrulousness until he was as still as a predator. Right now he felt like a fist, clenched and ready to strike.

Capello ran through his preparations once more to calm himself, but their meagerness offered little comfort. Besides himself and Harper, there was a man covering the service entrance and another on the roof. Capello knew that cornered men almost invariably ran upward. He glanced at his watch. Other agents should be there in less than an hour now. He wondered again if he should have police help but decided that he had been right to exclude them. The antipathy between the Bureau and the local police was deep and well founded. Capello was convinced that their heavy-handedness would give away the trap in an instant.

Finkbeiner tensed on the seat beside him. For the first time in half an hour he was silent. Capello looked at the sidewalk in front of the hotel. Coming east from the Avenue of the Americas was a group of tourists, German or Scandinavian, definitely Nordic. Their hair was closely cropped around the ears in the enduring Teutonic fashion and their clothes had the cut, the style, the pattern— Capello was not sure what it was, the subtle but recognizable difference—that labeled them European. The agent counted six of them moving in a loose group, their configuration changing and re-forming like an amoeba as they adjusted to traffic. They all seemed to be talking at the same time and they all wore their shirts open several buttons in concession to the heat. Except for the haircuts, which had been reshaped by American barbers, they all resembled Finkbeiner.

"Is he there?" Capello whispered, his voice sounding harsh in the sudden silence within the car.

"I am not certain," said the desk clerk. It was the first time he had sounded unsure of himself in the last thirty minutes. "He may be. On the far side. I cannot see him clearly."

Capello sought the man who might be Stitzer. He glanced at the composite picture on the seat, then at the man on the far side of the group. He sported a mustache, as the Swiss had said, but so did two other members of the group. Whether he was consciously trying to hide or not, Capello couldn't say, but his gait was perfectly measured to keep his face at least partially obscured at all times by the men next to him.

The knot of tourists approached the entrance to the hotel.

"Is it him, goddamn it?!" demanded Capello. He regretted his impatience immediately because Finkbeiner turned to face him, raising his voice, gesticulating.

"I am not certain! He is too far, he is not clear . . ."

"Look again, please," said Capello soothingly.

The tourists seemed to waver as they neared the entrance, as if they had suddenly encountered some unseen current.

For a second it looked as if they would enter. Capello lifted his radio handset to his lips.

"Harper," he whispered. "Suspect coming."

He knew at once that it was a mistake. The man on the far side was looking at Capello, his eyes flicking past the car, then back in an instant, taking in the radio, the stakeout, the whole situation. Capello could not be sure, of course; it could have been a random glance, it lasted so briefly there was no noticeable reaction from the man, no tensing, no hesitation. But Capello felt a sinking feeling in his stomach. Blown, he thought, and he cursed himself and Finkbeiner.

The tourists continued on, past the entrance and toward the corner. Capello knew he had very little time to make a decision. He could take the chance that the man was Stitzer and go after him right now, before he vanished into the city, but to do so he must abandon the stakeout and, if Stitzer was not the tourist but was staked out himself somewhere, watching his hotel for suspicious signs, then Capello would surely give himself away. The alternative was to assume that Stitzer was not that cautious, was not in fact the tourist, and that all that was needed to catch him was patience.

One of the tourists, shorter than the rest, stopped and turned, looking back in Capello's direction. He pointed up, laughing, at some aspect of New York life that struck him as funny. Four of the other tourists also paused, turning, following the pointing finger of the first. The sixth tourist continued toward the corner, never hesitating.

Capello squeezed the button on his radio as he leaped from the car and began to spring. By the time the man reached the corner and turned out of sight, all four agents were racing from their positions to join Capello.

As he reached the corner, Capello guessed himself to be no more than twenty yards behind, assuming that Stitzer had not broken into a run himself as soon as he turned. Capello hoped he was running, it would mean he had panicked and would make it much easier.

The only one running was Capello. He brushed against a businessman, pushing the man off balance. The man started to protest, then saw the gun in Capello's hand. He hurried away, and others coming toward Capello scattered to the side like swimmers who have seen a fin slicing the water.

Capello holstered the pistol and began to walk quickly, his eyes racing over the crowd that flowed on both sides of Broadway. No Nordic tourist, no suspect, no Stitzer.

At the far end of the block, the agent who had been covering the service entrance sprinted into sight, and running footsteps behind him told Capello that Harper had arrived. The pedestrians darted briefly to one side, jerking in unison, then back again into place as they adjusted to the sight of guns and running men.

A cab pulled away from the curb, the backseat empty. Capello leaped into the street in front of it, holding up an imperious palm and reclaiming his gun with the other hand. The alarmed cabbie slammed on the brakes, swerving to one side as his hands flew defensively from the wheel to his head, warding off the anticipated bullets with flesh and bone. Capello jerked open the back door. The rear seat was empty.

The agents began to search the stores as soon as Capello gave in and called for police help. Within minutes the street was sealed off, and the agents moved through the buildings like beaters through the bush, but Capello knew that it was an exercise in futility. Stroup had been right; Stitzer was as good as he had claimed. Only now, he was alerted. Capello had gotten lucky, had received one good chance—and missed.

Stitzer turned the corner and forced himself to keep walking briskly and not break into a run. A sudden dash might make him conspicuous enough for someone on the sidewalk to point him out when his pursuer arrived. He reasoned that he had at least twenty yards on the man, maybe thirty. Not much of a lead, but it should be enough. He had chosen his hotel carefully, scouted the escape routes before he ever entered the Marquise. It had been selected not only because of its anonymity, its comfortable position in the ranks of midtown mediocrity, but also because of its proximity to the warren of subway tracks that branched out from the Fifty-ninth Street station.

He turned into an office building and strode purposefully toward the bank of elevators, past the thoroughly uninterested Puerto Rican in the foyer who wore random bits and pieces of a uniform designed to give him authority. He waited, counting off the seconds in his mind as his lead time slipped away and the elevator doors refused to open. He kept his back to the outer door; he didn't need to look, he would know when the man entered. His pursuer would be in a hurry and incautious; Stitzer had already assessed him as a sloppy craftsman; the first move had proved that. The elevator opened and Stitzer entered, allowing himself a brief glance at the street. Pedestrians were agitated, roiling around some obstacle just beyond the doorway, like a stream eddying around a rock. His pursuer would have stopped after rounding the corner, and Stitzer could imagine him now, puzzled, planning his next move, waiting for his backup team. Stitzer figured his lead time was back to what he had started with, probably more. And in any event, enough, which was all he was concerned with.

In the basement Stitzer hurried across the concrete floor to the deep shadows. No one had yet bothered to replace the bulb Stitzer had removed on his initial reconnaissance visit, and so he was able to work in darkness, obscured if not invisible to any observers outside the shadow. He paused beside the giant furnaces, listening for the telltale grind and chuck of the descending elevator. This was the one phase of the escape where he felt he was vulnerable and he needed a few seconds. The signal lights on the elevator descended through the numbers, then stopped on the main floor.

Stitzer squeezed behind the boilers and worked his way through the deepening dark to the grilled doorway. The padlock was a very simple one, applied for formality, not security. No one was likely to want to gain access to the blackness beyond. Stitzer picked the lock with the kit he had acquired earlier from a pawnbroker in the Bronx. Everything illegal, he knew, was available from a pawnbroker. It was simply a matter of finding the right one and paying the right price.

Once through the grilled gate, Stitzer reached through the bars and snapped the padlock back on its chain. The entire procedure had taken less than ten seconds. Whatever lead time he had left was now entirely academic. He took one step into the blackness and was gone.

It took Capello and his team two and a half hours to find the grilled doorway. The building superintendent on duty had been unaware of it, and Capello had needed a subway maintenance foreman to locate it for him.

"They're all over the place this close to a major terminal," the foreman explained. "You need access to the tracks from different angles. You get a wreck, a derailing, whatever, and you might not be able to get through from the station. With these limited-access routes, you can come in from all sides."

"Access isn't all that limited, though, is it?" said Capello. He followed the stabbing beam of the foreman's flashlight as they passed through the gate and down the staircase.

"That's just what they call them," said the foreman. "There should be a light along here." He found the switch, turned it on, but the darkness remained obdurate. "There's supposed to be one every twenty, thirty feet," he said, puzzled.

"He would have broken the bulbs behind him as he went along," said Capello. The foreman's beam found a smashed bulb just as his feet ground shards of glass into the stairway. "Just to slow us down."

"He figured we'd be after him, then," said the foreman.

The foreman's use of the plural annoyed Capello and reminded him of Finkbeiner's proprietary attitude. Everybody wants to get into the act, he thought.

"He takes precautions," said Capello. The rumble of a train sounded in the distance, then rushed at him with terrifying speed and noise. The foreman clutched at Capello's arm and pulled him back against the wall. Capello turned his head as the engine raced past, iron squealing on iron as the brakes hit and the giant train decelerated.

"Easy," said the foreman.

Capello wrested his arm free from the foreman's grip. "The fuck you mean 'easy'?" he said.

"You looked a little shook."

"Where could he go from here?" Capello asked, struggling for his composure. The train had startled him and he was surprised by his response. Danger was frequently implicit in his work but seldom so close at hand. It was usually handled by the lesser agents, men lower on the command ladder with less time, less rank. More courage, Capello thought. He gathered saliva in his mouth and spat at the track. He hated being scared, hated being demeaned by his own body's reactions.

"Where couldn't he go?" the foreman shrugged. "The system opens up from here. He could walk half a block that way"—the beam stabbed toward the distant station—"and get on a train going to any part of the city. Or he could go that way"—he inclined his head toward darkness. "I wouldn't want to go after anybody in there. Anybody dangerous, I mean."

How about the most dangerous man in the elite corps of dangerous men, Capello thought. He wondered why he had drawn this assignment. Did it fall to him by lot because it was his turn? Was it a vote of confidence in his abilities from a higher-up? Or was someone out to get him? He perceived the political workings of the Bureau only dimly enough to be wary of them, not to understand them.

"Not many people know about these entrances, you said."

"I wouldn't think so. No reason to."

"How do you know about them?"

"Me? I work here."

"I know you work here," said Capello. He was getting very annoyed with the man. "But how did you learn? By osmosis? Did someone show you? What?"

"We got charts," said the foreman. "Maps, like."

"I know what a chart is," said Capello. "Let's get out of here and take a look at them."

As he left he glanced back into the darkness stretching downtown toward the Fiftieth Street station. Stroup had warned him, he thought. He said that Stitzer, once alerted, would go underground faster than a mole. As it happened, he had gone a whole lot faster.

# Chapter 11

THE ENGINEER ON DUTY at the Con Edison substation at Thirty-eighth Street and Seventh Avenue later reported having heard a muffled *pop* some minutes before the incident began. This recollection came only after intensive grilling by police and an FBI agent, and thus memory was suspect. There was speculation among the police that the man might simply have been asleep when the explosion went off. The engineer didn't like the police, but he was particularly put off by the agent and a dour, hawk-faced man who scowled contemptuously when not muttering questions to the FBI man, who then relayed them to the engineer. Unlike everyone else, who seemed harried and weary after hours of crisis, the hawk-faced man seemed angry, deeply, ineradicably angry.

As reconstructed later, the incident went like this. A person or persons unknown gained access—by a method unknown—to the level immediately above the Con Ed subbasement and attached an explosive device to the water main. The device, based on the best guess of experts who examined remaining scraps of evidence, was made of the malleable jelly known as plastique, a particularly murderous and versatile charge favored by terrorist groups. The plastique had been packed in a container made of cloth and leather—one expert suggested a money belt—and detonated by a timing device constructed of a stopwatch and batteries. The stopwatch sold for less than five dollars at any of dozens of discount camera shops in the city, and the batteries were even more widely available. The source of the plastique—like the identity and entry of the perpetrator or perpetrators—was unknown.

The explosion ruptured the water main but with a minimum of noise or extraneous blast damage—the experts were respectful of the technical skill involved—and within some ten minutes the water had entered the Con Ed substation. The engineer—awakened by wet feet according to some of the police cynics—was unable to stop the flooding and not blessed with enough presence of mind to shut off all power in the facility. The water soon took care of that for him. When water reached the transformer the system short-circuited and started a fire, which in turn caused a blackout that affected Manhattan's garment center, Macy's, Gimbel's, and the New York Telephone headquarters. The engineer escaped unharmed.

The incident took place one day after Capello's unsuccessful attempt to capture Stitzer outside the Hotel Marquise. The aftereffects of the blackout took six days to repair, and Carl Thorne, like most of the reportorial staff of his newspaper, was pressed into duty on the story. Carl's first assignment was a feature piece on the Con Ed workmen who went underground to locate and splice the affected electrical cables to cables leading from another substation.

After ten minutes underground he was escorted back to the surface by a Con Ed worker who was doing his best to keep from smiling.

"It happens sometimes," said the worker. Carl sat on the

street, the Men at Work sign behind his back, equipment littered around him, his feet still dangling into the manhole. Curious onlookers crowded around and stared as Carl sat in the sunshine and shivered.

"Shouldn't come down here if you're claustrophobic," said the worker, a trace of condescension slipping into his tone.

"I didn't know I was," said Carl. "I've been in tight places before, it never bothered me."

"This is different. Not everybody likes it."

Carl tried to laugh but the sound came out like a sob. The hole had been cramped, dark, airless, humid. He had felt as if he'd been buried alive, as if the very atmosphere had confined him, crushing his arms to his sides.

He wrote an article that received a scribbled word of praise from Helstrom—a rare accolade. The piece spoke of the grimy faces of the workers, the complexities of the splicing technique, the hard hours and difficult conditions. He did not mention that he had been led out, whimpering.

Two hours after he finished the article he was once more in Capello's office. Dr. Michaelmas was there, smiling uncertainly, and Stroup was there, standing behind Capello now, his arms crossed on his chest.

At their previous meeting the major had been seated across the room. He was now at Capello's shoulder and Carl took the move as symbolic of his increasing control of the investigation.

"Dr. Michaelmas has been good enough to supply us with a partial list of the books your uncle ordered from the library while he was at the sanitarium," said Capello.

"Hospital," Michaelmas corrected.

Capello smiled at the psychiatrist and nodded. "Hospital." Carl could see that Capello was the diplomat again.

The agent held up a computerized printout that closely resembled the accordioned ribbons that chattered their way out of the teletype machines at the newspaper. The sheet was over four feet long and it fell into pleats as Capello lowered it back onto the desk.

"A book a day," said Capello.

"For five years," said Michaelmas.

"Could he really read that fast?" Capello asked.

Carl shrugged. "He had a lot of free time."

"Eight hours a day," said Michaelmas. "Eight for reading, eight for exercise. He never varied."

"Some of these are technical manuals. Could he really read them and understand them that fast?"

One of Michaelmas's hands fluttered up from his lap to make a gesture. He glanced at it as if it were a disembodied apparition, unrelated to his body.

"I don't know what he comprehended, but he read them. I mean, he turned the pages, every page, and his eyes moved up and down. I assumed he was speed-reading."

"You watched him read?"

"On the monitor. Sometimes in person. It didn't seem to break his concentration if I stood outside the cell and watched." Michaelmas saw the others looking at him. "He was my patient. My most interesting patient."

Capello turned deferentially toward Stroup.

"He could understand what he needed to know," Stroup said. "You don't have to understand theory to know that water will short-circuit electrical equipment. All you need to know is where the water is, where the electricity is, and how to put them together. He already knows all he needs to know about explosives."

"Are you talking about the blackout?" Carl asked. "Are you saying my uncle did that?"

"We think so," said Capello.

"The water main was sixty-eight years old. It ruptured. We've been reporting that it ruptured."

"I know what you've been reporting," said Capello. "That's exactly what you're going to continue to report."

"Jesus."

"Yes, I know. Manipulation of the free press and all of that." Stroup snorted, but Capello continued, smiling, "Cooperation, Mr. Thorne, is what this is all about. More scare headlines aren't going to do anyone any good. Are they?"

"They would at least alert people."

"To what end? We are alerted. The police are alerted. His best weapon is panic. Panic could shut this city down faster than a hundred bombs. We have to keep him from using that weapon, and the only way to do that is to keep the public from knowing what is happening. It will not alarm them to think the city is falling apart. They're used to that. It will, however, scare the shit out of them to think one man is causing it intentionally. That's what we intend to keep to ourselves. Do you understand?"

Carl paused.

"Do you understand?"

"Yes," Carl said, finally.

"Good. Because your publisher understands perfectly well and wouldn't run anything to the contrary even if you were foolish enough to write it."

"It seems to me you could use the public to help find him," Carl said. "You could run his picture in the paper, on television . . ."

"It seems the same to us." Capello continued to smile but the sincerity was fading. "We intend to do precisely that, but with a little variation." The agent handed Carl a single typewritten sheet with a copy of his uncle's picture, the one with the mustache, clipped to it. The photograph was a glossy black and white, suitable for use in a newspaper. Carl glanced at the accompanying copy. It was a report, in newspaper style, of a bank robbery.

"This afternoon a savings bank in the Bronx was held up by three men with nylon stockings over their faces. A bank guard was wounded slightly and they stole something close to fifty thousand dollars," Capello said. "The police are looking for this man for questioning." Capello tapped Stitzer's picture. "His photo will go in every newspaper in the city and on every news broadcast for three days running. If anyone has seen him, we should hear about it."

"He robbed a bank? I thought he was alone."

"He didn't have anything to do with the bank," Stroup said impatiently. "It's just an excuse."

"Was there even a robbery?"

"There was," said Capello. "The three men were caught ten minutes later. Who benefits by knowing your uncle wasn't with them? Only your uncle."

"There's a name in the article," said Carl. "Lester Gorman."

"Thanks to Dr. Michaelmas." The psychiatrist sat up straighter in his chair. "He told us that your uncle would have to keep reading, that he'd be addicted to it . . ."

"Well, conditioned," Michaelmas corrected.

Capello shrugged, the cloak of diplomacy slipping. ". . . so we checked out the library and went through all the library cards issued since your uncle left the sanitarium." Michaelmas shifted but remained silent. "His handwriting turned up on a new card as Lester Gorman." Capello paused.

"And what has he been reading?" Carl asked, knowing Capello wanted him to.

"Among other things, every chart and map and diagram concerning New York City that the Forty-second Street branch has on file. And it has the blueprints for every piece of public construction performed in this city in the last one hundred and twenty-seven years. Do you understand the implications of that? He has access to information about the subway, the water lines, the sewers, the electrical lines, the reservoirs—I mean every nook and cranny and crawlspace forty stories up and eight stories below ground in this entire city. He has more information about this city than probably anyone else in it."

"Why are you telling him all this?" Stroup demanded. "He doesn't need to know."

"Cooperation, Major," said Capello. "We are cooperating with Mr. Thorne because we expect—we need—him to cooperate with us. It's important that he knows everything —especially how dangerous his uncle is."

"He hasn't hurt anyone," said Carl quickly.

"That we know of. Except for the man he murdered . . ."

"Coombs," said Michaelmas quietly.

"Except for Coombs. Or weren't you counting him, Mr. Thorne?"

"We don't know that he did that. There were the dogs."

"Yes, indeed, dogs. There certainly were dogs. Let me tell you about something that happened today, Mr. Thorne. We're reasonably certain that dogs didn't do it. You're a reporter, do you know where the city gets its water?"

"The reservoir in Central Park, I suppose."

"Wrong," said Capello, with satisfaction. "The Central Park Reservoir only serves as a temporary catchment. The water is pumped into it, via huge tunnels, from the Hillview Reservoir in Yonkers. Our water travels thirteen miles underground before it reaches Manhattan."

"I didn't know that."

"Neither did I, until today. Neither do most people who don't have any reason to know. Your uncle knows." Capello paused. His smile broadened as if he relished his tale. "Explosions were set off this morning that damaged the valves controlling the flow. I'm talking about valves to close a tunnel twenty-four feet in diameter, Mr. Thorne. The engineers don't know how bad the damage is yet, but they are not terribly optimistic. If they can't fix them, and fix them soon, we're in for a very nasty drought in this city. We are convinced the explosives were not set by dogs."

"Are you convinced that my uncle did it?"

"The explosive involved in the Con Ed incident and the

water tunnel incident was plastique on both occasions. On both occasions it was set off by a timing device. We know it was a stopwatch at the Con Ed plant—they're still looking for evidence at the tunnels. Now I'd say either it was the same man who did both jobs or we're under concentrated guerrilla attack. Your uncle is the simplest explanation, wouldn't you say?''

''I'm not your adversary, Mr. Capello, and I don't much like being addressed as one. I've already told you I'm willing to cooperate in any way I can.''

''I thought you were in doubt about your uncle's involvement.''

''Yes, I am. As far as I know, I mean really *know*, the only crime he's guilty of is escaping from the—'hospital.' I can hardly blame him for that. However, I still want to help. If he is involved, then maybe I can be of some service. And if he isn't, no harm is done.''

''But harm is being done.''

''You know what I meant.''

''Yes, and let me tell you what I mean. Your uncle could be anywhere, and, to be very candid, I don't expect to find him by running his picture in the papers. I was a bit overly optimistic about it all in the beginning, but I see now that Sergeant Stitzer is a competent man. Extremely competent.''

''He's a genius,'' said Stroup.

''He will make errors. He's human and he will make mistakes. Eventually we would catch him that way. But I don't think we can afford to wait. We have to go after him. Unfortunately, there is only one way to reach him. Only one lure we have to offer.''

Capello paused again, looking with expectation at Carl. Carl cleared his throat.

''Only one lure?'' Carl repeated.

Capello offered his largest smile. ''You. Or, more specifically, your column. That appears to be where he got his signal to begin this operation. That means he read it—we know that from his scrapbook—and apparently trusted it. We assume he is continuing to read it. At the moment it is the only line of communication he trusts—it's also one he might think we don't know about.''

"But he doesn't trust me," Carl said. "He tried to attack me at the hospital. You were there," he said to Michaelmas.

"He doesn't believe you are you," said the doctor. "But he must think that somewhere his nephew—his *true* nephew—is alive and sending him messages. I would have to assume that he believes your column speaks for the real nephew while you yourself he sees as an imposter like all the rest of us.''

"If I can reach him through my column—then I can help him.''

"At this point," said Capello, "I think you're the only one person who *can* help him—and the rest of us.''

"What do you want me to do?''

"We'll proceed by small steps. First, just have him make contact. Let's establish that he's listening. We want you to write a column asking him to respond to you. Have him give you some sign that he's out there and hearing you.''

"What kind of sign?''

"That's up to you. Something from your past, something you share with him that nobody else knows about. Don't press him too hard, let him respond to you any way he wants to. All we want out of this first one is to know he trusts you.''

"To know he trusts me and then what?" Carl asked warily.

"One step at a time, Mr. Thorne.''

"I want him to get help.''

"We all want him to be helped.''

Carl saw Stroup twist his face, contorting a smile into something bitter.

"I don't want him hurt," Carl insisted.

Capello smiled. "One step at a time," he said. "One step at a time . . . We want Stitzer to trust you, but we also must all trust each other."

"It's for the common good," Stroup said.

Looking from face to face, Carl could not remember when he had felt so much unease in the presence of smiling people.

# Chapter 12

PAULINE ANSWERED THE PHONE on the third ring. She knew before she picked up the receiver who it was, and for a second she debated whether to answer it. But the importunate ring of a telephone seemed to have priority of urgency that little else did. Like a crying baby, Pauline thought. Drop everything and pick it up, no matter how important your other work is, no matter that it's only someone selling something.

But it was no salesman. The silence on the wire stretched, broken only by a faint electronic hiss. She heard breathing, but she wasn't sure it wasn't her own.

"Mark?" she whispered, surprised at herself. The silence continued. She wondered what had made her speak her suspicion aloud. Why did she assume it was Stitzer and not some sexual deviant who was quietly abusing himself on the other end of the line? Or Marissa, Carl's leggy former lover, sending her own message of venom.

She decided she would not tell Carl about the call, she

would keep it a secret, just as she had done with all the
others. Any mention of his uncle disturbed him so—and
after all, she wasn't positive it was anything more than a
bad connection, some well-intentioned caller stranded in the
middle distance of electronic mystery. That happened often
enough these days.

And her relationship with Carl was not one that took in
the details of life. It existed on another plane, in a realm of
stylized fantasy where romance reigned supreme and ugli-
ness was banished. In each other's arms there was no rent to
pay, no tiresome days at work, no quarrels with colleagues,
no tales of rudeness and repressed violence in supermarket
lines. They spoke a language they seemed to have invented
themselves, filled with words lacking allusion and reso-
nance. Their love was their only common experience, and
everything they did and said referred only to that love.
Their conversation was simple, the theme unvarying: How
much do we love each other, how much more today than
yesterday? It was, Pauline realized, a fool's paradise. How
long could it last? A fever this high must ultimately abate or
kill the patient. But while it lasted—oh, my God, while it
lasted. The world would impinge upon their Eden soon
enough; meanwhile Pauline would protect it as long as she
could.

Carl would be home in half an hour and they would have
two hours together before she went to her night class.
Dinner was prepared and waiting in the oven. They would
eat, then make love, or, depending on the urgency that
emerged in their first embrace, they would make love and
then eat. She would offer him updates on the soap operas
she watched while fixing the meal. He would offer nothing
at all about his day but much about her, her eyes, her face,
her body, all paragons to him. Pauline is perfection, seen
by a vision as pink and hazy as a sunset. He would look into
her eyes and gradually that heartrending smile would creep

over his lips, tugging them as if they dared not move, until they parted and his whole face seemed to split with joy. She could feel his smile deep inside her. They would lie and look at each other and both would try not to think how strange it all was.

Waiting, Pauline spread his newspaper on the table and searched for his by-line. It was two days after the blackout and another watermain had broken, on East Twenty-third Street, flooding the streets and the subway tracks. The authorities were claiming the two incidents were unrelated. Aging equipment, an unusually high volume of water being used because of the heat, unfortunate coincidence, etc. The paper was filled with pictures showing New Yorkers coping with inconvenience. It seemed to Pauline that the authorities were rather strident in their plea for calm and cooperation. She skimmed through the pages, taking the gist of the stories from the headlines and the subheads, letting messages of looting and chaos impinge only on the fringes of her consciousness.

She found Carl's by-line on the fourth page. It was peculiar, a memory piece about the dog he had as a boy, the man who taught him how to train the animal, some confused explanation of how he had lost track of both the man and the animal, and a request for the man to get in touch with him. There was a strange sense of urgency about the article, casting an importance on the situation that seemed unwarranted. Pauline did not dwell on the strangeness, however. As always, she thought it was a superb piece of writing and she read every word. She was convinced that he had become a better writer since they had fallen in love.

Elaine heard him hang up the telephone and she started for the kitchen. She liked to give him privacy when he made his calls, and she thought again about the possibility of getting another telephone installed in the bedroom. It wasn't much, but it was something she could do for him, and she wanted very much to do something for him. He had done so much for her already in the few days since he moved in. Filled her life, that was all. Made her feel loved, feel worthy, feel *good,* goddamn it, and what was better than that? He loved her. At least he seemed to love her. Elaine had some trouble accepting it, but not because of him; he was wonderful, gentle, patient. No, he convinced her that he loved her—and Lewis, she could see that he loved Lewis, too; and why not? Lewis was a terrific kid—it wasn't any failing on Roger's part. She didn't think he *had* any failings. It was herself that was the problem. Elaine didn't really see how *anyone* could love her. Lewis's father had not. Her own father had not. Neither had any of the lovers—if that was the word for them—who had drifted so casually in and out of her life.

She glanced at her reflection in the kitchen mirror and put a hand to her hair. It was limp and stringy again. I look like yesterday's spaghetti, she thought. No amount of washing or conditioning or setting seemed to have much effect. She needed to go to a salon, one of those expensive ones, and get the very best money could buy. He deserved it. She knew he'd give her the money for it if she asked, but she didn't want to ask. He had spent too much on her already. And *Lewis.* He had poured money over Lewis as if the boy were his own son.

"You look lovely," he said. He had caught her looking at herself. She turned from the mirror and saw that grin that crinkled one entire side of his face.

"I don't," she said. "I look terrible."

He rose, holding out his arms. "What do you know about it?" She melted against him. She had never felt a body as strong as his. She had never felt so protected before, even though she felt a little frightened too. That was just because she wasn't used to him yet, she told herself. She still couldn't believe her luck. A stranger in the park, a conversation on a bench. The next day he was in her apartment, sharing her bed. It had been so fast, but somehow it had seemed exactly right.

It was only when she thought about it, when she tried to put it into words to explain it to others, that it seemed rushed. Elaine knew what her mother would think of it, of course, but then her mother didn't realize that the world had changed. She didn't understand what life had been like for her daughter. There would be no reason to tell her mother for weeks, and by then it would be a long-established relationship. Lewis's opinion was the only one she really worried about. She had taken him aside the morning after her first night together with Roger and asked him how he felt about it. She had already decided that Roger could stay as long as he wanted, as long as she could keep him, but she would have considered Lewis's feelings if he had disapproved—she was certain she would. Lewis had not disapproved; he had smiled and seemed almost as excited as Elaine was. Lewis liked him too. She couldn't imagine why everyone in the world wouldn't like him.

"Are you finished with your calls?" she asked. "I'll make us something to eat."

"All done," he said.

"Nobody answered?" she said.

His eyes seemed to tighten and the grin came much more slowly. She feared she'd said something wrong.

"Why do you say that?" he asked. His voice was casual.

"No reason. I just didn't hear you talking."

"That's right," he said. He seemed amused now, but she didn't know by what. "Nobody home."

"I wasn't listening. I mean, I wasn't trying to listen . . . I just didn't hear anything . . ."

He laughed and she knew everything was all right. "Ah, you're a real little *dobryj chelavyek*, aren't you?" he said.

"A what?" She didn't expect him to answer. He said a lot of things she didn't understand, and he never explained. His smile widened. She didn't know what she had done, but she was glad he liked it. He kissed her then, and she thought she would faint, it felt so good. When she pressed her cheek against his, she could feel the bristles of the beard he was growing. It was coming in a little bit grayer than the hair on his head, and she thought it would make him look so distinguished. And it made him look quite different than the mustache alone. Softer. Gentler. More like the man she knew he really was.

They ate dinner with the television news playing. It was a habit she'd acquired living without a man, and he didn't seem to mind. He kept up a constant chatter with Lewis while they ate, teasing him, instructing him, drawing him out. It was so good for Lewis to have a father figure. More than I ever had, she thought.

"That looks like you," Lewis said suddenly, pointing at the screen.

There was a photograph of Roger, staring blankly into the camera with the lifeless stare of a mug shot. At least it looked like Roger, Elaine thought, before the beard. Before she saw him smile.

"It does look like me, doesn't it?" Roger said. "Maybe I've got a twin somewhere."

The picture was replaced by a close-up of the anchorman, who said something about a bank robbery, something about a reward, some name she didn't catch.

Roger caught it, however. "Lester Gorman's going to get me into trouble if he doesn't watch out," he said. He turned to the boy. "Let's turn me in and get the reward," he said, flashing a wink at Elaine.

"It really did look like you," said Elaine, but Roger wasn't listening to her now. They were giving a story about a flooded subway and he seemed very interested. Elaine

186

paid no attention to such things. If you watched the city fall to pieces, it would drive you crazy.

The heat had abated for a day and a gentle breeze turned the morning into springtime in midsummer. New Yorkers seemed stunned by the change, as if the removal of an oppressive weight had left them still crouched and bent, uncertain whether to rise.

Pauline and Carl reacted to Central Park as if discovering it for the first time. On the Sheep Meadow he suddenly broke into a run, pulling her along behind him.

"Come on!" he called, running backward for a few steps, his face beaming. They were on the crest of the long, sloping hill, and he was propelling them down it. For a few halting steps, Pauline tried to hold back, but at first their momentum and then the infectiousness of his spirit caught her and she ran behind him, cutting in and out of the crowd of sunbathers, meditators, and Frisbee-throwers. She could hear his laughter ringing out and she too began to laugh, although she didn't know at what or why.

At the bottom of the hill he turned abruptly and held out his arms. She couldn't stop and raced into his arms. He held her, staggered back a few steps, still laughing, then they fell together onto the grass. He rolled atop her.

"I love you," he said. "I love you, I *love* you."

"Not here," she said, but when he kissed her she could no longer think why not there. They lay on the grass, scarcely noticed by the others, and embraced and kissed.

Like teenagers, Pauline thought, but without judgment. There seemed suddenly nothing wrong with acting like teenagers.

They lay for a while, his arm pillowing her head, and watched the clouds.

"You've given me my youth," Carl said.

Pauline laughed. "I'd say it was the other way around. You make me feel like a kid again. Or close to it."

"For you it's again," he said. "For me it's the first time. I never felt really young, until you. I always felt as if I'd been born middle-aged."

Pauline remembered him as the nineteen-year-old "man of the house," sober even then despite the hormones and frantic impulses of his age.

"Why?"

"I don't know," he said. "I've always felt responsible. For everything."

"And now?"

He rolled onto his elbows and looked into her eyes. "Now I feel loved," he said. "And happy." There was a note of surprise in his voice, as if even as he said it he could scarcely believe it.

They walked through the park, holding hands like children. Every few minutes Carl would stop, whirl her around, then grab her and press her to him, his face close to hers, his eyes wide with joy. They would both burst into smiles then, unable to contain the intensity of their emotions.

When they reached the bandshell, where a drunk was shuffling across the stage in an imitation tap dance, Carl spun her around again.

"I can't stop hugging you!" he said, but as he drew her to him, the smile melted. He stared over her shoulder with a look of fear and despair.

She turned to follow his gaze but saw nothing remarkable. "What is it?"

"Uncle Mark," he said in a tone of deep gravity.

"Where?"

He pointed but Pauline saw only the crowd, foreshortened by distance into an anonymous mass.

"I don't see him."

"He's gone," Carl said. His voice was flat and emotionless now.

"Are you sure it was Mark?"

Carl nodded. "He was with a woman and a boy." He paused. "They looked like a family."

Pauline glanced again at the bodies in the distance, then looked at Carl. The joy had been wiped from his face, and the boyishness.

"Let's go home," he said.

# Chapter 13

ELAINE STUDIED THE NEWSPAPER picture carefully. It had startled her at first, coming across it like that while looking for her horoscope. Suddenly there was Roger, staring blankly at her from the page. It was the same photo she had seen on television, but this time an artist had sketched in a beard. She stared hard at it until the black dots seemed to separate from the white background and swim in her vision. The haircut was shorter than now and the beard wasn't quite right, but it was impossible to say it *wasn't* Roger. Except for the bank robbery. He had been with her that day, she remembered it clearly. He had bought a video game for Lewis, an act of generosity so rare in her life that neither she nor the boy would ever forget it. So it could not have been Roger who robbed the bank.

Still, the similarity in the face haunted her. She studied the newspaper again, squinting deliberately to put the picture out of focus. The blurry image, details obscured, seemed to come to life and move on the page. Somehow, with the imperfections of the reproduction gone, it looked

190

more like Roger than ever . . . imperfections. She stared harder still, pulling the newspaper close to her eyes.

Roger and Lewis were playing Monopoly on the floor. Lewis, as usual, was trying to cheat and whining when he lost. She could hear Roger's patient voice, calmly giving way to the boy. Elaine admired his patience, it was so much greater than her own.

Roger looked up from the board to see her standing in the doorway. He smiled and winked at her. She felt ashamed of what she was about to do.

"Are you all right?" he asked.

"Fine."

She watched them play for a moment. Roger reached out and tousled Lewis's hair, and she felt like crying.

"I'm just going next door to see Mrs. Englander," she said, at last.

He glanced up at her, his eyebrows raised.

"Just to see if she's all right. Her arthritis is so bad. I like to look in on her every so often." She hadn't seen Mrs. Englander in a month, and the lie made her blush. Roger's eyes lingered on her for a moment, and she was certain he could tell she was lying, but he said nothing.

"I'll stay if you want me to," she said.

"We'll be all right, won't we, Lew?"

"It's your move," said Lewis, not bothering even to look at his mother. "Roll a seven and you'll land on my hotel."

Roger laughed. "I'll do what I can."

Elaine felt so guilty that she almost didn't go, but it seemed she was committed now. She started out the door, then remembered she would need her purse. She fetched it from the chair next to Roger and was starting out again when she felt a touch on her leg. She almost screamed before she realized he was just giving her an affectionate stroke as she passed.

He must have noticed, because he asked if she was nervous, but Elaine just shook her head and kept going. Her face felt as if it were on fire. She knew she didn't deserve him and she didn't understand what made her go through with it.

She forced herself to be polite to Mrs. Englander for ten minutes before she asked to borrow the magnifying glass the old woman used for reading.

When she came back to the apartment, Roger was making popcorn. She put her purse on the kitchen table, feeling as if it were bathed in a spotlight. He turned and came at her suddenly.

"Gotcha!" he said, then bent her backward in an elaborate kiss. The first exploding kernel of corn hit the pan lid and he returned to the stove. The newspaper was still on the kitchen table where she had left it, neatly folded and squared. She didn't remember if she had done that, it wasn't like her to be that neat. She thought she had walked out with it still open to his picture—to someone's picture—but she wasn't certain.

"Where's Lewis?"

"Washing up. I've got to do the same when I finish here." He held up his hands. Black smudges covered his fingers. "Newsprint," he said. He beamed at her like a little boy proudly displaying his muddy fingers.

He gave the pan one final shake, then poured the popcorn into a paper bag and salted it. "Popcorn tastes better in a bag, don't you think?" He was still grinning at her. "Give me your purse."

"What?" Involuntarily she put a hand on the purse.

"I need a stamp," he said.

"Oh." She realized she had been holding her breath. "I'll get it for you."

"I can get it," he said.

But she was already opening the bag, shielding its contents with her body. Her fingers fumbled around the bulky magnifying glass as she looked for her stamps. Why am I so frightened? she asked herself.

Snapping the bag closed, she tucked it under her arm and handed him the stamp. He put the stamp on an envelope on the table. The envelope was addressed to a newspaper. She noticed there was no return address.

"I'll get Lewis," she said and left the kitchen, taking the purse with her.

Lewis jumped when he heard her footsteps, then looked at her sheepishly, trying to hide the mess behind his back. The boy had gotten into the half of the closet she had cleaned out for Roger's use. The man scarcely needed that much space, he had practically no clothes, but the few things he did own were meticulously cleaned, pressed, and precisely arranged. She had nudged the cheap nylon duffel bags he kept lined up under his hangers once while searching for a pair of her shoes. They could not have been more than an inch or two out of line, but he had noticed it later that day and questioned her about who had been going through his things. He had been patient about it—he was always patient, always calm—but she could tell he was annoyed.

And now Lewis had done this. She grabbed him by the collar and yanked him out of the closet. He started to cry before she laid a hand on him, but she ignored him, kneeling instead by the duffels and trying to assess the damage. There were three bags in all, small red-and-white nylon sausages two feet long with a zipper along the top and two little pockets on each side. Elaine had seen boys carrying similar bags to the YMCA, stuffed with gym equipment. The first one in Roger's closet, however, was filled with a substance she had never seen before. It was an opaque gel, with the consistency of bread dough but smoother, not sticky at all, and with the neutral, cloudy color of dirty ice. It reminded Elaine of desserts she had seen in Cuban restaurants, overcooked, faintly gelatinous concoctions smelling of guava.

Indentations from Lewis's fingers were still on the top.

Elaine kneaded the material, trying to remove the traces of interference. The gel was firmer than it looked.

"I didn't hurt it," Lewis said from behind her, his voice building to a whine of self-defense.

"You'd better hope not," she said without turning. "After all Roger's done for you. What possessed you to get into his things in the first place?"

"I couldn't help it," said Lewis.

"Go on out and eat your popcorn," she said. "I won't tell him if you hurry up."

She poked carefully at the fingermarks a few more times, then zipped the duffel closed. Her hand came to rest on the pocket. She reached in and withdrew a stopwatch. The glass cover had been removed and a naked electrical wire had been fastened to the watch, the loose end hanging free across the minute and second hands.

Elaine replaced the watch gingerly, then looked back toward the open bedroom door. She listened for a moment, holding her breath, until she was satisfied that both Roger and Lewis were in the kitchen. She zipped open the second bag and found the same opaque gel. Again there was a stopwatch in the pocket. The third bag was identical. Past the third bag, pressed against the wall in the farthest corner of the closet, was a briefcase, old and obviously well-used but still presentable. The latch was closed and at the first attempt Elaine thought it was locked. She tried again, pressing the button and prying up on the latch with her finger. It snapped up suddenly and the briefcase was open. Wondering why she was doing it, Elaine peered in. The satchel contained batteries, at least a dozen of the long-lasting rectangular type with male and female terminals. There was nothing unusual about them, she had purchased them herself many times for toys and flashlights, but she did not understand why Roger would need so many of them. On the bottom of the case was a thick layer of cotton wadding.

Elaine listened again until she was content that both of

them were still in the kitchen, then carefully peeled away a layer of cotton. Her fingers found another layer and, beneath that, an oblong piece of Styrofoam. Holes had been cut in the Styrofoam padding, and in each hole was a device that looked to Elaine like a shotgun shell. She pulled one out of the protective case and held it in her palm.

"Don't move!"

She hadn't heard him come, but she realized he was less than a step away behind her back. She froze as if a snake would strike her if she budged. Roger knelt beside her and reached over her shoulder to gently take the blasting cap from her hand.

"These are dangerous," he said. "That's why they're wrapped like that."

"I didn't know."

"No, of course you didn't." He carefully replaced the cap in the Styrofoam, then wrapped it once more in the cotton. "Children are hurt every year playing with these," he said. "They think they're toys and they end up losing their eyes or their hands. We don't want little Carl to get hurt, do we?"

"Carl?"

He closed the briefcase again, then stood and offered his hand to help her up.

"What is it all?" she asked.

He smiled at her and touched her cheek. She could smell the popcorn.

"It's my work," he said. She thought of asking him to explain, but she felt too guilty already. He was so good to her and Lewis, how did she dare to question anything he did? For a moment she considered telling him about the magnifying glass in her purse, but she didn't want him to realize how unworthy she was.

That night they made love. For reasons she didn't fully understand, Elaine at first resisted giving herself over to him completely. She withheld emotionally, willing him to come while ignoring her own orgasm; but then it came upon her quite suddenly, all the more powerful for having been denied. She came, shuddering, calling out his name and digging her nails into his back. She wiped her tears on the sheet.

"I'm just so grateful," she said, when he asked what was wrong.

Later they spoke of Labor Day, which was two weeks away.

"I thought we could picnic in the park. There's a big parade, that's always fun . . ."

"No," he said abruptly. "No parade. I want you and the boy far away from that."

"He loves parades," she said.

"Not this one," he said. "Now listen carefully, Pauline. I will have to work on Labor Day, but I don't want you and Carl anywhere near Fifth Avenue, do you understand? We'll find something else for you to do that will be just as much fun."

She did not argue. There was something in his use of the strange names that chilled her blood.

Elaine lay still, her arms folded on her chest, trying not to move, while he fell asleep. She listened as his breathing became slow and regular and then she waited longer and longer still. She had gotten out of bed on other nights and he had always been suddenly, abruptly awake, no matter what the time of night. He would scarcely move but she knew that he was lying there in the dark, ready to move. It gave her an eerie feeling. At times she wondered if he ever really slept at all.

Moving an inch at a time, she eased her feet to the floor. She didn't make a sound, the springs didn't creak, the floorboards didn't groan. She was amazed at how quiet she could be when she really tried. Everything seemed to be on her side. Even the door opened silently. She glanced back and saw him lying on his side, his back to her, his breathing still slow and regular.

In the kitchen she spread the newspaper on the table and put Mrs. Englander's magnifying glass against it. Dots of newsprint jumped up at her with startling clarity. She moved the glass across the face of Lester Gorman, the bank robber, and up to the hairline. She looked closely, then closed her eyes, pinched the bridge of her nose, and forced herself to look again. There, faint but distinguishable under the power of the lens, was a dim shape along the hairline. It looked like a squirrel vanishing into a forest.

She felt his hand caressing her neck and turned to look at him. It occurred to her that she should have been startled to find him there, but she was not. In a way, she was relieved. Now that he had caught her with the magnifying glass, she wouldn't have to confront him, she wouldn't have to explain her suspicions. He would know and understand, as he seemed to know and understand everything. There was no question of her doing anything, of course. She had never thought of reporting him; she merely wanted to satisfy her curiosity.

His hand on her neck was gentle and he was smiling, but his eyes were sad.

"It's all right," she said, trying to drive away the sorrow. She touched his naked chest with her fingers.

"Certainly," he said. Elaine knew everything was going to be all right; there had never been anything to worry about in the first place.

"I love you," she whispered. She stood on her toes to kiss him and felt the pressure on her neck increase. The lights seemed to flicker, and she realized just before the darkness was complete that it was her eyelids that were fluttering.

Lewis awoke to see the man standing in the doorway of his bedroom. The man's eyes were red and tears were visible on his cheeks. He looked as if he had been standing there, silently weeping, for a long time. He was looking straight at Lewis, but the boy wasn't sure he was really seeing. Lewis looked around the room to see if there were any clues to Roger's tears. His gaze rested for a moment on the brand-new school supplies stacked atop his dresser, the crisply clean notebook with eight dividers, the plastic case of twenty pencils with a cartoon dog cavorting across the front, the erasers shaped like fruit, the pencil sharpener in the form of a balding boy. School started in three days, right after Labor Day.

"What's the matter?" Lewis asked finally.

"Hi, kid."

"Where's my mother?"

Stitzer took one step closer to the boy. He felt great compassion for him, orphaned by the war. He put a hand on the boy's neck to comfort him.

"Where's my mother?" the boy repeated.

"Don't worry, Carl," Stitzer said. "Uncle Mark will take care of you." The boy looked puzzled. Stitzer did what he had to do.

# Chapter 14

WHEN CARL ARRIVED AT work, the letter was waiting in his in-box. It was a plain white envelope with no return address and a Grand Central postmark. The address had been printed in block capitals. Inside was a single sheet of ordinary white stationery with one word printed on it: Skippy.

Ten minutes later Capello was seated across from Carl at a Formica table in the newspaper's cafeteria.

"Caffeine," he said, explaining the cup of tea he placed squarely in front of himself. "Too much coffee all day long. It eats on your nerves like acid. At the end of the day you feel like you're being massaged all over with fistfuls of sand. You know what I mean?"

Carl nodded, sipping his cup of coffee. He knew by now that Capello needed his few moments of pleasantries before business began.

"People will tell you that tea has as much caffeine as coffee, but don't you believe it. It's got something like a tenth the caffeine." Capello poured a packet of artificial sweetener into the tea, then added artificial cream. "It does have more tannin, of course."

"That's true."

"But what the hell is tannin, anyway? It's the caffeine you have to worry about." Capello tasted the tea, then jabbed a lemon slice with a fork and squeezed the juice into the gray liquid. He smiled at Carl as if in explanation. "The trouble with tea, though," he said, "is I never developed a taste for it."

"I think tannin is another name for tannic acid," Carl offered.

"Acid?"

"The same stuff they use to tan leather." Carl eyed the agent over his coffee cup, hoping his smile didn't show. Capello moved the cup and saucer away from him, using only his thumb.

"So," said Capello, after a pause. "You said something about demands?"

"I didn't say demands," said Carl. "I have certain requirements."

"And I have certain duties," said Capello.

"I appreciate that."

"I want to oblige you, you understand. The Bureau wants to be accommodating to everyone—within reason. But naturally there are limits."

"I don't want him hurt," said Carl.

"Uh-huh."

"He's out there. He trusts me. The only way to get to him is to use—or abuse—that trust. I'll go along with that only if I have your personal assurance that he won't be hurt."

"My personal assurance."

Capello stretched his chin toward the ceiling and scratched his neck. Carl saw a rash of tiny razor cuts from the morning's shave. Tendrils of hair, black as snakes, jumped from under the collar.

"Nobody wants him hurt," said the agent.

"This guy Stroup wants to kill him."

"Oh, I don't think so."

"He's practically drooling at the prospect. The son-of-a-bitch looks like one of the worst of the Gestapo. He belongs in a black trenchcoat."

"The man can't help the way he looks, Mr. Thorne."

"He can help the way he acts. I think he feels he's in some kind of competition with my uncle."

"Perhaps he feels responsible. He trained him to do what he's doing."

"Does that give him the right to destroy his creation? That's what he wants to do and you know it. I think it's some sort of last-gasp exercise of his machismo reflex or something."

"I'm afraid you'll have to explain that to me," said Capello.

"I get the feeling he sees it as Götterdämmerung. The final showdown of the Titans, with Stroup playing the leading role. The puppet and the puppet master fighting it out in the streets of New York. The last of the breed, legislated out of existence by an unappreciative Congress. He *wants* the confrontation. He wants my uncle to be bloody in tooth and claw so he can step in and kill him personally. It's a vendetta for Stroup, and he won't be satisfied until he draws blood."

Carl paused and reached for his coffee. His hand was shaking and he put the cup back on the table.

"Well, now," said Capello. "Either you've been spending a lot of time with Major Stroup that I don't know about, or you're letting your imagination get away with you. Writers do that, I suppose."

"I'm not that kind of a writer. I'm a journalist. I deal in facts."

"The *facts* are that your uncle is setting off bombs, not Major Stroup. As far as I know, Mr. Thorne, Major Stroup has no blood on his hands at all. Maybe you see some that I don't.''

"All right, I exaggerated."

"The *facts* would seem to indicate that Major Stroup served this country in the military for twenty-five years. He was awarded many medals for valor. He is continuing to serve now—completely voluntarily—by offering his help in apprehending a man who is a dangerous psychotic actively —actively, Mr. Thorne—attacking the resources and the residents of this city. There are no known links tying Major Stroup to the Gestapo . . .''

"I said I exaggerated."

"If he has been walking the streets with a Colt .45 strapped to his leg, looking for a shootout, you're the only one who has seen him."

"Let me put it to you another way, Mr. Capello. I love my uncle like a brother and a father combined. He has been more important to me than anyone else in my life, including my parents. Do you understand that?"

"Yes."

"I already feel a strong sense of guilt as it is . . .''

"Why?"

Carl turned uncomfortably in his chair, crossing his legs and studying the table top.

"I just do."

"You've done nothing so far, except to try to help him."

"I don't mean officially," Carl said. "Look, it doesn't matter. The point is I am the only way you can get in touch with him. Now, unless you assure me that you will not harm him, I'm out of it. I won't cooperate, you won't be able to use my column. You won't be able to do whatever it is you're planning to do."

Capello hesitated. He stirred his tea once more, then carefully placed the spoon back on the saucer without drinking.

"Is it Stroup we're talking about?"

"When it happens, when you lure my uncle into a trap—that is the plan, isn't it? Some trap that I'm supposed to bait for you?—when that happens, I don't want Stroup involved. Not at all, not in any way."

"Mr. Thorne, let me tell you a little bit about the Bureau. Do you know what the bulk of our agents do? I mean every day and every week and every year since I've been in it? They do not kick in doors and have shootouts with John Dillinger. They do not chase Capone through the streets of Chicago like Elliot Ness. Do you know what seventy-five percent of the agents really do? They try to prove tax evasion against suspected underworld figures—I'm talking about organized crime, Mr. Thorne. The Mafia, if you will, and I say suspected advisedly. We know who they are and what they are, but proving it is extremely difficult. So we have agents going through their records, sorting their trash, tracing their money. We have more accountants in New York alone than Price, Waterhouse, Mr. Thorne. Most of our agents never leave their desks except to pee.

"Then there are the men in the field. The ones who collect the trash and carry it to the ones at the desks. The ones who ask the judge for the court order, then install the bugs and the hidden cameras for the crooked senators and congressmen who want to take bribes. Then there are the handful assigned to New York and Washington who spend their days watching members of the Soviet delegation as they go about their daily business of spying. Spies tend to work electronically these days, Mr. Thorne, and so do our boys. They spend their time monitoring listening devices. We also have a few agents who hunt down ordinary criminals. Bank robbers, for instance. It might be disappointing to someone of your imagination, but the way that is done ninety-nine percent of the time is by bribing informants. It's just so much easier to find a criminal if his friends betray him.

"And that leaves what? A fraction of a percent, less than

a handful in the entire Bureau who have never fired a shot in anger. *I* have never shot at anyone, Mr. Thorne. I have never personally even seen a criminal whom I have regarded as physically dangerous . . . And now we have your uncle. A soldier; no, not just a soldier, an expert, perhaps *the* expert at sabotage, assassination, and mass murder. What sort of preparation do I have, does the entire Bureau have, for dealing with that kind of man? Damned little. Few people do. Major Stroup does. He's done that work himself. He trained the man we're after. You may know the man, Mr. Thorne, but Stroup knows the killer, he knows how he works and he knows how to deal with him. We are very lucky to have Major Stroup. We need him.''

''You also need me.''

''We also need you.''

''And I am telling you again that if Stroup is involved, then I am not.''

''You leave me little choice.''

''I'm sorry, it has to be that way.''

''Well, we all do what we have to. Very well, Mr. Thorne. We will proceed without Major Stroup.''

''And I want your promise that you will not harm my uncle.''

''My personal promise?''

''Yours personally and as a representative of the Bureau.''

Capello smiled radiantly.

''That one's easy,'' he said. ''You've got it.'' As if toasting the successful conclusion of a transaction, Capello lifted his teacup and drank.

Half an hour later Stroup and Capello met in the agent's office. This time there was no pretense of personal warmth, no show of civility or formalities. They were two professionals and they went to work immediately.

A detailed map of four square city blocks was tacked to

the wall. Capello moved in front of the map, holding a red grease pencil and making punctilious marks, like a surgeon cauterizing blood vessels. Each scarlet wound represented an agent. The map was dotted with them.

"He doesn't want you to be a part of it," Capello said. He put a red mark in the fourth-story window of an office building. "My command post," he explained.

"Who doesn't?"

"Mr. Thorne."

"Too bad." Stroup stood across the room and studied the map from a distance for an overall perspective.

"He thinks you want to kill Stitzer. He thinks you have a personal vendetta."

"Really?"

"That's what he thinks."

Stroup approached the map and took the grease pencil from Capello. "Put your riflemen here and here." He slashed crude X's on rooftops on both sides of the street. "Your best sharpshooters. They can give you enfilading fire from here. You have sniper rifles? Put those on the roof, the automatic weapons closer, down on the street level."

"There won't be any automatic weapons."

Stroup studied the map, tossing the grease pencil in his hand. "It would be better," he said, after a pause.

"I can't guarantee pedestrian flow on that street. You know that. It has to look like a normal situation."

Stroup dropped the pencil on Capello's desk.

"It's your show."

"Yes, it is."

"Are your sharpshooters any good?"

"The best we have," said Capello, trying to keep the annoyance from his voice. "They can hit what they aim at."

"On a target range. Have they ever hit a target that's breathing? I can get you some men with a phone call."

"I have men."

"It's your show."

"Are you expecting a minor war?"

Stroup sat in the chair opposite Capello's desk and crossed his legs. He picked at the crease in his pants leg, straightening it to a sharp edge.

"Have you ever been there when the shit hit the fan, Capello?"

Capello felt the heat in his face trickling down from his scalp like a viscous liquid. He didn't know if he was blushing from anger or embarrassment. "I imagine I can manage to cope," he said tightly. "It's only one man."

"It will be your only chance," said Stroup.

"Is Thorne right, Major? Do you have a vendetta against this man?"

Stroup paused, looking up at Capello from under his brows, moving only his eyes. Capello thought he looked like a hungry falcon eyeing its trainer.

"I want him, if that's what you mean," said Stroup.

"I want him, too. Mr. Thorne wants him. We all want him."

"Thorne wants him for sentimental reasons," said Stroup. "You want him because it's your job." He tilted his head to one side, bringing his nose into sharp profile. The resemblance to a raptor was even more acute. "I want him because I made him. I picked him, I trained him, I encouraged him. I taught him the way you teach anything you want to kill for you. I fed him a diet of blood and raw meat and then I withheld that diet until he was quivering with eagerness, and then I took off the leash. You should have seen him in the jungles, Capello. All my men, they were all savage, but Stitzer was the best. He was born to it, some men are, but society never gives them the chance. I made him, and I gave him the chance. That's why I want him."

Capello turned away from Stroup. The emotion in the man's face was embarrassing to look at.

"Well, naturally, I value your advice, but you're going to have to keep out of Mr. Thorne's sight. We need him."

"Yes, indeed."

"You agree then?" Capello had expected a fight.

"Certainly. It's your show. I suggest you put me in a position where I can watch and keep in touch by radio. Right here." He jabbed his finger at the map.

"The manhole?"

"You're setting it up with the agents acting as repairmen, aren't you? Put me in there."

"Why there?"

"Why not? Thorne can't see me." Stroup bared his teeth in a smile. "I'd feel comfortable there."

Capello tugged at his necktie. Continuing association with Stroup made him feel uncomfortable. He did not understand the man and did not want to.

"All right," he said. "You can have the manhole. Just make sure Thorne doesn't see you."

"And my weapon?"

"No weapon, Major Stroup."

Stroup bared his teeth again.

"This operation is being run by the Federal Bureau of Investigation, with the cooperation of the New York City police—under my supervision. We are not going to arm civilians."

"Civilian?" Stroup sounded as if the word were not familiar to him. "Is that what I am?"

"That is my understanding. Are we agreed about the weapon?"

Stroup shrugged. He seemed to have lost interest in the topic. "What about Thorne? Are you putting him under protection?"

"Why should I do that?"

"So Stitzer doesn't think he can walk up to him whenever he wants. If he has unrestricted access to Thorne, why should he come when we want him to? Let him see Thorne, then whisk Thorne away. Tease Stitzer. He's watching already. If he answered the column, he'll be watching. We don't want to lose Thorne prematurely; we have to use him first. He's our live bait.''

"Bait is the phrase he used about himself."

"Mr. Thorne has a better understanding than I would have thought. You can leave a dead carcass around to attract a lion, Capello, but for a tiger you stake out a live goat. Tigers don't eat carrion and they're attracted by the goat's bleating. The closer the tiger comes, the louder the goat bleats. It lets us know what's happening in the dark.''

Capello had a brief image of Thorne tethered to a tree with a rope around his neck while something malevolent moved through the jungle toward him.

*Chapter 15*

CARL FINISHED THE COLUMN by late afternoon and reread it with a sickening sense of disgust. It was a document of betrayal, treachery in writing, designed to put his uncle in the hands of his enemies. He was surprised he was so good at it. The writing had been simple, he seemed to have a facility for it. As he stood in front of Helstrom's desk, he wondered why he had needed no practice to sell out his uncle.

"Very good," said Helstrom when he had finished.

"Yes."

"Should do the job."

"Yes. That's the idea. What could be wrong? I just did my best to get my uncle back into a cell for the rest of his life. What could be wrong with that?"

"You don't have to do it," Helstrom said. "Someone else could write it and we'd run it under your byline."

"That's a fine distinction. How much less guilty does that make me?"

209

"It's not a question of guilt. He's got to be stopped."

"I *know* that," Carl said, his voice rising in sudden anger. "Treachery's a dirty business, but *somebody's* got to do it, right?"

Helstrom neatly squared the pencils on his desk, setting three of them at right angles to one another, forming an H. Dealing with fits of conscience was not his business.

"You're doing the right thing. The only thing, really. You'll come to see that in time."

"Yes, I know. I've become quite good at compromising myself."

Helstrom shrugged. "I'm going to call this in to Capello," he said. "Is there anything you want from him?"

"Sure," said Carl. "Tell him to send my thirty pieces of silver."

Carl took the elevator to the basement and walked out through the loading dock, which brought him onto the street a full block away from the normal entrance on Forty-third Street. As he had been instructed, he did not look around to see if he was being followed but walked quickly and directly to the corner, where he hailed a cab. He thought he recognized an agent who was studying the girlie magazines at the newspaper stand but made a point of not staring at him. The cab driver seemed surprised at the destination but dutifully drove Carl three blocks before letting him out. Carl overtipped, then walked two more blocks, heading west. It was an agony not to look behind him.

He passed another agent standing by a pay phone and was certain he recognized this one, but the man avoided eye contact and Carl passed on. At the corner, Carl entered the lobby of a hotel and went directly to the bank of pay phones. The telephone on the extreme right had an out-of-order sign on it. Carl stood by until it rang, then answered it quickly.

"Thorne," he said.

"All clear, sir," said a calm voice. Carl understood it

was the agent at the street phone who had been covering his back.

Carl left the lobby and took another cab, this time going directly to the hotel on Eighth Avenue where Pauline was waiting for him.

The column ran in the next day's paper. Pretty Polly was mentioned in the headline, in the lead sentence, and twice more in the body of the text. Superficially, the story dealt with the racehorse of that name that had been put to sleep after breaking its leg; but the encoded message was easy to read. Carl had woven the phrase "action terminated" throughout. Skippy was mentioned twice. According to the column, Skippy, son of Pretty Polly, was being viewed by prospective buyers at East Sixty-third, between Fifth and Madison, at noon on Labor Day.

If he was still reading the column, if he could still be reached within whatever maze his mind had entered, Stitzer would understand the message. Whether or not he would respond was another matter.

"You've done what you could," said Pauline. They were eating a room-service dinner of chicken cooled to room temperature, vegetables wilted by delay. A candle flickered on the tray between them, Pauline's effort to transform their unpleasant reality into something romantic. Even she felt the attempt was pathetic. No amount of candlelight could disguise the fact that they were eating in the hotel room because they were hiding from her former husband, Carl's uncle, whose homicidal tendencies were doubted only by Carl.

"I've done the easiest thing I could do," said Carl.

"It wasn't easy for you. I know how much you've agonized over it."

"I agonized over him when he was in the cell, too. I'm great at agonizing. Lousy at helping . . . He took me hunting once, did he ever tell you about it?"

"When was this?"

"Before he married you. I was thirteen, fourteen. We had a .22 rifle, which I think he bought just for that purpose. We drove upstate, into an area not too far from Pleasant, as a matter of fact. I was terribly excited, I'd never been hunting, never fired a gun, and the idea of roughing it in the woods with my Uncle Mark was just almost too much to take.

"We were after squirrels—there isn't a whole lot else you can kill with a .22, and they're easy to find. Much easier than rabbits. All you have to do is sit still for a while and they come to you.

"Sitting still was harder than it sounds, though, at least it was for me at that age, but he was like a stone. I thought he'd disappeared almost, he was so quiet. I swear he didn't move a muscle, didn't blink. He just said let's be quiet, then it was like he turned into a tree trunk. It calmed me down, I'll say that . . .

"The squirrels came. I watched them jumping around, chattering, chasing each other. We were both so still, it was almost like a trance and I was watching the squirrels as entertainment. Then I felt him touch my elbow; he was lifting my arm, lifting the rifle into place. I took aim the way he had shown me, squeezed the trigger, but the squirrel moved. I hit him in the leg and he fell but got up and started running, dragging the bad leg behind him. And he was squealing. I thought I was going to be sick. I'd never hurt anything in my life before. He tried to climb another tree. I didn't think he could make it with the bad leg, but he did, and then he just sat there on the limb, not doing anything. He must have been in shock. Uncle Mark told me I couldn't leave it like that and of course I knew he was right.

"I looked at Uncle Mark and handed him the gun. I can't do it, I said. Don't make me do it. He just looked at me and wouldn't take the gun. Nobody makes you do anything, he said. You do what you have to. You do what you should. It crushed me, just crushed me. He wasn't blaming me, he wasn't angry with me, he wasn't even disappointed. But he wasn't letting me off the hook, either. He was treating me like an equal, like an adult, maybe for the first time, and I hated it.

"I shot at the squirrel again, but I was shaking so much I missed it, missed the limb. The squirrel probably thought it was an insect whizzing by. It seemed to wake him up, though, and he started to bite at his injured leg as if he were trying to get the bullet out. There wasn't any bullet in there, of course, it had gone all the way through, but he didn't know that. I started to cry, watching him try to repair himself. I fired again, missed again, and the squirrel started to gnaw at his wound with those huge front teeth. I shot again and this time I hit the branch. The squirrel tried to escape, jumped toward another tree, but the injured leg wasn't strong enough and he fell to the ground. I ran after him, firing crazy, half blind with tears. The squirrel was running, limping, trying to get to the next tree, and I was digging holes all around him with bullets. He made it to the tree and scooted around the back of it just as I managed to shoot off part of his tail. By the time I got to the other side of the tree he had made it into the branches, but there was blood on the trunk.

"I fired some more times, not even aiming, just blasting away at the branches above me and yelling at the squirrel. I don't know exactly what I was saying, but I was cursing at it for making me do this thing. Finally I stopped crying. Uncle Mark was hanging back, just watching me, never saying a word. I walked back to where he was so I could get a better look into the tree. The odd thing was that I wasn't upset anymore, I was just angry. Furious, but with a cold rage. I wanted to kill that squirrel, I hated it, detested it. I had stopped shaking, the tears had dried. I used the side of the tree as support and took aim. The squirrel was gnawing itself again. The bullet hit it square in the head. When it fell

I walked over to it and emptied the gun into its body. When I was finished there wasn't much left but fur and blood; you couldn't tell it had been a squirrel. I didn't stop shooting until there weren't any bullets left, but I remember very clearly that I didn't feel much of anything while I was doing it. It just seemed right.

"Afterward, when we were driving home, we came to a bridge over a small river. Uncle Mark stopped the car and I got out and threw the gun into the water. He didn't tell me to do it, I never told him I wanted to do it, we just both seemed to understand. Then he drove home. I don't think either of us ever mentioned that day again."

"Why did you tell me that story?" Pauline asked, after a long stillness.

Carl looked at her, puzzled. He thought for a moment before answering. "I'm going hunting again," he said, then laughed bitterly. "And I'm not sure if this time I'm the hunter or the squirrel."

She comforted him as best she could, knowing he took her body not for love but for diversion. He sought a temporary anodyne for his guilt; she gave him love and hoped it would suffice. When it was all over, he would return to her, she told herself. Now his passion for her, that burning focus as concentrated as a laser, which had held Pauline transfixed as the center of his attention, his life, his being, was now scattered and diffused by events.

He was atop her now, straining hard, substituting effort for ardor. She knew his mind was no more aware of her than it was of the room that surrounded them or the bed that supported them. She told herself she should feel used, but she did not. It was a way of serving him, and she realized with surprise that giving completely of herself was what loving meant.

In that moment she let go of the last of her resistance to their unlikely pairing and loved him entirely. When he finished, she was weeping silently. When at last he noticed the tears, he misinterpreted them. "Don't worry," he said, "it will all be over soon. You'll be able to go home the day after tomorrow."

She clasped him to her. "I am home," she said.

Capello introduced Special Agent Merck with a certain awe, as if he were in the presence of a star.

"Agent Merck is with our counterespionage detail," Capello explained. "He knows more of the tricks of spying than most of the spies he watches. Isn't that right, Tom?"

Merck had a mannerism of pushing up the skin from chin to lips, as if he needed help from his fingers to smile. Carl thought he must have once had a beard and had never gotten over the habit of stroking it.

"I've put in a few years," said Merck. Carl guessed his age at forty. His face was going a bit to flesh, the hair surrounding a slight widow's peak was thin with a sprinkling of gray. He was the plainest man Carl had ever seen. His features lacked detail, as if coming from one pressing too many from a mold that had begun to blur. And yet there was a strange plasticity about the features, as if they could change, with the slightest of alteration, from one face to another. It was not as if Merck resembled no one but rather as if, with a little effort, he could look like everyone. Carl could imagine him blending into a crowd, even *becoming* the crowd with a change of shirt, a different hat, a businessman's briefcase, or a sportsman's racquet.

"Agent Merck is going to teach you what you have to know for the meet," Capello said.

"What do I have to know except to act natural?" Carl asked.

Merck massaged his face, seeming to smile. "There's nothing harder than *acting* natural," he said. "The real trick is to *be* natural, but you'll be too nervous for that."

"Why should I be nervous?"

Merck looked at Capello, one eyebrow raised quizzically.

"You'll be nervous," Capello said, "because you're not stupid."

Merck took him to Eighty-seventh Street and they walked the block between Fifth and Madison avenues together.

"This street is substantially like the one on Sixty-third where you'll meet," Merck said. "The composition of the stores is different, but the essential details are the same."

"Why don't we do it on Sixty-third?"

"Because he may be watching there. Now the first thing is not to try to make eye contact. A spy approaching a meet in hostile territory is extremely skittish. His nerves are raw. He's like an animal that doesn't know whether to run or attack. If you look him in the eye, he's going to feel pressured and make a decision. You don't want him to make decisions. You want him to give himself over to your will. He's prepared to do that, that's why he came. He's been summoned by a higher authority and he wants to give himself over to it, but he already feels every eye in the city is on him, so don't add your eyes to his burden."

"He doesn't think I'm a higher authority," Carl protested.

"You're the source," said Capello. "You gave him the trigger to start the operation, you gave him the order to come to this meet."

"*If* he comes," said Carl.

"He'll come," said Merck. "You're offering him a chance to let someone else do his thinking for a change. You're letting him off the hook, at least for the moment, and, believe me, there is nothing a spy desires more than to be let off the hook. He'll come. So, item one, don't look at him. You'll see him in the corner of your eye, if he wants you to, and that will be enough. In some instances you might need a recognition signal, but in this case, since you know each other by sight, you won't have to bother with it."

They approached the Fifth Avenue end of the block. Carl noticed a police department truck double-parked at the corner.

"The Labor Day parade will be going past on Fifth Avenue," Merck said. "There will be a lot of people on this end, watching the parade. That's good for him, the more people the better, he'll take comfort from it. We want him to feel safe."

"He *will* be safe," said Carl.

Capello smiled. "That's right. We're just talking about his perception."

"Could we have the barrier?" Merck asked. Capello nodded toward the truck and two policemen immediately placed sawhorse barriers across the street. A third policeman stood in front of the barrier, waving traffic away.

"It's a one-way street running west to east, so we only need to block off traffic in one direction and the street is sealed off," said Merck. "There is a perfectly logical reason for the barrier, so it shouldn't bother him. Most of the people will be at this end, watching the parade, but there ought to be enough pedestrian traffic to soothe his nerves. It isn't exactly a controlled situation, but it's partially controlled, and under the circumstances that's the best we can hope for."

The crowd at the barriers would also give Capello a chance to plant a dozen agents inconspicuously, but neither man bothered to mention that to Carl.

Merck stood with Carl at the barrier, watching the traffic as if it were a parade. "You'll be here half an hour early and take a position watching the parade. You may not be able to see, but don't worry about that, you're not here for entertainment. Now the timing is crucial. He'll come by once. If you're not here he might wait for a minute, no more than that. That's just basic craft. If you're not here, he'll assume something's wrong and he'll vanish. At twelve o'clock, on the dot, you will turn from the barrier and start walking, neither slow nor fast, toward Madison. Whatever happens, you must keep walking. He must be drawn away from the crowd, out into the open.''

''What if he doesn't follow?''

''If you do your job right, he will follow. That's what he came for. He assumes you have secured the area; he assumes you are taking him someplace safe. He assumes you are in command. He *wants* to assume that.''

''In other words, he trusts me.''

''If you do not act strange, if you do not panic and overplay it, he will assume he can trust you. If you do anything wrong, he will know it is not safe. In either event, he will take his cue from you. Now let's try it.''

While Capello acted the part of Stitzer, Merck watched Carl check his watch, turn from the barrier and walk toward Madison. Merck corrected his speed, the turn of his head, the rigid, self-conscious set of his shoulders, and made him do it again and again. Each time Capello came from a different direction, at a different speed, and each time Merck had Carl walk all the way to midblock before he stopped. Midblock, opposite the manhole in the middle of the street, was the area Capello had told Merck he would have his maximum forces. By that point Stitzer would be too far in the trap to get out, no matter what he did.

When they had rehearsed to Merck's satisfaction, Capello signaled the police and the barriers were gone in less than a minute.

''Will he be all right?'' Capello asked.

Merck thought for a moment. They had dropped Carl back within the protected maze of his own watchers.

''If he doesn't think too much,'' Merck said. ''If he doesn't start worrying about what he's doing, he'll be fine. The trouble with amateurs is they think too much about the wrong things, at the wrong times. If you're properly rehearsed, when the moment comes all you have to do is use your senses, let your instincts play it for you, not your mind. When your mind starts going, it only gets in the way.'' Merck paused and massaged his phantom beard.

"He'll be all right, if he doesn't think. It's the other guy you've got to worry about.''

"What if things go wrong?''

Merck looked at Capello appraisingly.

"For instance?''

"For instance, what if there's a shooting?''

"If there's a shooting, I'd expect him to panic.''

"I don't want a panicked civilian on my hands. He can only add to the problem. I want you to stay with him, Merck. As close as you can get without giving anything away. If the balloon goes up, it's your job to take him out of play and keep him there so the rest of us can concentrate on the business at hand.''

"I take it there's a little more going on here than I've been told about,'' said Merck.

"It's possible.''

"I've been on antiespionage for twenty years. I've never known a spy to shoot. I've only known one who even carried a weapon. When they're caught they give up and wait to be traded back to their country for one of ours.''

"This one isn't a spy,'' said Capello, "and there's nowhere we can trade him.''

"In that case,'' said Merck, "when the shooting starts, I shall do the only smart thing. I shall duck.''

"But on top of Mr. Thorne.''

"Fine, that will give me something soft to fall on.''

# Chapter 16

MAJOR STROUP SAT BY the window of his studio apartment overlooking West Eighty-seventh Street. The Hudson was half a block away and he could see it when he leaned out the window. On a warm night there was no need to see it, he could smell it. It was a warm night now, and, as always, there was a breeze off the river, bringing with it the particular odor of a dropping water level, a pungent mix of silt and decay.

Stroup was not looking toward the river but rather toward West End Avenue and, beyond that, to Broadway. An intensely lonely man, Stroup loved to watch people. He had been very much at home in the Army for that reason; he was surrounded by people day and night, and it was his business to watch them all—watch but not necessarily interact. Civilian life had been a hard adjustment, and his watching had been reduced to a more passive form. He no longer had a say in people's lives, could no longer influence events from one remove. The intermediaries who had permitted him to deal with people yet not deal with them, his captains and lieutenants, those unquestioning conduits who allowed him to manipulate hundreds of soldiers from a distance, had vanished with the rank and perquisites of an officer on active duty. Once a puppet master, Stroup had been forced, out of uniform, into the role of a mere spectator.

He watched, as always, several feet away from the window so he could look but not be seen. It was bad enough being lonely, it would be intolerable for others to know it.

Normally as he watched the people below he fantasized, joining into their little dramas of dropped packages, lost parking spaces, recalcitrant dogs. He had his regulars and his favorites, neighbors to whom he had never spoken but whose schedules were like old friends. Tonight, however, his mind did not register what his eyes took in. Stroup did not need to borrow the worries of others, he suddenly had his own again, and they frightened and exhilarated him.

He held a Browning B-80 shotgun on his lap and was laboriously cutting through the trigger guard with a hacksaw. When that was done, he would file the remaining nub until it was flush with the receiver. He wanted to be able to grab and fire the gun in a hurry, with nothing in the way to impede his finger. He expected to be in a split-second situation, and any fumbles could be fatal. He thought of the likely situation as being one of crisis or near-panic; but he knew he would still be in control of himself. He had based his life on being in control—he only hoped he would be fast enough.

When he was finished with the trigger guard he turned to the more difficult task of cutting through the barrel. He wanted the barrel no more than eleven inches long so the shot would begin to spread almost as soon as it left the weapon. He did not want to just hit his target, he wanted to splatter it. The Browning was a semiautomatic, which meant it could fire three three-inch shells of Magnum 20 gauge as fast as he could pull the trigger. That kind of load with that kind of barrel could blow the side off a house or knock a charging bear backwards. It would surely do the same for a man—assuming that Stroup had the opportunity to use it.

Lying on his bed was a .45 automatic service revolver which Stroup had brought with him when he left the Army, claiming, as most officers did, that it had been stolen. It was a common ruse, one the Army understood and condoned. After spending a career surrounded by weapons, most men did not relish the idea of going naked into the civilian world. A hunting knife was in a scabbard in Stroup's right boot. Like the guns, it was well oiled and would slip from the leather at a touch.

Stroup rested for a moment from his sawing and massaged his forearm where the muscles were bunching in protest. He estimated that he would have the shotgun converted to its most lethal—and highly illegal—form by two in the morning. A perfect time to lay his trap. The best time to hunt the tiger was when he was active. It was also the most dangerous.

After a further hour of sawing and filing, Stroup placed the shotgun on the bed beside the pistol. He paused for a moment, admiring his handiwork, then abruptly yanked the shotgun to his shoulder and drew a bead on a target in the street below. He gently lowered the gun back to the bed, shaking his head. He wouldn't have time to aim; he would have to fire as fast as he could, shooting from the hip or the shoulder or the knee, however he found himself. He might be off balance, definitely frightened, and too damned close to the target for comfort. It was the closeness that made the shotgun possible, of course, but it also multiplied the fear quotient. He would have to fire by reflex and trust the spreading shot to do the job.

He suddenly grabbed the gun again and jerked around a full 180 degrees. The hammer clicked as he pulled the trigger, and Stroup froze in place. He looked at the shotgun's line of fire. It was held level with his ribcage and pointing at an angle across his body. He sighted along the barrel to see if it would hit his target. His image stared back at him from across the room. The barrel of the gun in the mirror was aiming several degrees away from Stroup. If he had been firing a single bullet, he would have missed completely even though he was only ten feet away. But if he had been firing Magnum 20 gauge with this weapon, he would have cut himself in half.

Stroup smiled bleakly at his own face. "You're dead," he said, and watched his reflection glare back at him with malice. When did I start to look like that, he wondered, studying the harsh lines and sharp shadows on his bony face. The gun in the mirror wavered slightly, and Stroup looked down at the real weapon in his own hands. Was it age—or was he scared already? He didn't like either answer.

After loading the Browning with the maximum three cartridges, he worked the breech once, bringing a shell into the chamber, ready to fire. Using plastic food wrapping, Stroup began to seal the shotgun, pressing out the wrinkles over metal barrel and wooden stock. He worked with special care around the naked trigger. At the hammer he pulled the wrap away, creating an air space so it could work unimpeded.

When the gun was sealed in plastic film, he gently placed it in an extralong garbage bag. He closed the bag with a wire tie, then taped over the fold with waterproof tape. Using a razor, he gingerly cut a tiny slit and worked with care until the trigger poked out of the garbage bag, then sealed the opening with more tape. When finished, he had his weapon sealed in double layers of plastic with only the trigger showing. If he failed, it would not be because the weapon was jammed or the powder was wet.

He placed three industrial-strength bar magnets on the top of the barrel and felt them tug securely against the weapon. He lifted the gun by the magnets alone, shaking it. The weapon clung to the magnets, metal to metal, as if welded. It would take a very firm pull on his part to free the weapon when the time came, but the one thing he did not fear was lack of strength. Adrenaline would see to that.

Finally he placed the shotgun into a case hand-carved from blocks of Styrofoam and taped it in place before slipping the case into an olive drab Army-issue duffel bag. He debated for a second whether to take the .45 with him—it would cause him even more trouble than the shotgun if the police stopped him. The lethal metal felt comforting in his palm, heavy for its size, dense and smooth. He tucked the pistol into the belt at his back where no one could see it if his jacket flew open, yet within easy reach if he needed it. There was no question of making a quick draw with a .45. Stroup doubted that he would need the pistol; it seemed unlikely that he would encounter Stitzer tonight, but he had had the sense on a few occasions that he was being followed. Perhaps not a sense—a fear. He did not delude himself that the extra gun offered any impenetrable defense if Stitzer was stalking him, yet one took whatever precautions were possible.

Holding the duffel bag at his chest like a rifle at port arms, Stroup ran down the five flights of stairs in his apartment building. He made it a point never to use the elevator, going up or down. Conditioning was a matter of discipline, and taking the hard way was the only method to assure it. Comfort, Stroup understood, was insidious.

Broadway was never deserted completely, regardless of the hour, and Stroup walked briskly downtown, paying little heed to those in front; he was listening for any pattern of footsteps that fell into rhythm behind him. He resisted the urge to break into a steady double time—dressed in street clothes as he was, it would only invite the police to stop him.

224

At Seventy-second Street he took a cab crosstown rather than risk going through the park. On Fifth Avenue the signs of life fell off markedly, and when he turned onto East Sixty-third, he was the only one on the street. It was a commercial street with nothing to attract people after the shops and restaurants were closed. At 2:30 in the morning, with the dark and threatening park at one end, the street was as deserted as any place in Manhattan was apt to get.

If he had been followed coming out of his apartment— and Stroup still was not certain he hadn't been—he had certainly lost any pursuers during the ride through the park. No other lights had followed for over a minute, and Stroup felt secure.

The manhole was in the middle of the block, halfway between Fifth Avenue and Madison. Stroup had been there the night before and had loosened the cover so he could be certain to lift the heavy disc quickly when he needed to. He had smeared the edge of the cover with wax and it came up without hesitation, just as a car turned the corner and caught Stroup in its headlights. He dropped the cover and moved to the sidewalk, waiting for the car to pass, its driver eyeing Stroup strangely. When the car was out of sight, Stroup jerked the lid to one side and eased himself into the manhole. The recess was chest-high, which would allow him to see everything happening on the street yet be completely out of sight just by ducking his head. Stooping down now, he took two steps into the utter darkness of the hole, holding the plastic-encased shotgun in front of him. He felt for the pipe with his head, then let the magnets seek out the metal. The gun snapped securely into place against the pipe. Tomorrow he would draw the gun closer so it would be at his hand when he needed it, but for now it was safely and secretly out of sight, black on black, an amorphous shape in the darkness.

His work done, Stroup stood for a moment on the

sidewalk, assessing his trap—and his chances. He sighed. It was not what he would like, but under the circumstances, it was the best he could do.

He walked toward Madison Avenue, running through the operation again and again, no longer looking for flaws—there were too many to dwell on; it would work or it wouldn't—but rehearsing it so that by the time events actually took place, they would no longer surprise him. Stroup did not agree with Shakespeare. A coward may die many times before his death, but so do wise men. He tasted fear, rolled it over his tongue, anticipated it until he had conquered it. It was only when a soldier accepted fear as a natural and welcome part of the atmosphere that he could proceed as if it didn't exist.

Using the boy's crayons, Stitzer had traced the sewer map on plastic wrap he found in the kitchen, creating an overlay he placed atop the city grid. The street map he had made himself, again using the boy's crayons and craft paper, following the details of a smaller pocket-size version he had purchased weeks ago and enlarging it to the proper scale. With the overlay in place, he could see how to get to any location in Manhattan underground.

The sewer map was quite detailed, showing the diameters of the various tunnels and pipes as well as their locations and angles of drain. What they did not show was the flow rate. At the prime usage time early in the morning, when most of the city was showering, shaving, and flushing, and again at night time, as they prepared for bed, certain channels would be impassable. Stitzer had made estimates and knew which pipes to avoid when, but he wasn't going to be using the sewer during peak times anyway. The hours he had spent charting the danger zones were only for contingency planning, emergency measures.

He traced his route now for the tenth time, drawing his

finger along the green line that represented one of the huge
ten-foot pipes he could run through upright, then slowing
his finger as the green intersected with the red, a smaller
pipe where he would have to travel bent double. Where the
green met a blue line, Stitzer made the adjustment in his
mind and began to crawl, his hands and knees scraping
against the pitted sides of the pipe. He glanced at his
preparation list to make sure he had included a note to check
on the gloves and the kneepads. He had.

His first destination was marked with a blue X. The line
then continued in blue for fifty yards before veering to the
south and turning yellow. This was the area of greatest
difficulty—and danger. Stitzer would have to move on his
stomach like a snake, his shoulders barely squeezing
through the narrow opening. He would be at his slowest and
most helpless here, and although he had taken measures to
protect himself, the peril made his intestines tingle just to
think of it.

In effect, his route was taking him upstream, through
feeder lines of decreasing size until, in theory, he would
emerge in someone's kitchen from a two-inch pipe.
Roaches and water bugs did it, and the occasional rat.
Stitzer, however, did not intend to go upstream forever.
After one hundred yards in the smallest pipe he could
negotiate, the yellow intersected with another green line.
Once in the major artery, Stitzer could branch out into any
one of the seventeen possible tributaries. Given the time, he
could emerge virtually anywhere in the city, and effective
pursuit would be all but impossible.

A whole world exists in the sewers beneath the streets of
New York City, some of it much older than anything still
standing in the sunlight. The sewer system under Manhattan
is enormous, consisting of five feet of pipe for every foot of
roadway. The pipes snake into the system from every
house, every apartment, every office building, and every

storm drain in the city. The first pipes are small, ranging in diameter from four to eight inches. Where the systems from more than one city block converge, the pipes are three feet across, large enough for a man to crawl through. The largest pipes of all, the ones that hold the confluence of sections, are nearly ten feet across, large as a small bedroom and more than a mile long, sunk deep within the city's bedrock.

But the pipes are by no means uniform. All the pipes installed after World War II are prestressed concrete, but there are metal ones dating from before that, and even some ceramic ones, formed of fired clay, that lie under the older parts of the city and date to just after the Civil War. Underneath what is now Wall Street, twenty-five feet below the pavement, lies a wooden sailing ship, rumored to be loaded with Colonial treasure bound from the port of New York to London.

It is a staple of popular myth that baby alligators, imported in large numbers during a fad in the late 1950s and flushed down toilets when they grew too big or too troublesome, now flourish in the sewers. Huge and ravenous, the myth has it, these ancient reptiles roam beneath the city, ready to devour anyone foolhardy enough to wander by. It is not true. The climate in New York is too cold to support the subtropical alligator. But life does teem in the sewers. Mucus-slick algae coat the walls of the old tile pipes, serving as a breeding ground for millions of insects. Mosquitoes lay their eggs in the standing pools in summertime. Roaches scurry and scuttle everywhere, using the sewers as a refuge from exterminators, running down the drains when threatened and climbing back up again elsewhere. Dung beetles thrive, feasting on the innumerable small corpses that flow and rest and flow again, surging with the tides of water usage. Newts and blind salamanders feast on the insects, indifferent to the darkness. Huge rats, many of them albino after centuries of inbreeding, feed on the salamanders and the garbage and the human waste products. Every unwanted peanut butter sandwich flushed down the toilet by a child helps feed something underground.

To eat the rats there are cats, scarred and savage. Many of them were conceived in the sewers, their parents' howls of copulation reverberating under the city, but few are actually born there, for the cats prefer to escape their hunting grounds when not actually hungry, seeking the drier climes above ground. They come and go through innumerable leaks in the system. Stitzer was planning to do the same.

He took one last look at the maps, then burned them in the kitchen sink. When the ashes were washed down the drain, he went into the master bedroom and retrieved the duffel bags filled with explosives. The two shapes on the bed did not bother him. When he had covered the bodies with a sheet, he had erased them from his mind. People were killed in combat, and Stitzer had long since learned not to mourn the enemy.

He placed the duffels into two enormous suitcases. The cases were large enough to be comical yet not so huge that he couldn't handle them. It had taken him some time to find them and he worried slightly that the purchase might be remembered, but they were ideal for his purpose. They looked funny, but the cloth would not restrict the explosion and they would hold a tremendous amount of shrapnel.

He synchronized the watches carefully, then covered each duffel with broken glass, the result of smashing every bottle and jar in the kitchen. The shards were large to allow for the further shattering the explosion would cause. A tiny piece of glass traveling at great speed could do damage enough. On top of the glass he poured brads and tacks and nails. He would have preferred iron filings, which made much sharper, more lethal shrapnel, but the nails would serve. It had taken half a dozen hardware stores before he finally found one that sold them in bulk and not in sealed plastic containers.

When the suitcases were filled with their deadly cargo, he covered the shrapnel with a towel, then locked the cases and tied them with a length of rope. With the bombs sealed, Stitzer began to paint the cases.

He slept that night on the floor, as he had the previous night as well. He had been living in luxury too long. Sleeping with the woman had been wonderful, but it had dulled him, and it was time to prepare again for the hard way. Waking when the first rays of the sun touched his face, he lay for a moment, the dream still vivid in his mind. He had been playing with Carl when the boy was eight years old, tossing him into the air and catching him, but delaying the catch to the last possible second so the boy felt he was certain to fall. The expression on Carl's face was a mixture of both delight and fear, that marvelous childhood blend that possessed trust and uncertainty in equal measure, before maturity and experience would eventually eliminate the trust.

Stitzer's laughter rang and reverberated around them, as if they were in an echo chamber, punctuated by the boy's gasps, then squeals of pleasure. Stitzer loved that boy, loved the trust, the adoration in his little face. There was a sense of adventure in Carl that only Stitzer recognized. It was hidden from his parents by their overprotective concern for his health. With them, he was the child they wanted him to be; and with Stitzer, he was the child Stitzer knew he could be—brave, adventurous, aggressive.

The dream had changed subtly as a sinister note crept in. Carl began to age as Stitzer threw him, becoming ten, then a teenager, then a young man. As the boy grew heavier, Stitzer strained more and more. His laughter changed to grunts of effort and the possibility of dropping him became very real. As Stitzer woke, Carl had been nearly as old as

Stitzer and yet somehow the same little child, the same boy Stitzer had loved as no one else in his life.

For a moment the loneliness and longing overwhelmed him. He felt immeasurably sad. He wanted that little boy again, he wanted his own youth back, he wanted ease and comfort and the luxury of love. For that moment he thought he would do anything on earth if he could only regain those magic moments when a little face looked into his own, filled with love and delight. The longing was so strong that Stitzer felt immobilized.

With a major effort of will, he got to his feet. There was no way to have the child again; but Carl was still out there. The boy's spirit was still alive, he could sense that spirit in the columns, coming off the page to him. It had been that spirit that had sustained him for the five years of waiting at Pleasant Hospital. And now the boy was calling out to him directly. At least he prayed it was the boy and not the near-perfect imposter they had already been using against him. If it was the *real* boy, then all would be well. Stitzer would find a way out of their situation for both of them. If it was a trick and the imposter awaited him, Stitzer knew how to deal with that as well.

The hotel had become prison to Pauline and she prepared to leave it with a feeling of liberation, shrugging off the bonds of the little room, the long, narrow hallway, the tasteless wallpaper, the sparse furnishings designed for discomfort. There was an aura of desperation and loneliness about hotels that Pauline felt was still clinging to her skin like a film as she packed her overnight bag. Only being back in their own apartment would remove the residue of depression, and she hurried to get herself ready. Carl had left five minutes earlier, trudging forth with a grim and reluctant determination that no amount of cheer on Pauline's part could dispel.

The telephone was ringing as she let herself into Carl's

apartment—their apartment now—and she ran for it. As she touched the instrument, the last ring died, cut in two, as the caller hung up. She paused for a moment, remembering the haunting, silent calls that had seemed to her to come from Mark, but she dismissed the idea. Today was the day when the problem would be ended. Carl had promised as much. Capello, by letting her return home, had done the same.

They had left the apartment closed and the heat in the bedroom was stifling. The curtains were closed and the room was very dark. She knelt on the bed to part the curtains, and as she did so the closet door moved. Her instinct was to scream, but he had a hand over her mouth before she could finish inhaling. He jerked her back against his body, holding her with his great strength until the initial shock passed. His left hand was on her hip, the fingertips riding the edge of the pelvic bone, and her back was pulled against his chest.

Pauline reached up to claw at his face, but he did something to her hip with his fingers, and she felt a pain shiver through her pelvis that made her gasp.

"There's no point to that," he murmured. His breath fluttered the hair over her ear. It was strangely like a lover's whisper.

She realized it was Mark and felt the panic ease. Although she knew how dangerous they said he was, although she knew what he could do to her, she was less frightened of him than of an intruder who had come to rob and been discovered. Whatever else he might do, Pauline knew that Mark would not hurt her in panic. Whatever he did would be considered and deliberate.

As her body eased, he released the hand from her mouth but kept his fingers on her hip. Pauline slowly turned her body to face him. They kneeled on the bed, like two lovers.

"Mark," she said.

He smiled, his teeth flashing whitely in the gloom, and said something in a language she did not understand.

232

"What?"

"Lie down," he said in English. He placed a hand on her chest and gently pushed her backward. She could feel his palm pressing against her breast as she eased onto the pillows. He lifted his hand when she was supine, but his other hand never left her hip.

"Mark," she said again, starting to plead, but he pressed his fingers into her and again she felt the wave of pain in her pelvis. His right index finger was raised to his lips for silence.

"Speak when I tell you," he said, and she nodded to show she understood.

"Where is he?" he asked.

"I don't know," she said.

He pressed again and she gasped. The touch was so light she didn't understand how it could generate so much pain.

Stitzer waited calmly, his eyes on her face, while the hurt subsided. When her breathing was normal again, he spoke.

"Where is he?"

"Please?"

"Where?"

"Please, Mark. I don't know. I would tell you if I knew, but I don't. I'm not fool enough to think I can withstand torture."

She shuddered involuntarily before the pain came, which only made it worse. He waited once more until she was calm, then tipped his head to the side, asking the question without words.

"They're looking for you," she said.

He lifted an eyebrow, waiting. Pauline thought desperately of ways to stall, to tell him what he wanted, to keep the pain from coming.

"He left me this morning, he didn't say where he was going! I didn't . . ."

She screamed this time, but not loud enough to make him silence her. His fingers felt as if they were scraping sandpaper across an exposed nerve. She arched her back and twisted, but when she tried to pull away from him, she felt the weight of his hand pinning her to the bed. As she lay still, trying to recover, tears came. They rolled unheeded from the corners of her eyes down to her jawline. She felt them but did not bother to brush them away. All of her efforts were directed toward lying perfectly still, as if total passivity would save her.

This time they were both silent for many minutes. Mark sat perfectly still, looking down at her face. She did not think he looked angry or vindictive. He seemed at peace. After many moments the hand on her hip moved and she tensed, but this time there was no pain. His fingers had moved slightly down from the ridge of the bone toward the crease of her legs. They stirred once, like a small animal moving in its sleep, then were at rest again.

Pauline could detect no increase in pressure, but gradually she became aware that his hand seemed to be giving off heat. The room was hot but the warmth from his hand was different, local and intense. She felt the heat spreading throughout her groin.

Still he did not move and his expression did not change. A tension gripped Pauline and she longed to break it but was afraid to speak. The heavy, suffocating oppression of the room increased as the sun rose higher on the other side of the curtains. She had broken out in a sweat from fright, but now the perspiration came on its own and little rivulets ran from under her arms. The back of her blouse was soaked where it touched the bed and dark stains were appearing on her chest. Very slowly she moved one hand and undid a button on her blouse. His eyes never left her face.

When the discomfort became intolerable, she shifted under his hand. The fingers came to rest even closer to the inside of her thigh. He did not seem to notice, or care, but Pauline felt the heat spreading from his palm as if his skin were a casing for live coals. The warmth spread outward in pulses, and despite herself, Pauline felt the signs of her arousal.

Still he did not move, did not speak, but continued to stare at her like a statue.

"What do you want!" she cried suddenly, her voice hoarse. "You know I don't know anything!"

"Yes," he said softly.

"Then let me go. Please!"

Silence fell between them again. His eyes seemed to bore into her. She knew there was no point in trying to keep anything secret from him. He knew everything, knew what she was thinking, what she was feeling.

For the first time his expression changed. His face seemed to darken and become more sober. His eyes narrowed slightly. After a second Pauline recognized the expression. She had seen it often on Carl and remembered it now from her years with Mark. It was the same look for both men, the serious, intense look of lust.

He put his free hand under her blouse, atop her breast. The nipple seemed to rise of its own accord. He slid his palm across the breast, back and forth, scarcely stirring. His palm seemed to breathe upon the nipple, it moved so lightly.

Pauline resisted within herself for a moment, but the outcome seemed inevitable; it was as pointless to resist her own desire as it was to resist his force. She arched her back, pushing her breast to meet the teasing contact of his palm.

His other hand was so close to her sex now that her body cried out to be touched. She lifted her hips to meet his fingers.

"Please," she whispered.

His palm moved again on her breast, and then, so slowly, he lowered his lips to her nipple. Pauline shivered. He mouthed the tender flesh of her breast, his lips dry, barely touching the skin. Tentatively, like a blind man finding his way, he caressed the breast, the nipple, causing her to strain toward his mouth. She wanted to crush him to her and her hand hovered over his head, but she held back, at once afraid to touch him yet tantalized by the teasing ecstasy of his long delay. At last she felt the wet warmth of his tongue and she gasped.

Her hips lifted again as she rose to make contact with his fingers, which remained inches away from completion.

"Oh, please," she murmured. She felt that she would burst with need. His great patience and restraint were joyous torture. She strained again and his fingers brushed against her panties. She cried out as if she had been hurt. The fingers brushed her again, light as a feather borne on the breeze.

He lifted his head from her breast and she opened her eyes to look at his face. An expression of great wonderment spread across his features, as if he had discovered the answer to a plaguing mystery. His eyes were looking at her but didn't seem to see her.

One of his fingers insinuated itself under the pantyline and Pauline felt as if it had reached deep inside her. If he moved a quarter of an inch, she knew she would climax. She willed herself to lie still, to let him proceed at his own halting pace of discovery.

When at last he entered her, she could no longer control herself. She shuddered to a climax and then, almost immediately, to a greater one.

He climbed atop her, yanking at his clothing, suddenly feverishly urgent himself. He penetrated her fully and began moving rapidly, almost brutally, on her body. She heard her own voice screaming in a long, keening fall as she came for the third time and was only dimly aware that he, too, had reached orgasm.

Her skin continued to shiver for several moments longer, each touch of his flesh on hers sending a new tremor through her, even as he withdrew and stood beside the bed.

His fingers trailed across her chest, tracing the course of her sternum as he dressed himself with his other hand. At last, reluctantly, he withdrew even his hand.

"I'm going now," he said, his voice hoarse and subdued. "I'm going to get the boy."

Pauline struggled to make sense of his words.

"I don't want him to get hurt. If you have anything to tell me that will help the boy, tell me now."

"The boy?"

"Our boy," he said. "Carl."

"Carl!" She felt guilt as strongly as fear for Carl's safety. "Mark, don't hurt him!"

He looked at her, puzzled. "Hurt him? I'm going to save him."

"He's all right, Mark. He doesn't need to be saved. Just leave him alone. Leave us all alone."

For a moment his face had been open, innocent, but now it changed and a look of harsh reserve settled upon it. There was the look in his eyes of a man who knows better. He shook a pillowcase off a pillow and tore it into strips.

"*Stalchenki*," he said as he looped the first strip around her arms.

It took Pauline more than a hour to free herself from her bonds. When she placed the frantic call to Capello, it was too late, as she had known it would be. Capello was already staked out and the trap was closing.

# Chapter 17

THE MORNING WAS FIERCELY hot, and from his vantage point in his fourth-floor headquarters, Capello could see the dark stains on the short-sleeved policemen as they set up the barriers. His temporary office was without air conditioning, and Capello was already sweating by ten o'clock. When Carl was ushered into the office at eleven, Capello's shirt was unbuttoned to his waist and the hair on his chest was matted with perspiration.

He beamed a radiant smile of welcome and clasped Carl's hand warmly, as if the two of them were about to share an exciting, companionable outing together, but Carl could see the lines of tension already working around the agent's mouth and eyes.

"You look tired," said Carl.

Capello laughed. "Age," he said. "My wife has started telling me I look tired even on the days when I feel most rested. Actually, I've been here all night, setting things up."

Carl glanced out the window. At the corner he could see

a few curious pedestrians loitering by the police barriers. Otherwise everything on the street seemed perfectly normal.

"Setting what up?"

"Oh, there are a few agents out there. Someone has to coordinate them."

Carl looked again. He could see no one he would have thought was an agent. A mother strolled with her baby carriage. A yellow-helmeted worker stood up to his chest in a manhole. A young couple walked with their arms around each other. Two homosexuals carried groceries.

"I don't see any agents."

"Good," said Capello. "You might recognize a face or two later when you're down there. Pay no attention to them. Absolutely none. Do you understand?"

"Yes."

"If you're seen talking to anyone, he'll know you're not alone and that could kill the whole operation. If there's an emergency and you have to talk, lift your watch, look at it, then speak to the person next to you as if they had just asked you the time."

"Who will I be talking to?"

"Me." Capello held up a radio transmitter the size of a cigarette lighter. "Take your shirt off, please."

Capello taped the transmitter to Carl's chest and pushed a switch.

"It's on. Say something."

"Why is this necessary?" Carl asked. He heard his words coming out of a speaker on a table by the window. The table top was covered with a multitude of walkie-talkies and telephones.

"Just a precaution," said Capello. "You're going to be down there, I'm not. If anything happens that I can't see from here, I want to know about it. Now put this on."

He lifted an antiflak vest from the table.

"I don't need that!"

"Time is running out, Mr. Thorne. Please put it on."

"You promised me you wouldn't harm him!"

"Protecting yourself doesn't harm him," said Capello. "And it just might help you."

"Is this a goddamned ambush, Capello?"

"I'm putting the vest on *you*, Mr. Thorne, because we don't know what your uncle is going to do."

"You wouldn't be using it if you weren't—"

Capello grasped Carl by the arm and thrust the vest in his face. "Put the fucking thing on, mister! I've coddled your conscience long enough. Now it's time to get down to the street and do your job and let me do mine! If you want to take unnecessary risks on your own time, that's fine with me, but right now you're part of my operation and if you get hurt that reflects on me, so put this goddamned vest on!"

Carl left Capello's headquarters with his face burning. The vest was surprisingly light and seemed incapable of offering any real protection, but it weighed on his pride like a suit of armor.

Capello waited until Carl approached the barrier and took up his position amid the small crowd that was already gathering. Half of the crowd were agents, but not of the sort Carl would recognize as peace officers. There were two women, one of them a bag lady whose shopping bags contained a .38 automatic and a walkie-talkie that picked up her every syllable. Her lips were moving continually in a litany of invective aimed at the world—and an occasional word for Capello. The second woman, seemingly a suburban housewife, also had a .38 in the handbag she clutched to her side. Capello was particularly pleased with her. Her nickname was Suburban Sally, and unlike her colleague, the bag lady, she didn't have to act the role. Her persona reflected the prudish, nonliberated woman she really was. Like Merck, Sally was just naturally plain. The best kind of agent, in Capello's mind. He did not feel entirely comfortable with disguises. Anything that required too much artifice could go wrong. Like a reliable character actress, Sally was cast again and again in the same role and she always played it to perfection. Why she chose to spend her life with a gun in her purse was a subject of much discussion, some of it not very kind, among her male counterparts.

Capello watched Carl for a moment through his binoculars. He stood at the barrier, his eyes on Fifth Avenue, as if he were already watching the parade. At least he's not looking around, Capello thought. If he starts nervously checking everyone out, we're all in trouble.

Capello picked up one of the walkie-talkies and began to run through his checklist once more, making sure the agents he could not see were in place and ready. In addition to the six on the street who were within his view, there were six more at street level behind windows and doors, ready to spring forward at a moment's notice. The snipers on the roofs were the ones Capello felt sorry for. They had been in position since dawn, crawling out of their aeries in the last of the dark, then lying there in the sun as the heat grew. Poor bastards must be baked, he thought, and he hoped they had remembered to take their water flasks with them.

His checklist completed, Capello swept the street with his glasses again, stopping on the yellow hard hat that poked out of the pavement like a mushroom sprouting after rain. Stroup worried him, but he could not say exactly why. The man had seemed unusually docile when he took his position, as if all too eager to submit his will to Capello's. He had insisted that Stroup also wear a vest, and in the process had checked him for a weapon. If he had a gun on him, it would have been a small one, and that, too, troubled Capello. However, he had never been on a job that didn't trouble him somewhat, somewhere. If it had all been perfect, he would have known for sure that something was wrong. Capello lived with imperfection and called it security.

With a sigh he settled uneasily on the edge of his chair and continued to study the street. There was nothing more he could do but wait. At least, he comforted himself, this time the net was in place. He was still smarting from the fiasco at the Marquise Hotel, which had bruised his professional pride. That had been a hurried attempt at a snatch. This time Capello had planned for days and with the complete force of the Bureau at his disposal. There would be no excuse this time. Capello hoped he would need none.

The first band passed with a crash of cymbals and drums and a staccato stamping of feet. They were from a predominantly black high school and performed in frenetic double time. Even while marching in place, they pumped their legs like sprinters held back by invisible chains. It struck Carl as a weird amalgam of jazz and the goose step. The faces, shiny with sweat, gleamed against the fiery red of the uniforms.

A boy scout troop, speckled with the proud green uniforms and bandoliers of eagle scouts, strode by in a game but inaccurate attempt at unison marching. They were followed by some minor city officials in a convertible, waving to an audience that did not recognize them and did not care. The mayor and city council leaders would come later, heralded and chased by cheers and boos in roughly equal measure, but the first officials did not merit either praise or contempt. They appeared annoyed by their anonymity.

The first union walked by, caught between bands, with the strains of the one in front jangling discordantly with the one trailing them. The union officials, older, heavy men, straggled along slowly. The heat had formed stains under their arms and little deltas of moisture just above their paunches. It was labor's day, and for the officials their turn to walk in the sun. Their faces reflected a certain grim determination to enjoy it.

A clown worked his way down the side of the street, dragging two enormous suitcases and miming great weariness. He would lurch along for several yards, then sit atop the multicolored suitcases, mopping his brow with exaggerated strokes and flicking the imaginary sweat into the faces of the spectators. A huge crimson mouth painted into a permanent frown accentuated his woes with the weighty cases.

Carl had never thought clowns were funny. Their orange fright wigs and garish makeup had always seemed more frightening than comic. He had never laughed at one, did not remember ever seeing a child laugh at one. The one with the suitcases was no better or worse than any of the others, yet Carl found himself watching him with a curiosity he did not understand.

Another marching band approached and caught up with the clown, who had placed one of the suitcases on the curb amidst the spectators and was pretending he couldn't lift it. As the band passed, blaring out Sousa, the clown took a stopwatch from the pocket of his nylon jumpsuit and made a great show of studying the time. Late, late! he mimed, and, forsaking the one suitcase, he picked up the other in both arms and waddled, bent over, after the band. After a few yards he stopped and looked back. Some children were touching the case and he waggled an admonitory finger at them, started toward them, remembered the time, and hurried away again.

The clown approached Carl's barrier and crossed the street so he was only a few feet away from Carl. He plunked the suitcase down, his tongue lolling to show his fatigue. There was something intensely familiar about the man's pattern of movements, despite the exaggerations, that held Carl's attention steadfast. He moved like someone Carl knew, but he wasn't sure who. As the clown mugged for the crowd, Carl noticed his eyes flick through them all, taking in every face, then dart momentarily past the people and into the street beyond. Once more he mimed flicking sweat at the people, and when he did, his eyes caught Carl's and held them for a fraction of a second. Carl felt the skin on his neck leap into gooseflesh. The clown was his uncle.

The clown turned his back to Carl and sat atop his remaining suitcase, shoulders pumping hugely as he panted. Carl remembered his uncle clearly now, going through a similar act at home, minus the makeup, as he pretended to be various monsters and heroes. He would act out stories for the boy, taking all the outrageous parts and then bringing Carl into them to play the young boy lost in the enchanted forest, beset by beasts and trolls, and rescued, finally, by the strong prince with the magic sword. When Carl was younger, it had been a ritual of Stitzer's visits, better by far than any ordinary bedtime story. When he was older and Stitzer was acting as sole parent, the games had been banished by Carl's self-conscious adolescence, but Stitzer's pattern of movement, the way of placing a foot, the set of the shoulders, the tilt of the head, all remained, as indelible in Carl's memory as a fingerprint.

The man in front of him, the back of his neck exposed and vulnerable and almost within Carl's reach, was Stitzer. Carl knew it absolutely, and did not know what to do about it. He realized what he was expected to do, what he was there for. He had but to lift his watch and speak and his uncle would be betrayed. Very simple, and yet he could not do it. He realized at that moment how completely he did not trust Capello's pledge not to harm his uncle. As soon as he spoke, he knew that matters would be out of his hands. Whatever Capello had planned would happen, whether Carl wished it to or not, and no amount of good intentions would change a thing.

Carl thought desperately of some way to warn his uncle without exposing him. They could meet another time, under safer conditions, when Carl could guarantee his safety. If Carl could warn him now, surely his uncle would trust him in the future. The clown looked once more at the stopwatch. Displaying great alarm at the late hour, the clown grabbed his suitcase and headed up Fifth Avenue once more, locking step with a group of union officials who regarded him uncertainly. He left without glancing back at Carl.

Carl's concentration strained toward his uncle, urging him to run. To Merck's trained eye, Carl's reaction was as legible as a road sign.

"Where is he?" said a voice in Carl's ear. He turned and realized that Merck was standing next to him. Merck was wearing tortoiseshell glasses and a snap-brim hat. He looked almost like a different person from the one who had coached Carl the day before.

"What?" asked Carl. He turned away from Merck, watching the clown who made his way to the other side of the street and twenty-five yards farther up the avenue.

From his viewing post, Capello was yelling into the radio. "Annie, what the fuck is going on!? Has he seen him or not?" He swiveled his binoculars from Carl to the bag lady.

"I've seen fuck all," she muttered in her angry tones, interlacing her strings of invective with real information.

"Something's going on," said Capello. "What's happening down there?"

The bag lady rubbed the side of her head where the earpiece was hidden under a stocking cap.

"Yelling in my fucking ear," she said.

Capello had his binoculars back on Carl. He could see the young man's head following the antics of the clown as the white-clad figure moved up the avenue and out of Capello's line of sight.

Merck, too, was watching Carl.

"The clown," Merck said, his lips not moving.

Carl looked into Merck's eyes, startled.

"No," he said, the lie visible in every line of his face. Merck stepped away from Carl, who reached out and

245

caught his arm. "No," he said urgently. Merck jerked his arm free and hurried toward the bag lady.

Capello could hear Merck's voice over the background noise of the crowd and another approaching band. "The clown," said Merck, speaking directly at Annie, the bag lady. "Move in on the clown!"

Fifty yards away from the barrier, the clown had placed the second suitcase at the feet of the crowd. Throwing his arms up in distress at the time, he hastily waddled after the band, his oversize shoes flapping against the pavement.

By the time Capello had sent agents hurrying after him, the clown had already vaulted the fence and was into the park. One of the agents slipped and fell and another tripped over the fence, eliciting the only laugh of the day for the clown's act.

Stitzer shed the clown's shoes as he ran, loosing them with a kick. The wig was off when he hit the trees, and by the time he approached the zoo he had yanked free the Velcro strips holding the costume in place.

The entrance to the sewer was in the supply room of the lion house. With the stench of the big cats in his nostrils, Stitzer dropped into the darkness and scrambled down the ladder more than thirty feet. At the base of the ladder he stood in one of the huge main sewer tunnels that had been represented by a green line on his chart. He had underdressed in the clown's costume with blue jeans and a thin black sweater. He pulled a dark ski mask over his face, covering the white makeup and making himself virtually invisible in the darkness.

At the barrier, Merck had returned to Carl's side and he gripped his arm now, trying to calm him. Merck could see he was confused, alarmed, close to panic. The plan still had to be executed. There was no guarantee that the clown had been the target or that they weren't being observed even now by the real Stitzer. Merck's job was to see to Carl until he was ordered otherwise.

He looked now at his watch. It was fifteen seconds before noon.

"Go," he said, looking straight ahead and keeping his lips rigid.

Carl looked around, confused. Merck tightened his grip on Carl's arm, then released it completely.

"Go," he repeated. "Walk."

Slowly, Carl turned from the barrier and made his way through the crowd standing four deep behind him. He moved to the sidewalk and tried to walk naturally as Merck had coached.

On the rooftops, the snipers adjusted their holds on their rifles. Their sights, long focused on Carl, swept the street in front and in back of him.

From his position in the manhole, Stroup saw Carl begin the walk toward him. He reached up and felt the reassuring shape of the shotgun through the plastic bag. He gripped the stock, ready to free the weapon, while his eyes played the street and the crowd behind Carl, searching for his target.

Pedestrian flow seemed slow to Stroup. Everyone appeared sluggish, walking in a form of retarded motion because of the heat. Only the marchers, goaded by the imperative of public performance, moved with energy. Stroup could not see them from his street-level vantage, but he could hear the bands and the sound of many feet. All noises were accentuated by the echo-chamber effect of the open tunnel in which he stood. Sounds from the street seemed to swirl around him, colliding with one another and forming a featureless mix that sounded in his ears like a low groan. If he had been a fanciful man, Stroup might have felt as if he were standing neck deep in the den of an enormous sleeping monster, moaning in its slumber. Stroup had neither the inclination nor the time to be fanciful. His eyes searched hungrily among the pedestrians, across the doorways, into the windows.

Thorne was also looking. He held his head rigidly

forward, but Stroup could see his eyes flicking nervously about. When the gaze fell on Stroup, Stroup lowered his face, hiding his features in the lee of the shadow of the hard hat. The radio hooked to his belt crackled with static in that brief premonitory pause before a message, and Stroup listened for Capello's words.

When he heard them, it was too late. There came a sound from the sewer, closer and more distinct than the mingled reverberations of the background noise. A slight gasp seemed to come from the heavy air itself, startled by a sudden disturbance. Stroup reached for the shotgun as a tremor of fear seized his spine. Something huge and sinister was suddenly beside him in the darkness, and Stroup's finger clawed for the trigger to fire without looking. His hand was arrested in midair, and at the same time intense pain hit his kneecap. He felt a great pressure on his abdomen below the flak vest, as if he had been stepped on by something huge.

Stroup was yanked into the sewer, his head vanishing from street level like a fisherman's float at the moment of the strike. As he fell, the pressure on his abdomen moved upward, bunching the vest, and for the first time he felt a stitching pain, like a thorn in his flesh. It felt as if something were caught under his skin and was tugging to get out. It did not trouble him as much as the pressure, but Stroup knew immediately that it was the thing that might kill him.

Capello's voice had been crackling over the radio just as Stitzer struck, but the radio had gone dead abruptly, and now Stroup heard every sound of his assassin's efforts with an eerie clarity. His concentration seemed crystalline and every detail registered distinctly, despite the speed at which they were happening.

The sticking sensation continued to slice up his torso like a zipper. He knew the knife would touch his heart—perhaps already had—and he would die, so there was no panic. As the blade halted in its upward slash and stuck in the cartilage of the sternum, Stroup looked into the eyes of his killer.

"Stitzer," he said clearly.

The cool, disinterested look in Stitzer's eyes changed as he recognized the man he was killing.

*"Kak pozlivayesh,"* he said. The clown's crimson mouth under the dark wool of the ski mask smiled slightly.

"Stitzer," Stroup said again. He knew there was something more he should say to stop himself from dying, but his mind couldn't think of the words. The knife was caught in his chest and Stitzer was yanking to free it. Stroup realized with surprise that something had gone wrong, he was not dead, and instinctively his fingers groped for his own knife stuck in his boot. The handle was only inches away when Stitzer put a knee to Stroup's chest and pushed, catapulting the older man against the wall of the tunnel as the knife jumped free. Stroup's skull hit the bricks and he saw a brilliant light flash behind his eyes before he collapsed.

Stroup lay inert, wondering if he was really dead, but he could hear Stitzer pick up the hard hat and put it on his own head. He tried to open his eyes, but the eyelids were enormously heavy. He lay perfectly still, trying to think, to understand. The sticking sensation was gone, replaced by pain. He could feel the sticky flow of blood under the flak vest. Something metallic moved when Stitzer shifted his foot, and Stroup realized what had happened. He had been saved not by the vest but by the radio. Stitzer's knife had hit the radio, smashing through it, but the blade had penetrated the metallic backplate by less than half an inch. Stroup's wound was long but superficial, and he was in more danger from the blow to his head. As his senses cleared he slowly inched his right hand toward his boot until he felt the handle of the knife touching his fingertips.

Capello swiveled his binoculars from Thorne and his slow progress to the manhole. Stroup's hard hat had vanished for a moment, a movement of yellow in the corner of Capello's eye, but it was back in view again. He could not make out the major's face, only a dark mass under the helmet. He called again into the radio, but there was no response.

The two bombs went off within three seconds of each other, the first exploding as a carload of city officials were abreast of the clown's suitcase. The open car was blown onto its side, the frame riddled with holes by the flying metal. The sound of the blast was still reverberating when the second explosion erupted one hundred yards up the avenue. Bodies were still falling when the gas tank of the overturned car also exploded in a shower of flame, adding an inferno to the bomb blasts.

Carl fell to the pavement, instinctively ducking from the horrendous roars. He was shielded from the blasts by the buildings, but the shock wave concussed the windows and a shower of glass rained onto Sixty-third Street.

Merck had fallen on top of Carl, and Carl pushed him aside as he got groggily to his feet. The screams of the survivors pierced the air. Carl was halfway down the street, his vision blocked by buildings in both directions, but the sound alone was enough to suggest a nightmare of death.

The crowd caught between the two explosions burst through the police barrier and raced down the only avenue of escape open to them. They were atop Carl almost before he realized it, hundreds of panicked people, many of them bleeding from superficial wounds caused by flying glass, fleeing from the catastrophe in blind flight, as frantic as stampeding cattle. The street was filled with people running down the sidewalks and the street, desperate in their search for safety. He recognized a bag lady among them, coming toward him with surprising agility, and behind her a suburban woman who had been at the barrier almost as early as he had.

Someone grabbed Carl and lifted him off his feet. He was

yanked through the crowd that stumbled and clawed its way past him. He had the sense of something woolen pressed against his cheek and realized the person carrying him had no face, only a slash of crimson showing through the hole in the cloth and two more holes for eyes. He could not see the eyes. Then, in the midst of madness, Carl was stuffed into a hole. He fell on a man who was lying on his back in the sewer. The man did not cry out, and Carl thought he was dead. His abductor landed beside Carl and pushed his head down, doubling him over, then shoved him into the darkness of the sewer. As he passed the man whose face was lying in the pool of light beneath the manhole, Carl recognized Stroup. His eyes were open and alert but his skin appeared as white as the flesh on a fish belly.

As Stitzer stepped over Stroup's body, Stroup thrust upward with his knife, jabbing at Stitzer's groin. Carl turned to see the man in the ski mask lash out with his foot, smashing the boot into Stroup's face. Stroup lay still, but a sighing moan escaped his bloody lips. A knife hung from the inside of Stitzer's thigh, and he pulled it out and placed it in his belt as calmly as if he were removing a bramble caught in his clothing. Carl realized that the man was his uncle.

Stitzer jerked the shotgun free from the magnets and thrust the barrel into Carl's back, propelling him deeper into the sewer. As Stitzer followed, he blocked off the light from the manhole and Carl stepped into blackness.

Merck was the first to reach the manhole, and the bag lady was right behind him. They came down, weapons drawn, and Merck stumbled over Stroup's body. He started to call out a warning when the blast from the shotgun hit him in the chest. He was only ten yards away, but the shot group had expanded to fill the tunnel and Merck and the bag lady were felled by the same blast, their bodies shielding Stroup's.

Suburban Sally was hit by the second shot as she came

down the ladder. Her body landed on the others in a growing heap. By the time more agents reached the manhole and cautiously ventured down, Stitzer and Carl had long since vanished.

Carl staggered forward, prodded by the shotgun barrel in his back. His ears were still ringing from the shotgun blasts that had nearly deafened him. His first reaction was of total confusion, but as his eyes adjusted to the darkness he moved with a little more confidence, running bent over in the five-foot-high pipe. The sewer was very humid at any time, but now it was like a steambath. Carl was bathed in sweat before he had gone twenty yards. The floor of the pipe was moist, with an occasional small puddle where the pipe was not perfectly smooth. The walls were lined with cables and wires and small pipes, conduits of the telephone and power companies.

Ahead of him Carl heard a gasp of air that rumbled through the sewer like a blast of wind from a passing truck on the highway. He felt warm, moist air blowing on his face, then suddenly a gush of water burst through a side pipe leading into the main and hit Carl on the face and neck. Panting with surprise, he staggered forward, away from the sudden waterfall. The water smelled foul and clung to his skin like motor oil.

A welcome beam of light was visible in the distance, falling in a circular pattern through the apertures in the manhole cover. Carl ran toward it and reached for the cover. The barrel of the shotgun struck him on the elbow and his entire arm went numb.

"There," said Stitzer, pointing at one of the two pipes that forked in either direction. A thin trickle of liquid dribbled from each into the small pool at Carl's feet.

"It's too small," Carl said.

There was an updraft under the manhole cover as the pressurized, heated air of the sewer rose into the street, and it ruffled the ski mask where it hung loosely at Stitzer's neck. Carl could hear the pandemonium on the street above as people continued to run and scream just over his head. Stitzer reached inside Carl's shirt and ripped the radio transmitter from his chest, disdainfully dropping it to the floor of the tunnel, then he grabbed Carl behind the neck and forced him into the smaller pipe. Carl started forward on his hands and knees. He stopped after a few yards when he felt the darkness closing in on him, but Stitzer hit him sharply with the gun barrel and he crawled forward. The noise of the street receded.

Carl was crawling when he felt a tug on his foot. His palms and knees were scraped raw, and every inch of his skin seemed to be pumping out perspiration.

"There," said Stitzer's voice, deepened and hollowed by the echo.

Carl looked and saw nothing. All was a dark gray, the shade of his bedroom when he awoke in the middle of the night. Unlike his bedroom, however, there were no familiar shapes here, no paler colors to reflect what little light there was.

"There," Stitzer repeated. He turned Carl's head until it pointed toward a patch of dark on the side wall. Black on gray, the mouth of a cave on a moonless night. Carl's fingers tentatively explored the dimensions of the hole. It seemed too small for a man.

"I can't go in there!" he cried, terrified. His face felt chilled despite the heat. "I'll suffocate!"

His uncle's voice was calm and reassuring. "It'll be fine. You'll make it like a champ."

"Please! I can't go in there!"

"Now, Carl, you know I wouldn't ask you to do anything you couldn't do. I'll be right there with you. It will be fine."

Stitzer removed the ski mask and his white makeup shone

with a sudden, eerie light, like a ghost. The patch of dull white moved closer to Carl, the lips and eyes only areas of black.

"Once we get through here, we'll have a nice long talk," Stitzer said as soothingly as if offering cocoa and cookies.

"I can't. You'll have to leave me."

"Oh, I won't leave you." Carl felt a loop of rope pass under his arms and around his chest.

"For God's sake . . ."

"Just close your eyes. It won't take long."

Stitzer went into the pipe on his back. He pulled Carl after him until Carl's head was lying on Stitzer's waist. Carl felt the heavy weight of the shotgun being placed on his chest. Stitzer took each of Carl's hands in turn and placed them on the barrel of the gun, which pointed toward Carl's feet.

"Don't move your hands or you'll hit the trigger. It has no guard. You'll blow your feet off."

"Oh, Jesus." Carl's skin felt unnaturally cold and dry and he feared he was going into shock.

"Close your eyes now," Stitzer said, and he began to inch backward, wriggling like a snake, seeking purchase on the slippery walls with his heels, hips, and shoulders.

Stitzer dragged his nephew through the pipe that had been marked yellow on his map. He tried to keep his mind on the chart now, visualizing his progress along that line, only a few inches on the map but a hundred yards in reality. The rope across his shoulders bit into his neck with Carl's inert weight. Stitzer felt the pain in his inner thigh with growing intensity. With every thrust of his left leg the thigh muscles grew weaker. Stroup's knife had thrust deeply and slashed through parts of the muscle groups, and Stitzer assumed he had lost a good deal of blood. Sweat was seeping into the wound, and the salt exacerbated the pain.

He would bind the wound when he reached safety, but he had to get there first. He forced himself to keep his eyes open even though there was nothing to see. He yearned to give over as his nephew had, letting the fears of living entombment sweep away his consciousness. There was a certain comfort in giving in to terror; resistance was impossibly difficult and only added to the anxiety. But Stitzer had been there before. It was a fight he had won before and he would win it again.

Carl felt his uncle stop and opened his eyes. Blackness seemed to fall upon him like a weight, crushing his chest. He squeezed his eyelids closed and waited, counting his breaths, which came in quick pants. Still they did not move. Carl reached a hand toward the top of the pipe. His fingers touched the algae-slick surface before his elbow cleared his chest. The sides pressed against his shoulders. Liquid seeped through his clothing from the bottom of the pipe. His head rested on the buckle of his uncle's belt, and Carl realized he could no longer feel the rhythmic rise and fall of Stitzer's diaphragm. He wasn't breathing! He saw himself trapped in a slimy grave, strapped to a corpse. Carl could feel the walls squeezing in. He scrabbled frantically with his heels, pushing his body forward. Suddenly Stitzer began to move again. Carl continued to push with his feet, helping, and they moved faster.

Light struck his eyelids and Carl looked up to see a manhole cover directly above him. Light and air and freedom hung scant inches over his face. Several of the holes in the cover were plugged with dirt, but through one of them he could see the sky, fantastically blue, and then a pants leg, also blue.

Carl screamed and reached both hands toward the manhole cover. The rope under his armpits tightened, and Stitzer pulled him, yanking him away from the air. Carl tried to resist by digging in his heels while his fingers sought the holes of light. On the street above, he could see fragments of men as they pulled on the cover.

"It's stuck!" he heard them cry, and Carl saw an iron rod

secured across the cover, sealing it shut. Stitzer continued to pull on him, inching him away from the manhole.

"You locked it," Carl screamed accusingly at his uncle. "You sealed us in here!"

He clawed toward the bar that held him underground, but it was already beyond his reach. Struggling desperately, he twisted his body from side to side. The shotgun eased off his writhing torso, the barrel hitting the bottom of the pipe with a metallic clang. He was being dragged out from underneath the gun, and he felt the weight of it dragging across his body.

"Please, God, not the trigger! Not my feet!" He tried to reach the gun but could not lift his head enough to bend at the waist. The last of the gun butt tickled his fingers then slipped away as Stitzer tugged again.

The shotgun clattered into the sewer when the barrel was scant inches beyond Carl's feet and fired immediately, the lethal shot streaking harmlessly into the black tunnel through which they had just come. On the street above, men scattered, then went scurrying to send their reports to Capello.

Capello had reacted to the carnage by ignoring that which he could not alter and concentrating on his own immediate job. He turned his back on the slaughter of the marchers and bystanders on Fifth Avenue, leaving that horrible task to the police and emergency personnel. His own dead people, piled in a heap within the manhole, were also no longer his concern. He could not help them any more than he could help the hundreds of dead and dying along the parade route. All that he could do, he told himself repeatedly, was to catch Stitzer and prevent any further deaths. As the city reeled from shock Capello moved in his mind under the pavement and into the tunnels.

While the chief of police dealt with the aboveground

problem, the deputy chief in charge of operations was at Capello's side in the backseat of an FBI sedan. A police car ran interference in front of them, its flashing light twirling in urgency. There had been a moment of difficulty when the deputy chief had argued for riding in a police car, but Capello felt the operation slipping out of his hands and had insisted on his own auto. The moment had been brief but decisive, and he had won it with unassailable logic; he knew what the hell was going on—more or less—and the police did not.

Seated between Capello and the deputy chief was a beefy man with jet-black hair brilliantined so heavily that the individual marks of the comb's teeth were showing. His name was Mo Courtney and he was the civil servant who ran the sanitation department, regardless of the whims of political appointees placed above him. A map of the sewer system was spread across their laps and filled the backseat. In the front, Agent Harper sat next to the driver and worked the radios.

Harper turned now and jabbed his finger at the map. "They're right here, sir. He apparently secured the cover somehow, our men couldn't open it, but they could hear someone yelling."

"Thorne," said Capello.

"Probably. They said he sounded hysterical."

"Pardon me," said Courtney.

"What?"

"Someone has made a mistake. They couldn't be there."

"Goddamn it, Harper."

"That's the place they reported, sir."

"I'll have my men check it out," said the deputy.

"It was your men who gave us the report," said Harper.

"Why can't they be there?" the deputy demanded.

"I don't believe a person could get into a pipe that small. Well, into it, maybe, but not through it."

257

"If that's your only problem, forget it. Assume Stitzer can get anywhere he wants. Harper, how soon can we get there?"

"Two minutes," said the deputy.

"How far can he get in two minutes?"

"I'll send some of my men in after him," said the deputy.

"Sir, he still has the shotgun. There was a gunshot report right there."

"You send anyone in after them now and you're signing their death warrants," said Capello.

"If I might make a suggestion," said Courtney.

Capello smiled at him. "Don't be so polite," he said. "We don't have time."

"Two minutes is too long anyway. If he could get this far, then by the time we get there he will have reached this main sewer here."

"So?"

"This is one of the primary conduits. The feeder tunnels come into this one like spokes on a wheel. He can step into any one of . . ." Courtney counted the lines radiating from the main tunnel. His lips moved silently. ". . . seventeen tunnels. And those start to branch out again within a few hundred yards. My guess is that within three or four minutes he could be . . . well, you can see, it's hard to figure all the possibilities." Courtney spread his fingers across the map. The lines went in all directions like branches on a tree.

Capello sighed. The deputy refused to grasp the situation.

"You mean to tell me he could go anywhere in the goddamned city?"

"Well, in Manhattan, at this time of day, yes, sir, that's about right. He seems to have planned this very well."

Capello swallowed a bitter remark. He would need Courtney further and did not want to alienate him.

"Where can we have access to this major tunnel?" Capello asked.

Courtney placed his pinkie delicately at a spot on the map, like a man testing bathwater.

"Are we going in?" Harper asked.

"We're going to stop, look, and listen," said Capello. "Nobody's going in anywhere until I'm sure they have a good chance of coming out again. Get on your horn, Harper, and get me a mike, one of those high-powered jobs the anti-espionage people use. Get it to this intersection right away."

"I can't tell," said Harper. He pressed the earphones tightly against his head. Below his feet a wire led through the open manhole into the main sewer line, and on the end of the wire a highly sensitive microphone spun slowly in midair.

"What do you mean you can't tell?" the deputy chief demanded. "Can you hear anything or not?"

"I can hear too goddamned much." He handed the padded earphones to Capello.

Capello was reminded of the effect of holding a seashell to his ear. There was a droning background noise, not quite a roar, not quite a ringing. Gradually, as he became used to the background, Capello could make out individual sounds: water running, the squeak of a rat, scuttling noises. At one point he thought he heard voices, very faint, very far away, speaking in a conversational tone. And then a sound that may have been a footfall. Suddenly a sharp sound rang out, very distinct although distant, like metal on concrete.

"They're down there somewhere, all right," said Capello. "But we can't tell where from here." He spread the sewer map on the pavement. "Chief, I need your fullest cooperation. I want to set up listening posts all along here."

He drew a small circle that cut through the seventeen

feeder lines, then a larger one that sliced across the branches coming out of the feeders.

"Don't send anyone into the sewers. Do it this way, listen from the street. If you send anyone into the sewer, he'll kill them."

"I have some men who are not easy to kill," said the deputy.

"Good," said Capello. "Let's save them until the right time."

"Listen, Capello, the cowardly son-of-a-bitch has just murdered hundreds of people with a bomb. That doesn't mean he's superhuman. Any coward can kill with a bomb."

"He's got a shotgun."

"We've got shotguns."

"Chief, let me assure you this man is no coward. If he used bombs, he did it because they are efficient. It would take him longer to kill that many with his bare hands, but if that's what he had to do, I believe he would do it. I've been following him for weeks, and I respect him. I hate him, but I respect him. If you send a man down there, the man will die. If you send six men down there, I honestly believe all six will die."

"What do you intend to do, then?"

"First, let's locate him. Do you have the capability to set up these listening posts?"

The deputy bridled. "Of course I have the capability."

"Well, then, if you hurry, we can just get it done in time." Capello smiled.

When the deputy had gone to give the orders, Capello turned to Courtney.

"You said he could go anywhere in the city at this time of day. What did you mean 'at this time of day'?" Capello asked.

"This is a slack time," Courtney said. He ran a hand through his hair. His fingers left deep furrows. "There isn't any rain, there isn't a lot of water usage. If it was around

260

eight, nine o'clock when everyone is showering and bathing and whatnot, a lot of those tunnels would be flooded.''

"Impassable?"

"Well, more than impassable. Anything in there would get washed out. Flushed.''

"Flushed,'' repeated Capello. He savored the word. "Flushed. Tell me about it.''

Carl moved hunched over, the pain in his back so constant that he had almost forgotten it. They were moving on a downward gradient now and making good time, although Carl did not know where they were going. He felt better, more confident than at any time since leaving the barrier at the parade. When they emerged from the tunnel where Carl had lost the shotgun, it was as if he had had the fears scraped from him by the walls of the pipe. He had come through it, survived it, and felt stronger for it. He was still afraid, but the terror was gone. The fear now was normal and rational, and he could deal with it. He suspected that his uncle had known all along what the outcome would be.

Light streamed into the tunnel in front of him. Carl stood under a grating and let the sunlight hit his face, basking in the light. Mushrooms, long as a man's arm and just as thick, reached from tenuous footholds on the sides of the tunnel walls. There were hundreds of them, a small forest of ghostly white fungal trunks topped with yellow caps. The white filaments that spread the colony reached along the wall pipe in all directions for yards. Carl stared in wonder for a moment before he realized he was alone.

He held his breath, listening for a movement in the darkness from which he had come. The light through the grate streamed into his face. He had but to lift his hand to stick his fingers through the grate and into the street. As he deliberated, a cloud passed over the sun and the grate fell into shadow. A bus drove over the grate, the immense weight seeming to bear down on the very air in the tunnel and compress it.

Carl heard a sound come from his uncle's direction. He paused a moment longer, the idea of flight tugging at him, fluttering against the bars of his imagination. Then his mind registered the note of urgency in Stitzer's tone.

"Kid," Stitzer said. The hope of escape soared into the light and was gone.

Carl found Stitzer still standing in the tunnel, his back bent as if he were supporting the pipe on his shoulders. His left leg hung limply beneath him. He looked up at Carl's approach and smiled confusedly, then pushed the leg with his hand as if demonstrating something as strange and rare as the mushrooms.

"Leg won't work," he said, with the puzzlement of a man whose body had never failed him.

Carl helped ease his uncle to a sitting position. Stitzer started to slice away the pants leg with his hunting knife, and for a moment Carl feared he was going to cut off the leg for having offended him. When he had cut as far as he could, he handed the knife to Carl to finish the job.

Carl clutched the knife. He had never realized the size of the blade or the weight of the handle before. It was a killing weapon, and it felt lethal in his hands. The long blade, honed as sharp as it could get, was pointing straight at Stitzer's chest. The idea raced through Carl's mind, and flickered across his face. When he raised his eyes to Stitzer's, Carl saw him smiling, ironically. Confidently.

Carl tightened his grip on the knife and finished the job of cutting away the pants leg. The cloth was stuck to the skin, and as Carl peeled it away a clot came with it, and a gout of blood sprang from the wound.

"Press your hand on it," Stitzer said. Carl clamped his palm over the wound and felt the hot, sticky blood pump against it. He wondered at the amount of blood his uncle must have lost already. That he was still on his feet at all was remarkable, Carl thought, even without the useless leg.

Stitzer made a tourniquet with his belt, cinching it up high in his groin. When Carl removed his hand, there was nothing more than a seep of fluid from the wound, and then nothing at all.

Carl handed the knife back to his uncle.

"I knew you were the real one," Stitzer said with a chuckle. "You were too scared to be one of them. Even standing there watching the parade you looked like you wanted to hide your head in the ground."

"I'm not cut out for this kind of work," Carl said.

"You were never very good at killing things."

"Uncle Mark, I'm going to help you get out of here."

"I know you are."

"I'm going to get you away from the police. They'd shoot you on sight now, I'm sure of it. I'll get you someplace safe and explain things to you, you don't understand the way things really are, and then we'll negotiate your safe return."

"Return where?"

"Uncle Mark, do you realize how many people you must have killed with those bombs? They can't let you just go free . . ."

They heard the clatter of something metallic knocking against the grate. In the light that shone down twenty yards away, they saw a microphone at the end of a black cord being lowered through the grille.

Stitzer understood immediately and clamped a hand over Carl's mouth. Carl could taste the slime of the sewer against his lips.

They sat for several minutes without moving, scarcely breathing, then Stitzer released Carl's mouth. Gesturing for Carl not to move, Stitzer slowly unlaced and removed Carl's shoes, then his own, strapping the hunting knife against his bare ankle. The cautious movements made Carl think of a demolitions expert defusing a bomb. When the shoes were removed, Stitzer placed his lips against Carl's ear so that Carl felt the words as much as he heard them.

"Lie on my back," Stitzer mouthed into his ear. "Don't try to help, just lie there and hold on."

Aping the exaggerated care of his uncle's every movement, Carl climbed on his back. Stitzer crawled away from the microphone, supporting himself on his knee and fingertips. His left leg dragged behind uselessly.

It was like taking a ride on a spider, Carl thought. The only sound he could hear was the thumping of his uncle's heart through his shirt. In fifteen minutes they traveled only fifty yards, but they turned twice and put as many junctions in pipe between themselves and the microphone. Carl thought they had evaded danger when they rounded another corner and entered one of the main tunnels. At the same moment, a policeman descended a ladder a few feet in front of them.

Officer Drew Gibson, impatient, distrustful of the microphone, and eager for action, had disregarded the order to stay out of the sewers. His second mistake was to leave his gun in its holster while he climbed down the ten-foot ladder. When he saw the strange piggybacked beast crawl out of one of the feeder tunnels, his first thought was that it was a monster, some horrid double-backed version of the alligators he had heard of. He knew immediately that was wrong and clawed at the gun on his hip as Stitzer suddenly lurched to one side and shrugged off his burden. He reached for Stroup's hunting knife, which was in his belt, and threw it with a side-arm action. The knife penetrated Officer Gibson's sternum. Baffled by the pain in his chest, he managed to climb two steps toward the street before his lifeless body toppled back. The microphone, ripped from his wire, clattered onto pipe beside him.

"We've got 'em now, kid," Stitzer said. He chuckled and stood on his one good leg.

While Capello listened to Courtney explain the intricacies of the sewer system, Harper maintained communications with the agents and officers who were listening in two concentric circles across the city.

"They thought they heard something on Fifty-sixth and Madison," Harper reported. "But nothing for about fifteen minutes since then."

Capello made a circle on the map at Fifty-sixth and Madison.

"Can he stay down there without being heard?" asked the deputy chief.

"Not forever," said Capello.

"Forever? We've got traffic halted all over the city as it is. I've got men squatting in the middle of the street with their goddamned ears to the ground . . ."

"They're still alive, aren't they?"

"Until some motorist gets tired of this shit and runs them over."

"If you can't manage traffic control, Chief, I'll ask Washington to send a few men over to help."

"I can manage traffic control!" The deputy tried to cover his anger with a laugh, which fooled no one. "Look, Capello, I don't know how long my boys are going to be willing to sit tight. This maniac has just killed several hundred people . . ."

"And three of my agents," Capello said sharply. "You don't want him half as bad as I do. But I will not sacrifice anyone else to get him."

Harper turned to them, stunned. "Cap," he said softly.

Capello could see from Harper's face that trouble had started again.

"He killed a man on Fifty-fourth and Fifth."

"Who?"

"I don't know. A cop."

"Son-of-a-bitch!" said the deputy.

"Did he come up?" Capello asked.

"No. We're getting reports from all over now. He's right around in that area around Fifty-fourth between Fifth and Madison."

"Now!" said the deputy. "Send some men down now!"

"You don't even know what he's got down there with him besides the shotgun. What if he has another explosive charge?"

"You've got to do something!"

*"I'll* go down."

Stroup stood before Capello, a police shotgun in one hand. His flak vest hung open, revealing a swath of bandage and tape covering him from chest to navel. His face looked worse. The lips were hugely swollen and one eye was puffed nearly closed by a welt already turning fiercely purple.

"We thought he killed you," said Capello, feeling ridiculous even as he mouthed the words.

"So did he," said Stroup. The sounds were slurred through his swollen lips. "I just look bad, but the only thing hurting is skin."

Capello stared at the huge bandage, already soiled with sweat and blood.

"He cut me," said Stroup. "It's long, but it's not fatal." He shifted the shotgun in his hand. "I don't have to run a race. You know where he is, put me in there."

"No."

"I'm not *asking* you, Capello." They stood less than ten feet from a manhole, the cover off. "I can go in right here and take my chances, or you can do us both a favor and put me in in the best place." Stroup lifted the barrel of the shotgun and placed it on his forearm. It pointed in the direction of Capello's belly.

"I have another way of getting him out," said Capello. He tried to keep his eyes from looking at the shotgun. Stroup seemed crazed enough to use it.

"Good. That gives you two ways."

Capello paused. He glanced at Harper and the deputy, who were staring at the shotgun.

"I'm advising you not to go down there," said Capello.

"Okay, I heard it. They heard it. It's official, your ass is covered. Now put me down there."

Capello sighed and rubbed his hands over his eyes. He spoke from behind his hands.

"How much time do we have before we lose him, Mr. Courtney?"

The sanitation man glanced nervously back and forth from Capello to Stroup. "If he knows where he's going . . ."

"He knows," said Stroup.

". . . then fifteen minutes. Twenty at the outside. If he gets out of this ring, he can go anywhere, there's too much territory to cover."

"Right. Stroup, you've got ten minutes. If you're not up by then . . ."

"If I'm not up by then, I'm dead anyway."

Capello nodded and saw something like a smile contort Stroup's battered face.

A diversion was created by a clattering of manhole covers throughout the area, and Stroup slipped in amidst the din. Capello spoke before the major disappeared into the darkness.

"Bring Thorne out," he said. "That's why I'm letting you go in. This way you can get Thorne out."

Stroup looked up from the tunnel at Capello's face, which blocked the light. Capello could read nothing in the eyes. Then Stroup was gone. Capello did not hear him go.

The others clustered around him. Capello had felt their presence like a swarm of flies ever since the explosion.

Without initiative of their own, they clung to him. Capello wished he felt better qualified to play the leader.

He turned to Courtney and jabbed at the map. "Will it work here?"

"It should," said Courtney.

"Will—it—work?" Capello repeated slowly.

"Sir, I can't promise that it will work. I *can* promise that it will flood those pipes. Unless he's a salmon, it should work."

"Good enough," said Capello. "Chief, I want to turn on all the fire hydrants along this line."

Capello drew a jagged line across the map. It extended for three blocks in either direction of the last area he had circled.

"What for?"

"This area drains like a mountainside. Each one of these small pipes is like a stream feeding into a larger stream, which feeds into a still larger one, until all of them come together into a river and all of the rivers come together into one hell of a lake." His finger touched a large black circle on the map. "This underground basin right here catches everything that flows on this side of the watershed. If you spit into your sink anywhere between Wall Street and Ninety-ninth, it's going to end up right here." He jabbed the map again. "We're going to flush out those feeder pipes with all the water we can get, and we'll be waiting at this catchment basin to fish him out—if he's still alive."

"He won't be," said Courtney. "I don't see how anyone could survive it."

The deputy chief shook his head. "The water pressure is low as it is. If you do that, you won't have anything left in the system in case of fire."

"You've got about ten minutes to set it up, Chief. We want it coordinated so it will all hit him at once."

"But damn it, Capello, what if there's a fire?"

Capello rubbed the bridge of his nose with the back of his hand. "Harper, what's the latest report on the casualties?"

"Two hundred seventeen dead. About three times that many wounded."

"And how many peace officers?"

"Okay," said the deputy.

"Three agents. One policeman. So far."

"I'll turn on the water," said the deputy.

"In ten minutes," said Capello. "I want to pop him out of there like a cork out of a bottle." He stepped into the backseat and slammed the door. Harper jumped in after him as the car started to move.

"Cap, Stroup's down there," said Harper.

"Stroup's been warned," said Capello. "In ten minutes the water goes on."

"Cap, there's one other thing."

Capello turned back, annoyed.

"What?"

"Are you remembering that Stitzer's got Mr. Thorne down there with him?"

"I remember."

"Well?"

"Well what, Harper?"

Harper held Capello's eyes for a moment. The other man glared at him, challenging. Harper looked away finally, glad that he did not have the responsibility of command—or the conscience.

Stroup tilted his wristwatch so he could see the faint green luminescence of the hands. He had been waiting in the darkness for eleven minutes and Capello's time limit had passed. Whatever Capello had in mind did not concern him. The agent would do what he had to do, and Stroup was doing the same. He had stood without moving for the entire time, wedged into the opening of a large pipe, his back against one wall, his left forearm against the opposite wall, with the shotgun resting on top of that. It was a well-supported position, one that he could maintain for an hour or more without motion, and he was prepared to wait longer if need be. He knew he had to wait for Stitzer to come to him in any event. He was no match for the sergeant if he tried to chase him.

The pain in his chest was a steady burn now, exacerbated by the salty sweat that seeped into it. His face troubled him more; the pain came in pulses, and Stroup suspected that his left cheekbone was cracked. He blinked, then stretched his eyebrows upward, trying to force more vision into the eye that was swelling closed. In front of him the dark tunnel from which he hoped Stitzer would come swam slowly, as if the blackness were pulsing in time to his pain. Motion where there was none was a phenomenon of night vision; Stroup was used to it and discounted it. The motion he was waiting for would be positive and directly at him. He had missed it last time and nearly died, but this time, he told himself, he was ready. He slowly rotated his wrist away from his eyes. Whatever Capello had in mind was already two minutes overdue. Stroup just hoped it managed to drive Stitzer toward the waiting shotgun.

They first sensed a change in the atmosphere, a feeling of pressure as if something invisible were pressing against a membrane. Bent double in one of the pipes, they both stopped, listening. It was hard to identify the sound at first. There was nothing specific, just more background noise, as if the volume had been turned up. Stitzer leaned against Carl's back, holding onto the rope that now passed around them both. Carl, dragged on his back in the beginning, was now offering his strength to his uncle.

Carl felt something coming toward him, very fast, and threw up his arms to protect his face. A cat, teeth bared in terror, ran at them, its tail straight out behind it, its fur standing like spikes. Careening off the wall as it turned a bend, it scrambled against the slick surface for a second like a cartoon character, legs spinning beneath it, before it shot forward again, heading toward Carl and Stitzer as if it didn't even see them. In a mocking reversal of natural order, the cat was pursued by rats, dozens of them, their eyes gleaming red in the dim light as they raced under Carl's legs.

"Back!" Stitzer cried, and they turned as quickly as they could in the restraining space. Stitzer's dead leg was thrown to the side by the violence of his movement, and the knife strapped to his ankle clanged against the tunnel. The rats continued to flood between their feet, colliding with the men in their panic. Carl felt their claws clambering up his legs before leaping forward again, heard the panicked *screeee!* and the clacking of their claws against the tunnel like a chorus of castanets.

They were close to the end of the tunnel when Carl realized the water level was suddenly halfway up his calf. At the same time he heard the roar, a deafening sound that was racing toward him. The water was at his knees and propelling him forward, and he turned to see a flash of white as the river behind him was churned to spuming foam by its own speed. Beyond the white was utter blackness as the water swelled to fill the tunnel and shut off all light.

Carl screamed and stumbled, the water knocking him to his knees. He rose immediately.

"Hang on to the rope," Stitzer cried. Carl could hardly hear the words over the roar. He took one more step forward and the wall of water hit him in the back.

They were shot out of the tunnel into a larger one and bobbed up to the surface. Water was coming into the tunnel from all sides as twig fed to branch and branch to limb and limb to trunk. Carl and Stitzer were pushed in front of the flood like surfers riding a wave, but their river was only one of many. As Carl tried to swim he could see another river as huge as their own cascading into the tunnel from the side, and riding its crest was Major Stroup, a shotgun wavering crazily in Carl's direction. Stroup's feet flew over his head and the gun went off, its blast hitting the roof of the tunnel as the two streams of water collided and Carl was slammed under. He was spun again and again as the converging streams formed a vortex, whirling him around. Kicking frantically, Carl reached the surface, gasping for breath. The huge ten-foot tunnel was already nearly full. He had less than two feet between his gasping face and the top of the tunnel, and still more water crashed into the tunnel in front of them.

Stitzer's head bobbed to the surface next to Carl, his features strained with effort. Then Stroup emerged, his teeth bared, fingers clawing at Stitzer's face. Carl realized that Stitzer had Stroup by the throat. The two men struggled, only inches away from Carl, locked in each other's embrace, trapped in the swirl of the whirlpool, lost in the larger chaos. Stroup's eyes flashed briefly across Carl's face, bulging, frantic, demonic with hatred and desperation. The whirlpool, overcome by sheer volume, gave way to the current, and Stitzer and Stroup were suddenly swept away from Carl. The rope tautened and Carl was pulled along behind his uncle, less than a few feet away but unable to catch up.

They rose as they sped forward, lifted by the ever-increasing volume until their faces nearly scraped the roof of the tunnel. Carl was on his back, his neck straining to keep his face above the dark waters, and he realized he was crying out with each panted breath. There was light ahead of him, a strangely milky illumination, and as he raced toward it he realized it was filtered through yet more water coming in from a grate above. He tried to kick away, but he was too late. The water hit him in the face. He swallowed water and was struck beneath the surface.

The rope grew tight with a snap and Carl was jerked up

again. He arched his back, gasping for the precious air in the scant inches left. He thought for a moment that the rope was snagged on something because he was held fast, no longer going with the current. The water pushed at him angrily, his resistance an insult to its power. He felt the clothing being ripped from his body by the force.

They were not snagged, they were being held. Incredibly, Stitzer had managed to grab the grille above him. Carl could see his uncle's head reaching up into the water pouring down, like a man standing under a waterfall. His fingers gripped the grate. The rope that held Carl in place was looped around Stitzer's shoulder and chest like a bandolier. In the clouded light Carl could see the rope had already sawed into the skin of Stitzer's shoulder. Carl could not think how his uncle was breathing, but he was managing to withstand the torrent above and the raging sea below and the lethal drag of Carl's weight against the rope. Stroup had vanished.

Stitzer pulled on the rope, his bicep threatening to burst from the skin. Carl struggled to swim against the current, to relieve the pressure. The length of the rope shortened tantalizingly. Carl's hand was a foot from his uncle's, six inches, a finger-width. Stitzer's grasp stung Carl's hand with its power, the muscle in his arm quivered like a mountain giving birth.

Carl felt his feet touch the iron rungs of a ladder. He lunged for the ladder with both hands as the water tugged and threatened to spin him around. Stitzer had his good leg entwined on the ladder; the bad leg flapped aimlessly about in the current. Carl could feel it slapping at him underwater, the harsh metal of the knife knocking him with each blow.

Stitzer lowered his head from the torrent that poured in overhead. Unaccountably, he was grinning.

"We've got them now, kid," he said, yelling against the roar of the tunnel. His eyes were unnaturally bright, feverish in their intensity, and the grin had a ragged, savage look, as if ripped onto his uncle's face by the brutality of the situation. He's actually enjoying it, Carl thought, and in that moment he understood the depths of the madness that had sustained his uncle for the last five years.

"Going out!" his uncle yelled.

Carl could only nod his understanding. Something wet and soft slapped against Carl's mouth, and he shook desperately to remove it, not daring to release his grip on the ladder for a second. The water level was still rising and there was scarcely any room left in which to breathe. The air itself was thick with moisture and seemed to be moving at the speed of the water, pulled along in sympathetic motion. Carl feared that in any second it would be moving too fast for him to catch.

Stitzer put his head back into the waterfall coming through the grate. Both hands reached up into the torrent, like a man beseeching the heavens. Magically, the grate moved, then moved again. Stitzer had loosened it and opened a pathway to the street above. He had a hand out of the sewer, and then an arm. He was going to do it! Going to pull them both free! And Carl laughed in a maniacal burst of relief.

Something struck Carl in the chest and spun him around so his face hit the water. The animal was still living, for it struggled feebly even now. The water pulled it down Carl's body and it sunk its claws into Carl's flesh, as frantic to survive as Carl himself. The claws ripped at him but would not hold, and they dragged from his chest to his waist. When the raking talons reached his groin, Carl involuntarily put his hands down to protect himself. As he released the ladder the current snatched him and pulled him free. He slammed against the rope as a sail suddenly bellied by a gale wind snaps against its shrouds. Stitzer was yanked back into the sewer by the sudden blow.

Carl came to the surface, gasping, his face pressed against the top of the tunnel, trying to suck air from the concrete. The rope yanked and yanked at him as the water bounced him against the roof. He could not breathe and see at the same time because of the angle of his head. He filled his lungs, then lowered his head into the water until his eyes were looking through the tiny column of air toward his uncle.

Stitzer was clinging to the ladder only by his good leg. The rope had bent him double, and his head was pulled underwater by the drag of Carl's weight. The rope had slipped off his shoulders when he was pulled over, and Carl could see that his uncle held it in his hand. He was hanging on to his nephew as if he were his lifeline, and Carl realized that he would not release that iron grip even if he drowned in the act of rescue.

Carl arched back, tried to breathe, and took a mouthful of water. Sputtering and choking, he flailed wildly for a moment. He felt the rope slip, then tighten, and he knew he was killing his uncle. Carl kicked desperately toward him again, trying to ease the strain. He was exhausted already, drained as much by fear as effort, and he couldn't imagine how his uncle held on.

Stitzer's head burst through the surface, his eyes wild and demented. With a strength Carl could not understand, his uncle was pulling himself, pulling both of them, against the weight of tons of rushing water, back toward the ladder. Halfway there he faltered and the water sucked him under again, but then he was up, clinging to the rope like Ahab to Moby Dick as the white monster pulled him to his death.

Once more, stomach muscles stretched to the point of tearing, body screaming with pain, Stitzer pulled them both toward the ladder. His left hand clamped onto the rung. He tried to pull Carl to him, but this time Carl knew he would never do it. His uncle was spent, his mighty strength defeated at last. Carl could see the other man's body bucking against the strain as every muscle succumbed to exhaustion.

275

"Let go!" Carl yelled. He knew his uncle would kill them both before saving himself. "Let go!"

Still Stitzer tried, his teeth bared with effort, his head quivering with strain.

Stitzer's bad leg slapped against Carl, and he grabbed the foot. Stitzer could not help him, could not bend the leg, and Carl knew he did not have the strength to pull himself along it any more than he could negotiate the rope. He tore the knife free from his uncle's ankle and cut the rope. The last thing he saw as the current seized him was his uncle, still clinging to the ladder, screaming Carl's name, but Carl could hear nothing, and then he was sucked under the dark water.

Carl kicked toward the surface again, but suddenly there was no surface. His fingers clawed at the roof, but the water had filled the tunnel. There was no difference between up and down, no air anywhere. Carl felt his lungs burning and knew he was going to die.

He was tumbled head over heels, slammed against the walls of the tunnel as the sea that contained him rushed toward its destination. He could not see; he could not hear anything but a roar. For the longest moment he thought his lungs would burst and his entire chest split open. He could not think, his mind was filled with panic and his body lashed out desperately but futilely. Then the pain in his lungs ceased and he felt a sense of peace. He realized with surprise that he was thinking of Pauline. The thoughts had such a clarity, such a serenity, that he realized he was already dead.

Light of incredible whiteness burst into his head like a bomb exploding behind his eyes. The tide that had borne him through the tunnels smashed into the huge underground reservoir, and Carl was thrown to the surface like flotsam. He gasped, taking in spray, choked, then breathed again. His body shuddered all over with the sensation of breath. Intense lights hit him from all directions and he could hear human voices above the roar. They were yelling excitedly, and he sensed that they were yelling about him, at him.

Slowly, Carl took in his surroundings. As his eyes adjusted to the brightness, he realized he was in a reservoir that contained the flow of seven rivers as huge as his own. They spilled in on waterfalls, crashing against each other in the middle of the basin like opposing ocean currents. The surface of the water roiled with waves. On a walkway above the water were searchlights, at least a dozen of them, and beside each light stood men with guns.

Carl recognized Capello, who was stripped to the waist, his hairy torso drenched and dripping like the coat of an animal. Capello was yelling something, pointing at Carl, and Carl strained to call back, to yell for help.

Hands grappled at him, voices yelled indistinguishably; they pulled him out and he sagged to the walkway, unable to support his own weight. The rope was still tied to his body.

Capello knelt over Carl, took the rope from his hand.

"He cut it," Capello said. "The son-of-a-bitch cut it." The words made no sense to Carl. He knew he was blacking out. Capello shook him roughly by the shoulder. The agent was screaming, his face contorted with anger and frustration. "Where is he!" he yelled furiously. He seemed desperate, panic building in his voice, behind his eyes. "Where is Stitzer!"

Carl tried to speak but could only sigh with exhaustion. He rolled his head to the side and for the first time became aware of the body lying next to him. Stroup's mouth was open, the muscles slack, the eyes staring vacantly upward. His skin was gray, bloodless, except for the bruises, which retained their purple cast even in death.

Capello brandished the rope in Carl's face. "He cut it! He let you go! He didn't try to save you! You don't owe him anything anymore, do you hear me? You don't owe him anything because he betrayed you!" Other faces looked down over Capello's shoulders. Carl did not recognize them, but they all had the same desperate look as Capello.

"Do you hear, Thorne?" Capello held Carl's head in his hands, lifting if off the walkway, pulling it close to his own face. "I've got to know where he is! You don't need to protect him! You don't owe him!"

Carl wanted to say, You lied to me. You tried to kill him. He wanted to say, I don't owe you either. He wanted to say many things, but he could feel the clouds of darkness creeping over his mind.

"Where is he!"

"He drowned," Carl said. And he closed his eyes and slipped into unconsciousness.

Carl awoke in a hospital bed, his eyes gummy with sleep, his mouth stale and dry. He had been unconscious for nearly twenty-four hours, and the first face he saw was Capello's. Disheveled, weary, the agent had the look of a man who had been waiting for a long time for Carl to awaken. Carl watched him for several moments, debating whether to let the agent know he was alert. Capello was sunk within himself, unaware of Carl. When his gaze at last took in Carl's face, he seemed almost reluctant to deal with him.

"How you feeling?" he asked.

Carl nodded slowly. He felt tired, but beyond that he had no idea yet.

"The doctors say you're fine, just worn out."

Carl nodded again, waiting for Capello to continue.

"We haven't found your uncle's body yet," he said finally. "It could be anywhere, of course."

"Yes," said Carl. His throat seemed stuck together.

"He could be at the bottom of the underground basin. Courtney told me that's where he would have to be. They're dragging it now." Capello paused, his eyes not quite focusing on Carl's face. Carl realized he was talking to himself. "That's probably where the body is."

"Yes," Carl said again.

"Or it could have been swept through the basin and into the treatment plant. Or even the East River." Carl shrugged. "Those tunnels interlock in such a way . . . with the system that full, pipes could back up . . . a filter might have come loose and his body could have been swept in another direction . . . it's complicated."

"I'm sure."

"Or it might be caught somewhere in the tunnels, snagged on something."

Carl struggled to a sitting position. Capello leaned forward to help, plumping the pillows, strangely solicitous.

"I'm sure you'll find the body," said Carl.

"Oh, they will—but not me. I'm leaving. I've been transferred to Washington." Capello tried to smile but failed, his face coloring with embarrassment. "It's a career change," he said.

"I see."

"Analytical work. The Bureau's requirements are more and more in that direction."

"You explained that to me once."

"Um—" Capello lifted his head, then let it sink, as if even that much effort were too great.

"I don't ask officially," he said after a pause. "It's no longer my case. I just want to know from a personal point of view . . . Did you see him go under? Do you know for a fact that he drowned?"

"Could anyone have lived in that flood?" Carl asked.

"No," said Capello. "But you did."

"But you caught me," said Carl.

"It would help me to know," said Capello. His eyes sought Carl's and held them. For the first time Carl saw a weakness and a pleading. "Just to know, would help."

"I saw him drown," said Carl.

"I knew it," said Capello, without triumph. "I knew he had to." He mustered a pale version of his diplomatic smile before he left.

When Pauline came she took Carl's hand in one of her own and slipped the other under his hospital smock onto his chest. Her touch was warm and the heat seemed to spread throughout his body. They looked at each other for a long time without speaking, and when she lay her head on his chest, Carl felt as if he would burst with happiness. It took him a long time to realize what made this moment different, why having Pauline with him was suddenly untempered joy. Eventually he realized it was because for the first time he was with her without guilt.

Three weeks later, Carl's newspaper carried a front-page story about a subway train that ran out of control and collided with an oncoming engine. Officials blamed equipment failure.